GARDEN OF MYSTERIES

MISSELTHWAITE BOOK TWO

DRAKE LAMARQUE

GREY KELPIE STUDIO

This book was written while I have suffered from Long Covid. This has impacted my ability to remember words, my ability to focus on a task is severely diminished, and it's also reduced the amount of time I've been able to work each day.

I dedicate this book to any of my readers similarly afflicted by Covid-19, Long Covid, ME, CFS or any chronic illness. This is for you.

A catalogue record for this book is available from the National Library of New Zealand.

Paperback 978-0-473-65099-5

Epub: 978-0-473-65101-8

Kindle: 978-0-473-65101-5

PREFACE

Content note:

This book contains polyamory/ multiple partners, references to previous death of parents, cutting and blood letting, violence and bullying (not between the main characters).

CHAPTER 1

JULY 1901

There was nothing that made one quite as disagreeable as waiting for something one wanted. And right that moment, Alistair felt very disagreeable indeed.

Alistair didn't think he'd ever been so nervous before, and it was making him extremely grumpy. He paced the halls of his late parents' country manor, waiting for his friends to arrive.

The house was dark and dusty and miserable. He'd thought it a charming enough residence before he knew any better. And while Misselthwaite was also terribly dark, it had become the sort of home Alistair had always dreamed off through his lonely childhood. It was after all, a place of friends, of interesting teachers, and access to more books than he could ever possibly read. He even had his own room to retreat to when it all became too overwhelming.

Although, perhaps he wouldn't need a room of his own in the coming term, if William made good on his promise to furnish his apartments to accommodate them all?

But he was getting ahead of himself. Well ahead of himself. He paused to examine his appearance in the mirror. His golden brown hair was brushed neatly enough, and tied with a new black ribbon. He had shaved that morning and managed to not nick his skin. However, his eyes looked too wide, too staring, and even with all the time in the Garden at Misselthwaite he was still unpleasantly pale. How he wished to tan the way Thomas did. His skin was always warm and beautiful looking.

Or to be blessed with Samal's perfectly golden complexion... now that would truly be something.

Instead he had to make do with what he was. Which was, to his own eye, rather off-putting.

Thankfully, they had seemed fond enough of him despite his obvious shortcomings. He had to trust that they wouldn't have suddenly changed their minds.

The university holiday was only two weeks, and he'd seen them not less than ten days before. The days since then had been busy, first travelling from Yorkshire to London, and then out to the countryside to check that the family house hadn't burned down in his absence. The skeleton staff had kept most of the rooms shut up. Although they had welcomed him back and cooked his meals, the large house felt horribly empty still.

Alistair had gone through his father's study for the first few days, finding precious little about his past in the magical world. He had hoped for... he hardly knew what.

A locked box perhaps? Stuffed with photographs of Alistair and his twin Ambrose as boys. Notes from magical research, newspaper clippings of the curse breaking successes, perhaps?

But there was nothing. If [Mr Lennox] had kept any records at all, they weren't in his study. Or perhaps he had kept them but they had all since been destroyed.

Alistair eyed the fireplace, a modest thing, which took up a part of one wall. Even the ashes had been swept away. He wondered, for a moment, if there was anything hidden up inside the chimney, as things were wont to be secreted away in mystery novels, it seemed entirely ridiculous, and hardly the kind of thing he ought to be doing if he wanted to make a good impression on his .. boyfriends? Lovers? Chosen soul mates for the rest of time?

Alistair sat down suddenly and wished for guidance.

The very idea that he could host them all here, in this huge house which felt nothing like a home any more, suddenly seemed like the worst possible thing he could have attempted. He didn't know how to run the house. The gardens here were pathetically boring, tailored lawns and lines of poplars, and barely anything even in the kitchen garden. He felt disconnected from the things which made him understand who he was, and he curled forward, cradling his face in his hands as tears flowed from his eyes.

"Ambrose, how I wish you hadn't died," he mumbled into his hands. Perhaps it was a good thing Ambrose wasn't here to see him, pathetic as he was being. He hadn't spoken to Ambrose at all since leaving Misselthwaite, and he missed the strange, ghostly presence almost as keenly as the company of his lovers.

He sighed, tired of his own dramatics, wiped his face and got to his feet. Collecting his journal and pen, he left the room.

He might as well wait for them in the parlour, so as to be close to hand when the coach arrived. Perhaps a cup of tea would soothe his frayed nerves a little.

There is perhaps something wrong with me and the way I think about things. I grew so accustomed to being in school with William, Samal and Thomas by my side at all times that now I mourn their absences. I had lived my entire life without them up to this point, and although I was lonely, I feel I was at least somewhat content.

Now, I feel dramatically bereft.

I know what I am missing out on. I know the joy and warmth of companionship and I miss it so terribly it's a constant ache. Although the servants are polite enough they are not companions.

Are others this much affected so quickly? Surely not. Surely there is some defect in my heart or mind that means I have formed too great an attachment?

Or, perhaps, it is simply that the lonely life I led previously made me extra voracious for the company of others?

Whatever it is, I am practically beside myself in anticipation of their arrival.

I fear this kind of clinginess, a need that seems disproportionate to any other need, is off-putting. That when I am reunited with them they will see that there is nothing special about me at all. That I am strange and unlikeable and they will leave me to enjoy each other's company instead.

CHAPTER 2

*A*listair was on his second cup of tea, reviewing the notes he'd made last term in History of Magic, when the approaching sound of horse's hooves roused him from his reverie.

He set the book down, carefully marking the page with a ribbon, and stood up to watch out the window. The coach pulled up outside the front door and the groom rushed out to assist as the door opened and first Samal and then Thomas stepped out.

It was as if they had brought the sunshine with them. The day had been dim and cloudy, uncharacteristically cold for summer, Alistair was sure, but now there seemed to be rays of light, warmth and the promise of a bright and mild evening. He couldn't help but smile, watching as Samal dusted off his trousers and looked around. Thomas was just behind him, speaking to the coach's driver, and laughing as he hopped nimbly down without using the steps. Samal was dressed in a simple but elegant pale beige suit, and Thomas more informally in brown trousers and a simple white shirt, but they both looked perfect to Alistair.

Alistair went into the main entranceway and out, unable to patiently wait indoors a second longer.

"Tom! Sam!" he cried. Walking was too slow, so he ran, slipping a little on the gravel but determined to get there. He hesitated then, suddenly worried that he'd read things wrong, and he's being too enthusiastic, when his friends maybe don't want him to be so effusive. His breath caught in his throat as he realised he had no real idea how to act around him.

Sam turned and smiled, stretched his arms out as if to catch him. "Alistair!"

Relieved, Alistair sped up again. He closed the distance between them to throw his arms around Samal's neck and kiss his cheeks, allowing Samal to lift him off his feet with the strength of his embrace. All his sense of hesitancy had gone and he let himself feel the way he felt. "I missed you so much!"

"I missed you too." Samal laughed under the barrage of kisses and then set him down.

Alistair turned immediately to Thomas and gave him the same treatment. Thomas laughed and kissed him back, his hand immediately going around Alistair's waist to pull him closer.

Alistair pulled back finally and smiled so wide his cheeks hurt. He hadn't been smiling much in the last few days, if at all.

"William's coming separately," Samal said. "He and his father were deep in some deadly serious conversation when we left. He said he'd take a later train."

Alistair nodded. He looked back at the door, realising too late how shabby and neglected the house looked, before summoning up the courage to invite them inside.

He cleared his throat. "Please, do come in." He felt oddly formal and stiff, gesturing for Samal and Thomas to go before him. "The house, it's been shut up, so it's not very impressive at the moment, I apologise."

"It's still impressive," Thomas said. His eyes were wide, looking around at the entranceway. "You could fit my family's whole cottage in here."

Alistair felt ashamed then, as if he were showing off his

family's wealth and prosperity, perhaps he was being crass. "Ah, I hadn't thought of that," he said.

Thomas smiled, as if nothing in the world could ever bother him. "It's very nice."

Alistair felt the knot of shame loosen a little as he watched Thomas's face. He genuinely wasn't bothered by the show of wealth. Alistair supposed perhaps it wasn't exactly a shock to Thomas, to see how large the country house was.

"Right, well, would you like to see your rooms first or shall we go to the parlour for tea?"

"Rooms?" Samal touched Alistair lightly on the shoulder. "I sort of expected we'd be rooming together."

"Oh?" Alistair felt off-footed all over again, but a swell of pleased anticipation rose in his chest. "I'd like that too, I just didn't want to make any assumptions of what this visit would be. I didn't want to- to presume."

"Presume away," Thomas said, blithely. He was examining the large portrait of Alistair's maternal grandparents. "I missed you, and I want to sleep in bed with you tonight, if that's all right with you."

Alistair blushed, looked around at the servants bringing in Thomas and Samal's travel things, but they didn't respond in any way.

"Right, wonderful," he said. "Then uh, let's go to the parlour and have afternoon tea and you can tell me about what you've been up to."

The servants brought hot scones, butter, jam and whipped cream to go with the tea. Alstair hadn't felt particularly hungry before, he found himself ravenous now that his friends were present.

He was also grateful for how he didn't have to talk while he was eating. He was able to leave the bulk of the conversation to Thomas. Thomas told them about his week at home, helping with his younger siblings, doing chores around the cottage and assisting in his mother's garden.

It was pleasant to listen to and Alistair felt himself relaxing, imagining the cottage, and feeling vaguely guilty that he'd never asked if he could visit it.

Samal, as was his tendency, didn't say much. He watched Thomas and Alistair with a soft gaze and sipped his tea.

The afternoon passed in what felt like a moment, and soon enough night was falling. They were sitting down to dinner when William's coach arrived. He smiled wanly as he walked into the dining room. He was dressed elegantly in a charcoal suit with a black and silver brocade waistcoat under it. His travelling cape was presumably already being brushed down and hung for him.

"Evening, all."

"William! You're here!" Alistair leapt to his feet, again feeling the pressure to host correctly, although he wasn't sure he knew how to. "How was your journey? Was it pleasant? I hope it was pleasant, please have a seat. Have you eaten already?"

William waved his hand and sat in an empty chair with a place setting laid out. "I'm all right, please relax."

Alistair sat down again, his cheeks warming. "Sorry, quite."

"The journey was fine," William said. "I had a private cabin and it was perfectly pleasant."

Food was served, large platters of mashed potatoes, a side of ham and plenty of green vegetables and dinner rolls at Alistair's request. He thanked the servants as his guests helped themselves.

Alistair relaxed slowly. It was like being reminded what it felt like to have friends, as if just a week on his own had been enough for him to forget. He had gone back to his old self, and now he was relearning how to relate to people.

The four of them got more lively as the evening went on and

the servants brought out a wonderful dessert of Victoria sponge cake and the four relaxed into each other's company.

$\mathcal{W}$hen it was time to retire, Alistair led them to his room. He hadn't learned the spell to enlarge the bed, so he and Thomas moved the side tables while William and Samal wove the spell together. It was strange to watch, Alistair stood back, holding his journal to his chest. This was the bed he had slept in for his entire life before Misselthwaite. There were so many memories of it, and now it was being changed to something new, more adult, to accommodate his lovers. He felt uncomfortably grown up, suddenly. Uncertain of what it meant for who he was, or if it had to mean anything at all.

"Are you all right?" Thomas asked, sidling up to him. At some point over dinner Thomas had partially shifted form so he had fox ears and a tail. It was so endearing to Alistair that he put his arm around him and pulled him close without thinking.

"I don't know," Alistair said. "I'm not unwell, just feeling sort of..." he searched for the word. "Uncertain. Nostalgic for something I don't even really miss."

Thomas nuzzled into Alistair's neck, the tips of his pointy ears tickling Alistair's chin and making him smile. "That's to be expected. Things are different, now, after all."

"They are, indeed."

William and Samal finished the spell on the bed. Thomas and Alistair changed into night things, and climbed inside. In a moment Alistair was engulfed in limbs and the warmth of bodies.

"You can talk to us about what you're feeling," Samal said. "If you want to."

Alistair shook his head. "There's not a lot to say. I spent some time in my father's study, trying to find any records or things, something that might explain why they concealed magic from me, why they cursed me. But he doesn't seem to have kept anything anywhere I can find it. Perhaps he burned it all?"

"Or he hid it under a floorboard," William said. Alistair blinked at him.

"Why would he hide anything under a floorboard?"

"I don't know," William said. "But it's a jolly good place to hide things. No one ever thinks to look at the floor, let alone under it."

There was silence as they all considered this for a moment. Then Alistair made a move to leave the bed but was prevented by several hands pressing him down.

"You can look in the morning," Samal said. "We're in the middle of a reunion right now."

"Hmm," Alistair grumbled, but he didn't really mean it.

Samal's hand tugged the ribbon out of Alistair's hair and then he was combing his fingers through it. Alistair felt the tension he'd been holding in his neck and shoulders for the last two weeks ebb away.

"So, what did you all miss the most about me?" William asked.

Thomas laughed softly.

"Did you really just ask that?" Alistair said. He raised an eyebrow. "You can't just ask things like that."

"Of course I can," William said. "This is a reunion, and I missed all of you. No one has doted on me for ten days and I have been lonely. Tell me you missed me, too."

Samal paused in his combing of Alistair's hair and Alistair huffed. "Fine. Of course I missed you," he said.

"Yes, but what did you miss *the most*?" William pressed. "For example, I believe I missed Alistair's gentle and tactful way of speaking."

Alistair suspected he was being made fun of, so he stuck his tongue out at William. "I expect then, it won't be a surprise to hear that what I missed the most was the dinner rolls at Misselthwaite."

William pressed a hand to his chest, mock-outraged. "What about the roast duck?"

Thomas laughed and flopped across the laps of the other three. "I prefer the sweet potatoes, myself."

Alistair reached out to rub at one of Thomas's fox ears. He felt a surge of affection for all three of them, so relieved to be able to joke and laugh and cuddle in this way. "I did miss all of you," he said, softer this time.

Samal left off playing with his hair and tugged him in closer by one arm, pressing his back to Sama's chest. Alistair reached out to William and pulled him in. The affection made him feel bold and a little giddy. "I missed your handsome face," he said, looking William in the eye.

William stopped pretending to pout and preened instead. "That must have been terribly difficult for you."

"Oh it was," Samal said. "I too suffered from the lack of staring at your face."

"Of course you did," William sniffed. He sat up, shuffled around on the bed and faced all three of them. "I shall graciously allow you to gaze upon me now. Please make the most of it."

Thomas turned fully into a fox and leapt onto William's chest, tackling him backwards. Alistair and Samal joined the fray, tickling William's sides. He squirmed, trying to get away, but they were all laughing too hard.

CHAPTER 3

*A*listair slept better that night than he had since leaving Misselthwaite and he woke up warm and feeling safe. He didn't feel the aching loneliness that he realised had dogged his days, and instead felt gloriously at home.

They had a pleasant breakfast in the parlour, overlooking the house's gardens such as they were, and then the conversation turned to what they should do with the day.

"I'd like to have a look at the grounds," Thomas said. "But I don't really mind what we do."

"There's not much to see on the grounds," Alistair said. Unable to keep the glumness from his voice. "It's boring. I want to make it into a proper garden, but there's hardly time for such a large project. Even with magic."

"Best left until the long holidays over Summer," Samal said, nodding.

"I wanted to check under the floorboards of Father's study..." Alistair remembered suddenly.

"Right you are." William nodded. "There's a project which should take up a good portion of the day."

So, they finished off eating and made their way up to Mr Lennox's study. It seemed smaller with all four of them in it.

Thomas abruptly shifted into his dog form and started a thorough sniffing of the floor, starting in the corner nearest the door and working his way out.

"The rug will need to be moved, to start with," William said.

Samal crouched to roll the corner of the dusty Persian rug and Alistair knelt down to help, sneezing as the dust got to his nose.

Together they rolled the rug up and moved it to the hallway. The floorboards looked perfectly ordinary and unimpressive, and Alistair felt a sudden pang of guilt.

What was he doing? Defiling his father's sanctuary just to satisfy his own curiosity? It felt ghoulish... his parents. He hadn't been close to them, especially not his father, but they were the only parents that he had.

Perhaps he should let it be. If his father had hidden things, then perhaps there was a good reason for it. Perhaps they should let sleeping dogs lie. But there were still so many mysteries unsolved.

William looked behind the picture frames then started pulling books out at random from the bookcase to look behind the.

Samal was at the desk, looking through the papers.

Thomas the dog was sniffing the floorboards which had just been revealed.

Alistair opened his mouth to tell them all to stop when Thomas wuffed and sat down. He thumped his tail against the floor, sending up puffs of dust.

"You found something?" Alistair's misgivings all vanished in the face of a possible discovery.

Thomas wuffed again and tapped a floorboard with his front paw.

Samal and William both left off what they were doing to watch as Alistair knelt next to Thomas and felt around the edges of the floorboard he had tapped. It looked just like the others, except perhaps, now that he was closer to it, there was the slightest discolouration in the finish of the wood. It was worn at the corners, as if it had been handled.

His fingers slipped under a hidden finger hold in the wood and he lifted, feeling a faint echo of magic lift as the board lifted. His nose picked up the faint hint of his father's favoured brand of tobacco.

William helped him remove the floorboard and the one beside it. Underneath was the sort of treasure trove Alistair had read about uncovering in numerous mystery novels. He started lifting the things out. The others didn't touch any of the items until Alistair had examined them and handed them on and Alistair appreciated the gesture of respect.

On top were stacks of papers tied with string.

"These look important," he said, and handed them to William. Underneath was a shoebox, when the dusty lid was removed it was revealed to be filled with letters, filed upright, and filling the box. Alistair pulled out the first one, and quickly skimmed the contents. It was a letter asking for the curse-breaking twins' assistance with something.

A hard lump formed in Alistair's throat, but he ignored it. "This is correspondence asking my parents for help with a possession curse," he said. He rifled through the rest of the letters - each had a different sender, and each seemed to be requesting the same thing. There had been such a need for curse breaking... Was it still the case now? Had any other curse breakers filled the void which had opened when the Lennoxes left magical society?

"So many requests," Samal said, echoing Alistair's thoughts. "It must have been hard for them to resist."

"I don't think we'll find anything useful here," Alistair said. His voice sounded strained. Thomas had turned back into his human form, and commenced rubbing his hand in wide circles on Alistair's back.

He sorted through the letters, flipping each over and checking the return address, meaningless names. He had no idea what he thought he was looking for, until he saw the name "Birch" on the back of one letter.

"Look at this," he said. "A letter from a Birch."

"Read it out, Allie," Thomas said. "It's probably important."

Alistair nodded, and realised his hands were trembling ever so slightly, as he unfolded and smoothed the paper. He cleared his throat and read aloud.

"*D**ear Mr. and Mrs. Lennox,*
I hope this letter finds you well.

It was truly delightful to meet you at dinner with the Bazines, I admit to being truly charmed by your company, it was a lovely evening.

I am writing to you now in the hopes you may grant us a favour. Our youngest child Elmer has inadvertently cursed himself on a visit to a haunted house with some of his friends. Although the others seem to have been able to shake off their afflictions or otherwise walk away unscathed, we are concerned that the curse on Elmer appears to be worsening. My husband and I have tried various spells and counter-curses ourselves but it is resilient to all attempts.

Please, I know you have a busy schedule, but I am requesting that you visit and take a look at Elmer's case.

We would, of course, be able to compensate you generously for your time.

Yours in anticipation of a favourable response,

Viscountess Alice Birch and her honourable husband Viscount Birch

.   .   .

"Well," Samal said. "That certainly answers something."

"What's the date on the letter?" William asked, frowning.

Alistair read it out and realised with horror how close it was to the date of his brother's death. "They must never have answered," he said, slowly.

"They had their own family tragedy to attend to," Thomas said, softly. He moved closer to Alistair and leaned against his shoulder, warm and solid.

"The Birches may have still hoped they'd send Alistair..." William said. "But after an event like that." He sighed. "I'm sorry, Alistair. If it hadn't been for me and my awful-"

"William, none of this is your fault," Alistair said, quickly. His voice sounded rather dull and flat. He was still processing the idea that Eulalia, Eleanor and Everett had tried to kill him because of... because of what? Because his parents hadn't answered a request?

"Did Elmer live?" Alisair asked. "Elmer Birch?"

"I've never heard of him," William said. "He has certainly never been to Misselthwaite, and if the others attended, I'd assume he would have as well."

Alistair frowned, read over the letter again and then folded it back into its envelope.

"I suppose we'd need to check the records, the family registry books at the library would tell us," Samal said. "But I think the assumption that he didn't make it might be accurate. It would explain the Birches being bitches to you."

"I suppose it would." Alistair stowed the letter in his chest pocket.

"What kind of language is that?" William asked, looking severely at Samal.

Samal shrugged. "It's accurate."

Alistair's head suddenly felt heavy and sore and his hand went to his forehead.

"Perhaps it's time to knock off the investigation," Thomas said. Alistair hadn't seen him change back to his human form, but the frim hand on his elbow hauled him to standing. "Let's rest, have something to eat."

"Yes," Samal said. He replaced the items into the nook under the floorboards and slid the board back into place. "This was a lot to learn all at once."

"With my parents being the way they were," Alistair said. His words were sluggish, but he persevered. "Do I have any chance of being successful? What if it's in my blood to simply run as soon as things get hard?"

"I think you've already proved that's not the case," William said.

"I don't think you care as much about what society thinks as your parents seemed to," Samal added.

"And just because they're your parents doesn't mean you'll be exactly like them." Thomas urged Alistair out of the study with a firm hand. "You are you, and you can choose how you act and react. Look at William, he's not exactly like his father."

"That might be a poor example," Samal said. William kicked him in the shins.

"I suppose you're right." Alistair reflected that he had thought he knew his parents but he had been so surprised by so many things since they'd passed. His friends, his lovers' words were something of a comfort, but it wasn't enough to convince him.

Alistair's head pounded until he went for a nap in the afternoon, and the rest of the evening was rather subdued.

CHAPTER 4

*T*he next day William made a suggestion as they finished up their breakfast of bacon, eggs and fried slices of potato.

"How about we head into London and get some shopping done?" William said. "I have some things I need to pick up before the new term, and honestly, Alistair, when was the last time you purchased new clothing?"

Alistair looked down at what he was wearing. It was a serviceable if plain charcoal suit he'd had a few years, with a white linen shirt which was, admittedly, purloined from his father's wardrobe. But it was in fine condition.

He felt somewhat caught out by William's question though, and felt his cheek warming.

"I... I can't recall. Mother didn't often take me, and usually I'd wear Father's old things, or the tailor would come to us..."

"That settles it," William said. He wiped his mouth delicately with a napkin and folded it on the breakfast tray. "We'll go shopping."

"The only issue is," Alistair said, slowly. "I don't have access to any spending money beyond what's used for the house's upkeep. The university is all paid for already, I don't... it's all locked until I complete a year of study, and it's barely been one term."

"I'll pay," William said. He waved his hand, indicating all three of them. "I'll pay for anything any of you want. We have a lot of family money and I haven't spent hardly any of it since I've been sick. And Father, well, he travels a fair bit but there's plenty of money coming in from tuition and alumni donations."

"There's really no need for that," Samal said, stiffly. "I can pay my own way."

Thomas looked steadfastly down at his breakfast tray. Alistair knew that Thomas didn't have any of the family wealth or privilege the rest of them had. He probably also didn't have new clothes very often, and an opportunity like this would be invaluable for him. If Alistair refused, then Thomas's honour would mean he had to refuse as well.

Alistair wanted Thomas to have nice new things. Far more than he wanted anything for himself, he wanted it for Thomas. He had to agree if he wanted this for Thomas.

So, Alistair swallowed his own pride and cleared his throat.

"That's very decent of you, William. I'd be happy to accept." Thomas looked up, a fleeting hopeful look which turned into a warm smile when he saw Alistair watching him. Alistair didn't know if Thomas had guessed the reason he'd agreed but either way, Alistair felt good, as if he'd done him a favour.

They took William's coach into London, trunks and suitcases loaded on top with the plan to move into the Lennox townhouse until it was time to return to Misselthwaite.

William seemed very comfortable taking control of the itinerary for the day and took them first to visit a tailor down a dingy side-street.

"I'd have thought you'd be one to stick entirely to High Street," Samal said. He was walking in the back of the group, in what Alistair had come to think of as his protective position, keeping watch over all of them.

William shrugged. "Father has been visiting this store for a long time, it gets passed down from parent to child and so on, and the quality of craft cannot be beaten. However, their range is rather limited." He led them to a small, unassuming looking shop front which seemed to shimmer slightly as Alistair looked at it. The paint was peeling, a sort of warm mid-green, and there was a faded sign lettered above the front door. *Fortescue's dress fitting and clothing repairs.*

"Fortescue's? Is it a magical tailor?" Alistair asked, feeling rather foolish as he said those words together.

William paused outside the window. The window itself gave away nothing of what was inside, being so dingy and grimy that Alistair could barely make out the shapes of the shelves.

"Indeed," William said. "They weave spells into everything they make, it does make it rather time consuming and that's why they charge more, but it's absolutely worth every penny. My favourite travelling cape is from here."

"Oh," Alistair said. "That cape is very impressive." Privately, Alistair thought the cape made him look just a little ostentatious, but then, that did seem to be William's aim a lot of the time. At least it suited him. And he did find William impressive when he wore it.

"Indeed." William brushed an imaginary piece of dust off the front of his suit jacket and led the way into the shop.

Inside, Alistair didn't immediately see any difference between this and any other clothier. But there was something about the bell over the door's tinkling that seemed to linger in the ear, an extra resonance, perhaps.

The walls of the shop were papered in a slightly dated blue and cream stripe, but here and there Alistair could discern tiny runes sketched alongside the stripes. There was a large wide desk at the far end of the shop, which was covered with an unrolled bolt of fabric and a woman stood at it, using shears to cut around a paper pattern piece. She looked up when the young men filed in.

"Young master Carlisle!" She exclaimed. She set her shears down and patted her hair. She didn't look as young as a student, but Alistair thought she couldn't have been more than thirty. She had a warm face, and sparkling eyes. "It's been some time since I've seen you, and you've brought friends? How unusual."

"Hello Wilhelmina," William said. His voice had a warmth to it that Alistair seldom heard in public. "I'm sorry, I was sick for a time, but hopefully those days are largely behind me now."

"Well, that is excellent news," she said. Wilhelmina walked out from behind the desk and gave him a critical look up and down. "Indeed, you're looking very well. Aren't you going to introduce me to your friends?"

"Of course," William turned, a little flushed, and gestured to them each in turn. "This is Alistair Lennox, Samal Bancroft-Dalton and Thomas Sowersby. They're all students at Misselthwaite with me. Boys, this is Wilhelmina Fortescue."

"It's a pleasure," Samal said, bowing a little from the waist.

"Yes, a pleasure," Alistair said.

"Lennox here has never been to a magical tailor before." William slipped an arm around Alistair and coaxed him forward. "And he's rather likely to get into trouble if he's not careful, so I was wondering if you might have something suitable, I was thinking of a general protective ward kind of thing."

"Hmm." Wilhelmina looked at Alistair with an even more critical eye than she'd cast over William. Alistair felt suddenly exposed, and had to suppress the urge to turn and hide his face against William's chest.

"With those eyes, I think he'd suit the jacket I finished last week perfectly." She turned on her heel, skirt swirling, and went to one of the long rails which lined the walls, sorted through some jackets and pulled down a fine dark blue brocade. To

Alistair, he imagined it was the colour of the ocean after a storm. He had never seen the ocean, but he had read about it in books.

It was finer than anything else he owned, and he wasn't at all sure he would suit it, but he did desperately want to try.

She handed him the jacket and nodded to a curtain in the corner. "You can change into it there, if you'd like a little privacy."

Alistair smiled, pleased she'd guessed correctly, and hurried into the curtained off space to shrug off his woollen charcoal jacket and pull on the beautiful brocade. It slid on sweet and easy, and fit as if it had been made precisely for him. There was a murky looking glass hanging on the wall and Alistair turned this way and that, admiring himself.

Perhaps he wasn't as off-putting looking as he'd feared, or perhaps some of the jacket's magic was to make its wearer look a little more handsome? Either way he decided he liked what he saw, and he wanted the jacket.

"Well, are you going to show us how it looks?" William called.

Alistair pulled the curtain back and stepped back out into the store proper. William nodded with approval. Samal's eyes opened wide and he started to smile, and Thomas made a soft low whistle. Alistair felt his cheeks warming.

"Ach, yes, perfect," Wilhelmina said. She tugged the shoulder on the right hand side to make sure it was sitting correctly, and smiled. "Just a perfect fit, and the colour. The sizing for this one, in fact everything about it came to me in a dream, so I expected something in the universe knew that you'd be coming in and sent me directions."

"How do you like it?" William asked, before Alistair could respond to that.

Alistair swallowed and nodded. "I like it very much."

"Excellent. Then please add it to the tab, Wilhelmina," he said. "Now, Sowersby needs something fine to wear to dinner occasions." He turned to Thomas who all but shrank back from the sudden attention.

The next hour passed in this way, with each of them picking out something from Wilhelmina's stock and finding that it fit perfectly, or just so happened to complement their skin tone or the colour of their hair.

"It's a very specific sort of magic isn't it?" Alistair said, as Samal tried on a pale beige suit which hugged his figure in a very lovely way.

"Mm, fibre arts," Wilhelmina said. "Family gift. For the longest time it wasn't recognised as a true form of magic, although it's nothing near as dangerous as blood magic or void summoning."

Alistair blinked and made a mental note to look up those types of magic when they got back to Misselthwaite University. He didn't think he'd ever heard either of them before.

"I'm glad it's recognised now," William said. "My family has enjoyed the benefits for generations. You ought to be world-renowned!"

Wilhelmina laughed a little, caught Alistair's gaze and rolled her eyes affectionately. "The Carlisles have always been too kind to us."

When they were all outfitted, William paid for the entire tab, Wilhelmina wrapped their purchases, and then they were off to High Street. Alistair quickly tired of William's shopping style, which seemed to be to try absolutely everything he liked on, deliberate for a time and then eventually buy almost all of it anyway. They seemed to trail up and down the shopping district for hours, and his feet were getting sore.

"Are we nearly done?" he asked, finally.

"Are you bored?" William sounded genuinely surprised. Alistair nodded.

"I'm getting a bit bored of carrying all these bags," Samal said. "Couldn't we have them sent back to the house?"

"But half the fun is carrying bags of the things you've purchased," William said.

"I do note that you are carrying only the bag with cufflinks in it." Samal looked pointedly at William's hand.

"It's still a bag," William said. He shrugged and looked back at Alistair. "Well, we can go to dinner, unless there's something in particular you'd like that we haven't seen yet?"

Alistair thought for a moment, thought of the pairs of trousers he had ruined in the previous term kneeling in the garden, and how he'd had to learn a dirt removal spell just to try and salvage them. And even then it hadn't really worked.

"Gardening clothes!" he exclaimed. "Something sturdy, that will withstand the mud and so on. Like Professor Weatherstaff wears."

Thomas chuckled. William simply stared at Alistair, his mouth a thin line.

"We're on High Street," William said, slowly. His tone clipped. "All the best fashion houses have stores here. You can buy anything at all, the finest linens, cotton imported from Egypt, the cutting edge fashions from Paris, wigs, designer shoes, anything at all. And you want to dress like the school gardener."

"He's also a professor." Alistair lifted his chin and stared into William's eyes, refusing to be ashamed.

"Fine, the professor of gardening." William scoffed and rolled his eyes. "I don't think anyone sells *that* kind of clothing."

"Didn't you just say I can buy anything at all?" Alistair asked.

"I think I know a place," Thomas piped up. "But it's a couple of blocks away."

"Fine," William said. He sighed, as if they were asking him a huge favour but he waved his hand to indicate Thomas should lead on.

And so they visited rather more practical clothiers and

Alistair got himself a pair of sturdy overalls and a few other things to wear while in the garden.

William sighed, but still picked up a pair of heavy gloves for pulling weeds and a broad brimmed straw hat.

They loaded their purchases into the coach and rode a few blocks up the Strand to dine at the restaurant of one of the high end hotels there. The sign said "The Savoy."

CHAPTER 5

*T*he restaurant at the Savoy was beautiful. The kind of place Alistair imagined his parents must have frequented when they were still alive. He wondered if they had ever eaten here, met up with friends, or clients. He felt the shadow of them hanging over him, and he tried to shake it off.

The tables were spaced out so that it gave the air of privacy. They were seen to a table near the back of the restaurant, and William ordered a bottle of Chablis to arrive with their first course.

Once the wine had been poured into each of their glasses, William lifted his. "I'd like to propose a toast."

It all made Alistair feel rather more grown up than he had ever felt before. He lifted his glass, mimicking William.

"What are we toasting to?" Samal asked. "That we all survived a shopping trip with you?"

"We are toasting to our joyful reunion," William said. He appeared to have ignored Samal's jibe, but Alistair saw a vein twitching on his temple. "To the four of us being together again and for the foreseeable future, and in fact-"

"To friends!" Thomas cut in. He reached his glass against the table and tapped it against Alistair's. Alistair clinked his against Samal's and Williams, and then took a generous gulp of it. He hadn't tasted wine since his mother had last given him a drink at dinner. That was back before she'd died, months ago now.

He wondered at the crisp taste of it, which was at once familiar from previous tastes, and different. This wine was fruity to be sure, but it had a bitter taste as well. He wasn't entirely sure he enjoyed the first taste, but he took another sip all the same.

"To friends," Alistair said and drank again. The wine taste seemed to grow on him. Samal, he realised, had only allowed the waiter to pour him a small wine, barely half the glass. Alistair wondered about that. Perhaps, he speculated, that it had something to do with his angelic side. Perhaps he wasn't supposed to drink alcohol in case it wasn't pure enough?

But then, he hadn't been at all shy when it came to the more lascivious activities the four of them got up to sometimes, so perhaps it didn't have anything to do with sin.

"What is it, Allie?" Samal had caught him staring.

"They give everyone red wine at Catholic Mass," he said. As if they had been in the middle of a discussion about wine. It seemed as if he had little control over his tongue all of a sudden.

"Yes, I suppose they do," William said. His tone was dry.

"So you really needn't worry about it." Alistair patted Samal's hand.

"What are you on about?" Thomas asked, laughing a little.

Alistair smiled at him, feeling a warm wave of affection for him. "Sam's not less holy for drinking wine."

There was a short silence at the table, and then Samal started to laugh. "Oh, Allie."

William's laugh was less free, more of a suppressed chuckle, but his eyes were dancing.

"Oh, I see. Well, it should be even better to know that this is Italian wine, then," he said. "Practically from the Vatican."

"That *is* excellent news," Alistair squeezed Samal's hand. He wasn't entirely sure why they were all looking at him with such amusement. "Now you may drink up, Sammy."

"I simply... don't particularly care for the taste of wine," Samal said. "But I appreciate your concern."

Alistair nodded and poured himself some more wine from the bottle which had been left on the table. William deftly removed the bottle from his hand. "Perhaps you ought to have some water before you drink more wine, my dear."

Alistair had a sudden horrible flash back to the night he had first met William. He had drunk too much beer at a public house, and then embarrassed himself on the street. He certainly didn't want to repeat that mistake.

Alistair's cheeks were already flushed from the wine and now from the unusual term of endearment from William. He folded his hands in his lap and nodded. He was horribly aware of how little experience he had in being in society circles. He didn't want to embarrass his friends with sloppy behaviour, not when William had bought him so many things that day, and the dinner promised to be so good.

"All right."

The waiters soon brought their meals and the four of them relaxed into easy banter. The wine which had somewhat clouded Alistair's mind was abandoned and he stuck to water for the rest of the night, feeling a certain amount of relief when he felt the wine's effects lessening.

It was enough just to be there, eating good food in London with his dearest friends, the people he cared most for in the world. He felt at peace.

CHAPTER 6

They spent a pleasant few days in London, staying at Alistair's townhouse. Some days they stayed in and talked, or read books, or played cards. Some days they took in the sights, the British Museum and the National Gallery, lunching at fine restaurants with William always paying their way. Finally, it was time to pack up and return to University.

The train ride out to Yorkshire was far more pleasant than the last time Alistair had taken it. The previous time had of course been fast on the heels of his parents' funerals. It had been a real shock to his system, a change in life. Besides that, it was the middle of the school term, and the train had been largely empty.

Now the train was busy with students returning from the Summer break. The train felt packed to the gills, and Alistair was glad that William had a private compartment reserved that was large enough for all four of them. The sheer volume of students laughing, trying small spells and exchanging gossip was enough to give him a headache, but the compartment's door thankfully muffled enough of the sound.

They passed the time alternately playing cards together or

resting quietly. Alistair read one of the novels he'd managed to convince William to buy for him at the newsstand at London station.

They were most of the way to the school when William brought up a serious subject.

"You've all chosen your directions of study already, I presume," he said. His voice was artfully bored, which Alistair knew meant he was trying to pretend he didn't care as much as he did. "Father has begun to pressure me to settle on something."

"Haven't you been at university for years and years?" Thomas asked. "I'd have thought you'd know."

"Well, with all the interruptions and so on, I haven't actually settled on any one major." William shrugged. "But now I can focus my energies and complete a degree, finally."

Thomas looked a little worried that he'd crossed a line, but William didn't seem to be vexed.

"Mine's rather obvious," Thomas said. "There are so many possible forms I could learn, and each of them has their own particular set of complications. So I definitely want to focus on shape-shifting. Mind you, I do love Botany, so of course I'll still take classes in that as well."

Alistair was pleased to know that he'd still have Thomas as a partner in the Greenhouse.

"Mine is fairly self-evident as well," Samal said. "Healing is in my blood, and I couldn't ignore it. Besides, I've started to think I want to be a nurse, for my career."

That startled Alistair.

"A nurse? I had expected that if you were entering the medical profession it would be to become a doctor."

Samal shrugged and smiled. "Well, with my gift I'm sure I'll do something of both, and I won't go through mundane medical school, or work in a public hospital. But lately I've felt a pull towards nursing. Nurses, well, they have more time with the patients, they get to follow through the course of care and get to know people more than a doctor does."

"Odd," Alistair said. "You barely spoke three words to me when we first met. I didn't think you would be the kind of person who wanted such a person-centric job."

Samal sighed, slipped his arm around Alistair and pulled him close. Alistair suspected he'd been a little too blunt, again. He wondered if there was a way he could learn how to speak in a kinder way. Stop accidentally upsetting people with his words.

"Maybe that was because I was shy of you," he said. "And confused by how drawn to you I felt. I'm less shy around you now, and it's all your fault."

He leaned in and licked Alistair's earlobe, making him startle and then laugh at how it tickled. It also utterly distracted Alistair from his ponderings.

William's gaze, when Alistair looked back at him, was a curious mix of desire and amusement. It sent a delightful thrill down Alistair's spine.

"And what about you, Allie?" William asked.

"Curse Breaking and Botany," Alistair said, without thinking. "It's just obvious, really. Those are the two things I have talent for. And, well, I love botany and I suppose I like the puzzle of curse breaking well enough."

"I should say you do," Thomas said. "We had to drag you away from it and force you to dinner a few times last term."

"And we know how much you love dinner, especially the rolls," William teased.

Alistair's cheeks warmed again but he knew they were simply teasing him and didn't mean anything malicious by it. He hoped that would always be the case. He had felt out of sorts now and again ever since discovering the letters in his father's study. As if his family legacy would inevitably be upset and exile from magical society. He tried not to dwell on it, and instead turned the question back on William.

"So, William, what do you think your specialised study will be?"

William shrugged and sighed, tilting his head back. "Perhaps I'll look into divination, but I'm sure Father would prefer I choose something that's well, impressive to boast about to his friends. Not that he really *has* friends, but he likes for the family name to be upheld and all of that tosh."

"Is divination not impressive?" Alistair asked.

Samal tilted his head first one way and then the other. "It's impressive enough if the person has a talent for it, but a lot of it, well, the mundane society makes plenty of shows of it, and I supoose that makes it less desirable for those who prize magic above all else."

Alistair leaned closer into Samal's side, although it was a hot late Summer day, there was nothing as comforting as being under his wing. Even if his wings were currently hidden.

"Thankfully Misselthwaite is largely free from the people who think that way," Thomas said. "I mean, there are obviously still some who would wish I wasn't there, but the worst ones are gone." He leaned back in the seat opposite Alistair and crossed his legs.

"Father's no tolerance of bullying policy has done a lot of good for the school and for the larger community," William said. "But wider society... well, there's still plenty that can be looked down on. Some talents aren't even allowed to be used."

That was news to Alistair as well. "What sort of talents? Like the void summoning thing you mentioned, before?"

"Yes, that's one of them. It's simply too dangerous." William tipped his head back. "I suppose allure is a big one, people have used it for all sorts of terrible things, making others into slaves and so on. Same with blood magic, it's simply too powerful to be able to control another with magic."

"Necromancy as well," Thomas said. "There's not much good that can come from raising the dead."

Thomas's fox ears had poked out of his hair again, some time during the conversation and William reached over to scratch them absently.

"But that's why none of it is taught at Misselthwaite, and those who break the rules are banned," Samal said.

Alistair felt something unpleasant in his stomach, this talking around something that they were doing. "The Birches, they won't be able to come back to Misselthwaite, isn't that correct?"

"Correct," William said. "Father set many spells on the ground when he first opened it up as a college, wards against innocent mundanes walking in, protection for those within the grounds from wars and suchlike. When a student is expelled, their magical imprint is added to the wards."

Alistair nodded, thinking of the pure hatred Eulalia, Eleanor and Everett had shown him, based on his name and his family history. "Even though Everett is a shapeshifter? He could just choose to look like someone else couldn't he?"

William shook his head. "The spell would know. Just as it knows to protect Thomas in his fox form, or Sam in his angelic one. It would see the essence of his magic and know he was barred."

Alistair took a slow breath and let it out slowly, feeling some of the unpleasant twisting in his stomach ease off. "That's good to know."

Thomas made a dreamy sound and flopped over William's lap, smiling. William's ear scratches had apparently hit the correct place.

"So, nothing to worry about this term except for school work, breaking William's curse once and for all and keeping the Secret Garden a secret then." Alistair said. He counted them off on his fingers.

Samal squeezed him a little, leaned in and kissed the top of his head. "Well, one more thing. If you want to keep using the same dining table, we probably need to snag it as soon as possible," he said.

"Of course I do," Alistair said. "That's *our* table."

"The new students won't know or care," William said. "But we can go to dinner early just to be sure."

"How many new students are there?" Thomas asked, his words distorted as he yawned around them.

"I think just a handful. It's not technically the new school year. There will be a far larger influx in August."

Alistair pulled a face. He had barely got used to the faces he knew at Misselthwaite, and now there'd be more of them? He hoped they weren't awful.

He also hoped none of them had heard of the Lennoxes.

*W*hen they arrived at the station they piled into the coaches the school had provided and made the way up into the moors.

They passed through the small village of Misselthwaite, and started on the winding road up to the grand old house.

Alistair watched out the window, not for the view of Misselthwaite Manor itself, but for the gardens. The walled gardens were around the back of the building, so there was no chance at all that he'd be able to see *his* garden, but there were still pleasant gardens and trees in the front.

Misselthwaite loomed as ominous as ever. The window shutters all open, under the bright summer sun, but somehow the aspect of the house was dim and gloomy as if it were the middle of winter.

All the same, it sparked hope and excitement in Alistair's chest. This was the place where all the good things in his life had come to him. Magic, his ghostly brother, his friends and lovers... all the things he'd been missing during the break.

The number one thing Alistair wanted to do on return to school was make his way straight to the Secret Garden, to check on how the plants had fared in his absence. What had sprouted? What had bloomed? The questions were forefront in his mind.

However, as they disembarked from the coach things didn't go according to that plan. William was met by Medlock at the door, and whisked away to a private audience with his father. Thomas and Samal had to wait in line to see Professor Barlow about some class changes.

For his part, Alistair had to join a line of students at a temporary registration desk in the main hall, to ensure his bags were sent up to the correct room. The other students in the line with him were returning students confirming their room numbers and collecting keys, or new students being issued room assignments and keys for the first time.

The wait seemed to take hours. Alistair shifted his weight from foot to foot, wishing as hard as he could that this would be over with. He found he kept glancing over his shoulder towards the back way out of the building, and the way down to the gardens. How could this be taking so much time?

Perhaps he ought to go to the garden first, and then return to sort out his luggage and so on? Only, he didn't know what would happen to his bags, or those of Thomas and Samal, if he didn't stay in line and confirm they would all be rooming with William for the term.

What if the bags were sent away again? Or left in the huge pile outside for when it inevitably started to rain?

Alistair suppressed a groan of annoyance and looked to the front of the queue. The person standing at the front was a short girl with long hair and a strange pointy little hat perched on top, that seemed to be fussing over something.

Alistair made an impatient noise, and the person in the line directly in front of him turned to him with a sympathetic look.

"It's taking a while isn't it?"

"Rather a lot of a while," Alistair said. He eyed the other person. He didn't think he recognised him. He was tall and thin, and his jaw seemed a little too big for him. His head craned forward and down, as if he were aware of how awkwardly tall he was and was trying to make up for it.

"I'm Alexander," he said. He stuck out a large hand for Alistair, who took it somewhat reluctantly and shook it. "Alexander DeStafano."

"Alistair Lennox," he said.

"Is it your first term here?"

"No, my second," Alistair said. He decided to try and make an effort to be polite. "I'm studying botany and curse breaking."

"Lennox, curse breaking, yes, that makes sense," Alexander said. "I'm hoping to hone my skill in potions making."

"You've heard of my parents?" Alistair said. Perhaps being polite wouldn't be the best idea after all. He looked past Alexander and saw that the line had moved up, and Alexander hadn't noticed because he was talking to him. "You can move up now."

"Right."

Alexander stepped forward and so did Alistair. Alexander, undeterred, looked all around the grand entrance. "Look at that chandelier. It's an antique, you can tell from the design, but it's in such exquisite repair."

"I expect the household staff have spells to facilitate the ease of cleaning it," Alistair said. He felt incredibly awkward, although Alexander hadn't said anything rude about his being a Lennox. He seemed to be trying to be polite as well. Perhaps Alistair should give him the benefit of the doubt?

Thankfully the line moved a little quicker, seemingly none of the other students had so many questions as the girl with the pointy hat had. Alexander didn't seem bothered by Alistair's inability to hold up a conversation and instead continued to chat about the pleasant weather and other things he noticed about the hall and the building.

Alistair made noises of agreement but wasn't entirely sure how to contribute. Silently he was panicking. How did one make friends? And if he did make friends, and started to care about Alexander, then wasn't that just another person to worry about? How did people have scores of friends without staying up all night, afraid that they might come to harm, or start disliking them?

Finally, Alexander got his room assignment and hurried off, waving a friendly goodbye. Alistair waved back and attempted a smile, but he feared that it was more of a manic grimace and that he'd certainly frightened Alexander off.

Alistair explained the situation to the desk attendant who nodded and ensured that the correct luggage was sent to the correct room.

"Master Carlisle will have to give you keys though," they said. "I don't have those."

"Quite so," Alistair said, and thanked them before finally he was free of the cursed line. He checked the grandfather clock in the corner and saw he had a little time before he should change for dinner. He made his way to the back door but Thomas caught his arm.

"Allie, hi, we're all heading to William's rooms now, so we can get changed."

"I need to get to the garden," Alistair snapped.

Thomas smiled softly. "It will still be there after dinner, and besides, didn't you say you wanted to reserve our table?"

"I did but..." Alistair snatched his hand back from Thomas, who had been holding it in one of his and patting it with the other. He felt pressed in, somehow. He tried to explain. "There are new people, and the place doesn't feel the same, exactly. I don't want to have to deal with new things or unpacking right now, I want to get to the garden."

"Fine," Thomas said, after looking deep into Alistair's eyes. "Let's get you down there. The others are perfectly capable of reserving the table for us."

CHAPTER 7

*T*homas and Alistair walked briskly down the path to the ivy covered wall which concealed the door to the Secret Garden and the wellspring inside it. Alistair's stomach was tense, but it felt like his chest was stuffed with caterpillars crawling and writhing. What if he'd been away from the garden too long and it had lost some of its magic?

The wellspring couldn't have dried up, could it? He was relatively sure it wouldn't have. Everything he'd read about wellsprings indicated that although one could use magic to channel a lot of the power out of them one could never actually dry them up. But then, it had come into his life so easily, so perfectly when he needed it. It felt like it was liable to vanish from his life just as easily if he wasn't careful. He hadn't tended the garden in so long, hadn't pulled the weeds from around the plants, hadn't trimmed the rose bushes... There was so much that needed regular attention and all he'd done was sit around at home and read, and fret, and wish he was back here.

Now that he was back, he felt afraid, nervous of what he'd see. Reluctant to go inside.

Thomas seemed to have no such compunction, and shifted into golden retriever form so he could lollop ahead.

Not wishing to be left behind, Alistair hurried his steps until he was almost jogging. The wind *shushed* off the moors and his hair came loose from its ribbon. That felt better. The wind, the scent of heather and the late roses coming to him on the breeze. The feeling of moving his body felt freeing.

He was out of breath when they reached the passage with the hidden door, and he had to fumble to withdraw the key from his trouser pocket. Maybe he ought to run more often, then he wouldn't get so out of breath when he did.

Thomas yipped, dancing back and forth and not being too careful about colliding with Alistair's legs or thumping him with his plumy tail. Alistair smiled, paused to scratch behind his ears, and then opened the door for them both. Thomas barrelled through first, Alistair followed, locked the door behind and they both ran down to the water fountain.

The Garden felt right.

The Garden hadn't become overgrown in his absence, and nor had it all died away. It was much as he'd left it in fact, although the flowers were taller. As they got closer to the fountain Alistair couldn't keep the smile off his face.

The magically oversized flowers that he'd grown when the four of them had celebrated the start of spring together were still there, almost as tall as the trees, with leaves larger than dinner plates. The fountain presided over it all, the beautiful image of William's mother, Melusine, with her gentle smile and the small fawn carved out of marble. The late sun warmed his face, and Alistair got the feeling Melusine was pleased to see him.

The water made a soft sound, soothing to the ear, and to Alistair's soul. He went right up to the water and rested his hand on the stone frog he always gravitated to.

"Good afternoon, Melusine," he said, softly. "Are you here too, Ambrose?"

There was a mild gust of cooler wind and then he heard the sound of his brother's voice.

"I'm here."

"I've missed you," Alistair said.

"Missed you too," came the reply. Barely a whisper, but welcome all the same. The ghost of his brother was a strange thing to find comfort in, perhaps, but he was the only family Alistair had left. He smiled, let out a breath and felt his shoulders relax. Ambrose had never done anything to be ashamed of, unlike their parents.

Behind him, Thomas was bounding back and forth, no doubt soaking in the essence of power that flowed through the overgrown meadow. Alistair could feel it as well. He was itching to remove his shoes so that he could dig his toes into the grass and really connect.

How long did they have before William and Samal would miss them?

He could probably stand to linger a little while longer. He sat on the edge of the fountain and bent to remove his shoes.

He was bent to his task when he heard a rustling getting closer. He looked up just in time to cry out before the running dog form of Thomas tackled him and they both fell backwards into the water with a loud splash.

Alistair barely had time to open his mouth to shout his surprise, and got a mouthful of water instead. He scrambled to sit up, pushing his wet hair off his face. The fountain wasn't deep, but he had been totally submerged in it. Sitting up, the water came to his mid-torso.

"Thomas!" He shouted.

Thomas, still in dog form, yipped and surfaced nearby, shaking off so that water flew out of the fur around his neck, droplets hitting Alistair in the face.

"You've ruined my suit!" Alistair said, spluttering. But he wasn't angry, not really. Thomas's enthusiasm and the magic of the garden made everything seem funny. He sat back on his hands and laughed.

Thomas hopped out of the water, shook all over and shifted back to human form. He offered Alistair a hand.

"Sorry," he said, his face bright with a smile.

"You're not sorry," Alistair said. He took his hand and let Thomas tug him up and out of the water. "But it's fine, that was funny. We should do it to William the next time we come down."

"Oh stars, he'd slaughter us," Thomas said, through giggles. He helped Alistair out and over the ledge onto the grass. Then he said a quick spell, and the water drew itself off Alistair and out of his clothes, forming into a floating blob of water, which Thomas deposited back into the fountain.

"It might be worth it," Alistair said. He adjusted his clothes and dusted himself off. "Thanks for the dry off."

"Sorry, Melusine," Thomas said, turning to the statue and giving the statue a slight bow. "I meant no disrespect."

Alistair, on impulse, wrapped his arms around Thomas from behind and rested his chin on his shoulder. He wanted to say something, thank Thomas for being so sweet, or for making him laugh, or tell him how much he cared for him perhaps, but the words wouldn't form correctly. He didn't want to sound silly or trite, he wanted Thomas to understand how precious he was to him.

Perhaps Thomas could tell, just from the way he was holding him. He leaned back against Alistair's chest, and they both gazed at the statue, feeling the way the magic of the wellspring flowed through the ground and into their bodies and simply being.

Alistair sighed, the caterpillars in his chest were gone, his stomach had relaxed enough that it now was reminding him it was almost dinner time.

"We should head back up," he said.

"I expect so," Thomas said. "Especially if you want to change for dinner?"

"Eh, I don't think I can be bothered changing," Alistair said.

Thomas turned his head to kiss Alistair and Alistair tilted his head to meet his lips. The kiss was warm, sweet and affectionate. Alistair wanted to prolong the moment but the longer he did the more likely his stomach was to start grumbling audibly.

"Let's head back in," Thomas said. He tugged out of Alistair's hold and turned to look into his face. "Are you feeling better? You look better."

"Much better," Alistair said. "I heard Ambrose. I feel..." Alistair paused. It was never easy to express what he was feeling out loud, far easier to journal and tease it out in words that way. But Thomas wouldn't judge him, and genuinely wanted to know. It was worth trying to make that effort. "I feel like since I left Misselthwaite, I'd left a part of me behind. Like I was an incomplete person, and I didn't know entirely how to function. Or at least, I wasn't functioning correctly. Now I feel complete again."

"Good. That's really good to hear." Thomas kissed him lightly on the nose. Alistair slipped his shoes back on and they made their way towards the entrance of the Garden.

Thomas took his hand after he'd locked up the garden and they walked back up to Misselthwaite together.

"I worried about you a bit, off alone in that big old house," Thomas said. "Maybe I could come and stay with you next time we go on break? If you'd like that, I mean. If you like the quiet I'd understand completely."

"I'd..." Alistair was taken aback. Part of him wanted to tell him there was no need, and he should stay with his family, but part of him longed for Thomas's company at all times. He swallowed a sudden lump in his throat and nodded. "Having you stay would be very nice."

Thomas bumped his shoulder against Alistair's and they both lapsed into contented silence.

CHAPTER 8

*T*he first dinner of the term was more formal than Alistair was used to. He had started Misselthwaite partly into the term and hadn't been present for the start of term before.

The table which was usually frequented by teachers and professors was covered with a white formal cloth, and the headmaster, Lord Carlisle sat at it, in a high backed chair. Professor Barlow, the head of Magic and Magical Theory, sat to his right, along with the other professors, most of whom Alistair recognised. Even the librarian, Kincade, was seated there, beside Professor Weatherstaff, the grumpy man who ran Botany courses.

The buffet was stocked even better than usual with three different roast meats, a variety of fresh garden vegetables, potatoes roasted, mashed and boiled as well as several large loaves of bread of different sorts. A huge selection of long thin loaves, hearty round rye breads and of course a basket of Alistair's favourite dinner rolls. However no one had served themselves yet, and the food sat steaming and smelling divine as the last students took their places at tables.

William, Samal and Martha had reserved their usual table

and Alistair and Thomas joined them. No one seemed at all confused by the state of things, so Alistair tried not to fret over not immediately getting his plate of dinner.

Once the last student had taken their place, Lord Carlisle stood up and the room went quiet.

"Welcome back to the Summer Term at Misselthwaite." Lord Carlisle's voice was impressive, low but carrying easily to the back corners of the room. "I trust you are all well-rested, and ready to begin your studies anew.

"Students, I would like to introduce you to Catherine Winterbourne, a visiting professor. She is a specialist in curses and the breaking thereof, and will be in residence for at least the next two terms."

All eyes turned to the unfamiliar face as she smiled politely and nodded at Lord Carlisle, before looking out at the tables.

Catherine Winterbourne looked like the sort of person Alistair would assume to be a kindly aunt. She could have stepped out of one of the cosy family based novels he'd read as a child. Her medium brown hair was streaked with silver and worn in a thick braid that she'd pulled over one shoulder. Her eyes were deep brown, but sparkled with intelligence behind small wire-framed spectacles.

Alistair realised Lord Carlisle was looking directly at him. A visiting professor specialising in curse-breaking... Lord Carlisle must have invited her especially to spend some time with Alistair and hurry along his progress with William's curse. Well, at least she looked like she'd be easy to get along with.

Lord Carlisle was still staring at him so Alistair gave a nod of understanding. Lord Carlilse looked away and continued his speech.

"Welcome to those students who are joining us for the first time this term, and of course welcome back to all returning. Now, please help yourself to the wonderful dinner."

Medlock took over the proceedings by inviting each table to go to the buffet and help themselves in turn.

William sighed and Alistair turned to see him rubbing the bridge of his nose.

"What is it?"

"Winterbourne," he said. "This isn't the first time she's come to examine my case. Perhaps it will be easier with you involved, Allie, but... let me simply say that I didn't miss her company."

"Oh." Alistair looked over at the new professor again. She was smiling and chatting to Ben Weatherstaff, and they both looked happy enough. "Why not? Was she one of the ones who promised to heal you and then couldn't?"

"Did she do terrible experiments on you?" Thomas asked, leaning forward with wide eyes.

"Probably she just tried to make him take care of himself better and he didn't like it," Samal said. He was smirking a little, clearly trying to wind William up.

Martha smothered a giggle behind one hand. "Maybe she suggested he eat some green vegetables."

Samal laughed. "Or exercise for his health?"

William glared at Samal, his eyebrows drawing together in a fierce manner although his mouth quirked in a sly smile. "It doesn't matter what she did, we simply didn't get along. And if you keep making remarks like that, young Sam, you're going to get a spanking."

Just at that moment Medlock indicated it was their table's turn to go to the buffet. Alistair leapt to his feet, cheeks burning red at the idea of William spanking Sam. Of William spanking anyone at all really. It was such a silly and ridiculous threat, but it was having a strange effect on Alistair that he couldn't quite understand. He decided to puzzle it out later on, and focus on dinner for the time being.

CHAPTER 9

Over dinner, Martha regaled them with stories of the whirlwind trip she'd taken to Paris over the break to visit a cousin. The stories were very amusing, and Alistair enjoyed the camaraderie of listening and laughing along with the others. He wondered, fleetingly, if this was what normal families did when they had dinner together. His own dinners with his parents had certainly never been this fun.

Finally, the last food was eaten and people began to yawn.

The dining hall emptied as students made their way up the stairs to the dormitory rooms.

It felt strange to Alistair, to climb the steps and turn right towards William's rooms, instead of left to the room he had used last term. He felt a pang, wondering if his room had been let out to one of the new students, and then told himself off for that.

Of course it would have been. He had only lived in it for a matter of months, which hardly constituted ownership. There was no reason at all for anyone to have reserved it for Alistair's exclusive use.

The hallway that led to William's rooms had been cleaned up, and Alistair was surprised to see students letting themselves into rooms closest to the stairs.

"Since I haven't had night terrors or bouts of... my condition, father agreed there was no need to treat this as an abandoned hallway any longer," William said, when Alistair asked.

"So there hasn't been any relapse at all?" Samal asked.

"Well, I wouldn't quite say that, I've certainly had some days where I've felt I had no energy to speak of, or some aches," William said. "But nothing like the onslaughts I used to get, and every morning I've woken up again, which is a relief."

Alistair grabbed William's hand and squeezed it, feeling an almost overwhelming desire to laugh or possibly cry. He felt so proud and so happy for William. Alistair hadn't at all been sure that the spell they'd woven together to ward William from his own curse would work, or that it would hold, but so far, so good.

William stopped in front of his door and pulled out a handful of keys. He stuck one in the lock and then handed out the others to each of them.

"Since you're going to be living here, I thought it best that you could actually unlock the door and get in," he said. Alistair closed his fingers around the key and smiled. It was a symbol of William's trust, and he would do everything he could to be worthy of it.

William opened the door and ushered Samal, Thomas and then Alistair in before following them.

The rooms had changed since the last time Alistair had been in there. There were more couches, and a desk on each wall, enough for each of them to have one. The room was brighter as well, there were some recessed lights added. The portrait of Melusine smiled benevolently down on the room, and there was a new artwork as well, a rendering of the Secret Garden itself.

"Who did this?" Alistair asked, approaching the Garden painting to examine it.

"I did," William said. "It was a pleasant way to spend some of the break."

"It's lovely."

Thomas was in the corner by the door where their bags and trunks had been stacked. Samal was standing in the middle of the room, turning slowly, taking it all in.

"Is it all right?" William asked from the door. His voice wasn't his usual self-assured tone and Alistair glanced back to see he was watching them all with a strained expression.

"It looks good," Alistair said quickly. "I like the desks."

"Quite a Gothic sort of style," Samal said. "It suits you."

"I don't mind if you want to bring in more of your own decorations," William said, stiffly.

"I might want to open the curtains from time to time and let in some sunlight," Samal said. William rolled his eyes.

"You know perfectly well why I have such heavy curtains and why they've always been drawn."

There was a thump as Thomas dragged a trunk off the pile and started to open it up.

"The bedroom was a bit more difficult..." William pushed himself off the door and led the way to the connecting room. This room, Alistair had never seen before so he followed, curious. Samal was right behind him.

The room was almost as large as the sitting area. Against the far wall was the bed, magically grown to fit all four of them, the same as Alistair's old bed had been. There was a pile of pillows and cushions in familiar, flower-like colours, and a lush grass-green satin comforter. The bed was a four poster, with delicate white mesh curtains pulled back with pink ribbons to create a pleasing effect.

The walls were papered with white and blue, a gentle delicate stripe that evoked a summer afternoon, and even the floor was carpeted in a soft grey green, complementing the bedspread.

The whole thing was so sweet and pretty that it made absolutely no sense to Alistair for William to have put it together.

He looked at his boyfriend with an incredulous look. "Do you have a secret little sister who you brought in to decorate this room?"

"No, it's...all my work. I... " William wrung his hands together. "I wanted to evoke the Secret Garden, since it links us all, and it's where... where we all first... you know." He bit his lip. "Do you absolutely hate it? Is it too feminine?"

"No, I don't hate it." Alistair's feet took him to William without a thought and he put his arms around him. He was stiff, and didn't react. "It's really, really pretty, and I can see the garden in it, but...it just took me by surprise."

"It doesn't exactly match the rest of your style," Samal said. "But it is delightful."

William relaxed a little. "Do you really mean it?"

"Yes," Alistair said. He planted a kiss on William's cheek. "This was very thoughtful of you."

Thomas bounced into the room and gasped, clasping his hands together and beaming. He looked at William with wide, sparkling eyes. "This is incredible! It looks just right, just like we were talking about, and look and these..." he leapt up onto the bed and grabbed a pillow in each hand. "These are the exact colours of the flowers in the meadow."

"You and Thomas talked about it?" Alistair asked. It pleased him to think of them meeting up without him and planning the room decor.

"Yes," William said.

William relaxed further, and turned to wrap his arms around Alistair and give him a firm kiss. Under his hands Alistair could feel that William was trembling a little. He'd truly been concerned that they hated what he'd done.

"It's really beautiful," Alistair said again. William met his eyes, pressed his forehead to Alistair's and nodded.

"Thank you," William said, soft as a whisper.

"Maybe we ought to get ready for bed?" Samal suggested. He

pressed his chest against Alistair's back and kissed his shoulder. Alistair shivered lightly, thoughts suddenly more salacious than they had been a moment before, pinned between the two of them.

"Maybe."

"Are you really going to spank Sam?" Thomas asked from the bed. Alistair sputtered, getting hotter by the second, and William's eyes darkened.

"I wouldn't be opposed to it," William said. He gripped Alistair a little tighter, and Alistair's body responded with an electric shiver up the spine.

"No," Samal said. His voice low in Alistair's ear. "I'm not going to let him spank me."

Alistair was unaccountably disappointed. Thomas flopped back on the bed and stared at the canopy of the bed for a moment before speaking.

"You could spank me, if you wanted?" Thomas said. The three standing looked over at him. Alistair's heart was racing now. Was this really going to happen?

William let go of Alistair and stalked towards Thomas. Samal pulled Alistair close against his chest, his arms strong, almost restraining. Alistair's trousers were so tight... he dropped a hand to rub at himself through the fabric.

"Are they really going to..." Alistair couldn't complete the sentence, the words were too outrageous to say, too much like one of the really daring novels Alistair had read in his time. He felt almost light headed, and he wasn't even the one who might get spanked.

William loomed over Thomas, who grinned up at him, fox ears twitching.

"Don't tell me you're all talk and no follow through," Thomas said. His eyes twinkled and his freckled nose scrunched up as he goaded William. "You just like to act all tough and mean, but really-"

William took hold of Thomas's wrist and sat on the bed, manhandling Thomas over his lap. Thomas went quiet, he was still wearing his trousers, and his fox tail was poking out the top of it. William pushed the tail down, pinning it to Thomas's back with one hand and brought the other one up to slap hard on Thomas's round rear.

Alistair moaned softly, he couldn't help himself, it simply slipped out. Samal chuckled and nipped his earlobe. "You like that do you?" he murmured, dark, sinful.

Alistair spluttered through his reply. "I, yes, I didn't expect.. They'd really... it's very..."

Samal pushed Alistair's head to the side a little and kissed his neck. His hands moved to undo Alistair's waistcoat and shirt, hands trailing softly over his skin and making him moan some more.

"I think," Samal said softly. "That you're very, very interested." His hand trailed down to press against Alistair's hardness. "The question is are you imagining yourself in Thomas's place or in William's? I'm sure if you asked you could take either of their places."

The noise Alistair made in response was akin to a strangled gurgle. Samal chuckled again and palmed him through his trousers. His other arm clamped over Alistair's chest, and Alistair gripped it with both hands, not to get away but to have something to hold onto so he didn't just fall to the floor.

William had spanked Thomas several times now, and Thomas had stopped squirming. His face was bright red, and his eyes half closed as he panted, looking entirely debauched and wanting. Alistair wanted to know what it felt like to have William hit him in such a way. He wanted to know how it felt to spank someone as well, but the main part of him wanted to be in Thomas's place. Samal was waiting for an answer, wasn't he? Alistair just had to get the words out.

It was humiliating to admit he wanted something like that,

but it was happening right there in front of him, so at least he knew no one would judge him for saying it.

"I want..." he hesitated again and Samal slipped his hand inside his trousers and squeezed him. Alistair moaned, the pleasure of it giving him a little bit of courage. "I want to know how it feels... in Thomas's place."

Samal hummed and kissed his neck again, the act so gentle it brought goosebumps up on Alistair's arm. "There now, that wasn't so hard."

Samal didn't waste any time, he pushed Alistair towards the bed and yanked Alistair's clothes open almost at the same time. Alistair stumbled forward, kicking off his trousers and underthings. William looked up, his eyes dark. He had paused in spanking Thomas to pull his trousers down and was rubbing a palm over his rear. Thomas was practically purring, his eyes half closed, and his cheeks bright red. It set Alistair's heart on fire.

"Hello Alistair," William said, his voice low and rough. "Enjoying the show?"

"He's just told me he wants a turn," Samal said, his voice low as well. They were all so turned on, Alistair could feel it, a faint echo of the aroused connection they'd had when they first all consummated their relationship in the Secret Garden. Harder to detect now, and not as strong, but there all the same.

"Hmm," William let go of Thomas, although he didn't immediately move off his lap. "But someone will have to keep Thomas occupied. He seems rather worked up."

Samal climbed onto the bed and leaned back against the pillows, beckoning. "Thomas, come here," he said. A soft order, but an oder none the less.

Alistair felt as if all the blood in his body was in his cheeks and his cock. William leaned forward, slipped his arm around his waist and pulled Alistair in. His mouth fastened onto Alistair's nipple and Alistair keened with pleasure. Then before he knew what was happening, he was slung over William's knees, and there was a hand on his bare arse. Alistair's breath was gone, and he had to work to heave a breath, he was so excited to be in position like that.

"Tell me if it's too hard," William murmured. He waited for Alistair to nod his understanding and then his hand came down on his rear with a resounding slap. It stung, and the surprise of it had Alistair jolting, but the sting translated instantly into arousal. Alistair had thought he was already as aroused as he could be, but now he felt even more heightened. As if his body had an unlimited capacity for feeling attraction to his boyfriends, to wanting them...

William spanked him again and Alistair didn't bother to try and hide his moan. He loved it, and he wanted all three of them to know. He realised he'd closed his eyes, and he turned his head to look over at Samal and Thomas. Were they watching him? Were they seeing what William was doing to him?

They *were* watching. Thomas was in Samal's lap, his clothes pulled open but not off, and his cock stood out from him, enticing. Samal had pulled his arms behind his back and was holding them there with his hand, the other teasing, stroking his lower belly, and his thighs, circling his cock but not touching it. Both were watching him with hungry eyes. Alistair's arousal spiked again.

William spanked him again, much harder this time, and Alistair cried out at the sting. His own cock was rubbing against William's trousered leg and it wasn't nearly enough friction. Alistair's arms hung down beside his head, and he groaned, needing more.

"Please," he said, breathless and barely audible. William rubbed his palm over the hot skin of Alistair's arse.

"Please what?"

"I need more, please touch me, I want more," Alistair said. "Please."

William pulled him upright and onto the bed, stood up and undressed himself. Alistair, uncertain what to do with his neediness or his yearning for William, helped him tug his shirt off but found balancing hard on his wobbly knees.

Thomas whined, his fox tail was gone now, and he was rubbing himself against Samal's cock. His clothes had been cast aside while Alistair was otherwise occupied. Samal reached for a pot of oil and slicked up his cock, pulling Thomas onto it with a slow, deliberate movement. Thomas keened. "Bit fast," he gasped.

"Sorry," Samal said. He reached in front to stroke Thomas so he'd relax into it.

"Oh god," Alistair said, watching.

In a moment he was face down on the bed, William's hands moving him there deftly, before his body covered him a moment later. His skin was delightfully cool against Alistair's flushed body. He felt the hardness of his cock teasing at the hot skin of that had been spanked.

"Is it all right if I try something to prep you?" William asked, his voice low. Alistair was needy and impatient.

"Yes, get on with it, please!"

William murmured a spell Alistair didn't recognise, and suddenly Alistair felt slick and warm, loosened up. He yelped at the change in his physicality. Magic for sex? There were spells for sex?

Alistair had never even considered such a thing, he wondered wildly, if there was a place in the library for books about it, but the thought evaporated when William pushed himself slowly inside and he was flooded with arousal and intense desire for William.

"Just something new I learned," William murmured in his ear. "How does it feel?"

Alistair gasped, pushing back so that William would fill him faster. "Amazing, surprising, but amazing," he said.

William's hands found his wrists and he pinned them above Alistair's head. Alistair's body responded with more heat and need, and he moaned, tugging against William's hold just to see how securely he was being kept in place. Thrilling when he found William's grip to be strong and unrelenting. William growled in his ear.

"Mine. Now. Be still."

Alistair's eyes rolled back and he melted into the bed. "Yes."

Thomas was moaning, and Alistair battled to look over at them. Thomas was bouncing on Samal's lap. Both of them were flushed, their pupils blown, and they looked so beautiful, so perfect together.

William started to move faster, pulling part way out and then slamming deep inside of Alistair, hitting a spot inside him which felt utterly divine.

The unfolding of the desire for a bit of pain, and to be held down, flooded Alistair's mind, and he felt himself desperate for more. He wanted William to bite into him with his vampire fangs, or to wrap his hand around Alistair's throat and choke him. Or for him to tie Alistair down with chains and tease him for hours. The possibilities were overwhelming and each one more attractive than the one before. Alistair pushed back as best he could as William thrust and panted.

"More," he gasped. William reached around to stroke Alistair and he came almost instantly.

William groaned, lightly bit Alistair's shoulder and shoved himself deep inside as he orgasmed as well. Perhaps spurred on by them, and the faint connection of magic and arousal, Thomas and Samal completed as well.

William pulled out and did a quick clean up spell, cleaning up their bodies as well as the bedclothes. Alistair tried to catch his breath, lying still on the new, soft green comforter and reeling from all the sensations and ideas that his mind had supplied.

"Come here, Allie," Samal said. Alistair felt hands on him and he was half dragged into a warm pile of limbs with Thomas and Samal, William settled in as well.

"That was rather illuminating," William said. He rubbed a hand through Thomas's hair. Thomas grinned and then leaned over to kiss Alistair on the lips. Alistair felt warm tingles from the kiss, that spiralled out from his lips and warmed his entire body.

"I thought it was good," Thomas said.

"Yeah," Alistair said. He felt rather embarrassed again, now that it was all over, and rather grateful that none of his boyfriends had any kind of mind reading magic.

William ran his hand slowly down Alistair's back, letting his palm settle on the abused skin of his rear end. "I am surprised and pleased that you're interested in less... conventional styles of lovemaking."

Alistair blushed and hid his face in Thomas's neck. He had no words for how to respond to that. Thomas drew him close and held him, and William slotted in against his back. Samal's cool hand stroked the hair back from his face.

"I think you've embarrassed him," Samal said. William replied with a soft chuckle.

"There's nothing to be ashamed of, we're all consenting adults having fun."

"Please can we just go to sleep and stop talking about it?" Alistair begged, although his voice was muffled in Thomas's shoulder.

His boyfriends took pity on him, and extinguished the lamps. "All right, goodnight you three. We can talk about the possibilities this opens up on another night," William said.

CHAPTER 10

*T*he next day was administration day - full of checking of schedules, swapping classes if needed, meeting with tutors about special areas of study and the like.

William had attended to all of his administration done before the start of term, so after breakfast he excused himself to the library to investigate the book selection for his upcoming courses.

The doors to the ballroom were open, and Thomas, Samal and Alistair went through, with their schedules in hand. The room was lined with tables on each side, and behind each table a professor or a student recruiting for a club or activity.

Thomas and Samal had experienced all of this before, but to Alistair it was a confusing array of options and noise. The talk of the students and professors seemed to fill the room, echoing back off a ceiling meant to enhance the music of a string quartet.

"Oh, there's Professor Waxleaf," Samal said. "I should confirm this extra class with her, it's down on my schedule for four in the morning and I'm very much hoping that's not correct..." he hurried off towards the short line in front of Professor Waxleaf's desk.

"I had a note to speak with Barlow on my schedule," Alistair said. Thomas nodded and swooped in to give him a quick peck on the cheek. Alistair's heart gave a couple of extra beats at the casual affection.

"I'll take a look at the clubs and things," Thomas said. "Maybe there'll be something interesting."

Alistair joined the line to speak to Professor Barlow, but he followed Thomas with his eyes. He'd never had the opportunity to join a club, although as with so many things, he had read a great deal about them. Perhaps it would be nice to meet some new people and share a common interest. Perhaps it would make him feel like less of an impostor. At least he had access to magic now, those first few weeks at Misselthwaite before he'd discovered the Secret Garden had been utterly dismal.

The line moved quickly, which Alistair was thankful for, and soon he was face to face with the friendly Professor Barlow. He had black hair with a hint of grey at the temples, and a very handsome face.

"Good morning, Lennox," he said. His eyes brightened and he smiled as he looked up at Alistair. "I'm glad to see you've returned."

"Yes, well, I didn't really have a choice, between trying to break William's curse, and the condition on my inheritance."

Barlow blinked at him for a moment, and Alistair worried he was supposed to have been more polite than that. Then Barlow laughed and nodded.

"Indeed, indeed. I'm sure you noticed that Lord Carlisle has invited Professor Winterbourne to the Manor to teach some targeted courses on curse breaking?"

"I, yes, I did," Alistair said. "I believe I have a course with her twice a week?"

"That's correct. What wasn't announced last night is a second visitor to the school you may be interested in." Barlow clasped his hands before him on the table and his smile faded slightly. Alistair wondered why that might be. "We have a postgraduate student from a school in the Americas. She contacted Lord Carlisle and asked if she might complete her doctorate here, with access to the library, although I rather suspect she somehow got wind of the ingenious spell you did on young mister Carlisle. Her name is April Quinn, and I'd like to introduce you to her you have some time around your classes."

Alistair swallowed and nodded. "Of course."

"Her area of study is highly unique, but I expect that you may be able to learn something from her. And perhaps, she can learn something from you as well. She is due to arrive later today."

"Of course," Alistair said again. He unfolded the paper his schedule was recorded on and saw he had a wide gap over lunch time. He showed it to Barlow. "Perhaps after lunch tomorrow?"

Barlow made a quick note on a pad of paper he had beside him and nodded. "Thank you Lennox. Was there any other adjustment you wanted to make to your courses?"

Alistair shook his head. "No, Botany and Curse Breaking are the... the fields I'm most interested in and I have those."

"Excellent. Well, good luck then."

Barlow was already looking past him to give a wide smile to the next student, so Alistair sidled away and tried to find Thomas in the crowd of queues and people fussing with paper schedules.

He spotted Thomas and Samal at a desk with a student behind it and made his way through the shuffling crowd to them. There was a hand painted sign on the front of the desk "Student Association"

"What's a Student Association?" Alistair said. Thomas laughed and tugged him forward.

"Alistair, this is Zeta Blake. She runs the Student Association."

"Well, I'm one of the people who run it," Zeta said. She had a bright expression and sharp, intelligent eyes. "The student association organises mixers, club nights, all sorts of meetings and things for students to get to know each other. At the moment we are recruiting, and if you'd like to sign up we'll be able to invite you to all the events. The first thing we have planned is a picnic in the garden on Friday night. A kind of celebratory, welcome back sort of event."

"That sounds lovely, doesn't it?" Thomas tugged on Alistair's arm.

""Uh, yes, it does," Alistair said. "I like... gardens."

Zeta positively beamed as they pressed a clipboard into Alistair's hand along with a pencil. "Please write your name and room number here and we'll be in touch."

Alistair took the clipboard, saw Sam and Thomas had both already signed their names, and added his own. It couldn't be too awful to attend if two of his boyfriends were involved.

Martha hurried up and gave Samal a side hug. She looked over Alistair's shoulder and slapped him on the shoulder.

"Look at you! Signing up for things. It will be good for you to make some new friends," Martha laughed. "I'm proud of you, Allie."

Alistair wasn't sure if he should be offended by this statement, but mostly he thought she was probably correct so he didn't say anything.

Martha took the clipboard off him and added her name under his. "Hey Zeta, are you taking Advanced Inanimate Objects this term?"

Zeta grinned at Martha. "Yes, wouldn't miss it. I signed up for the curse breaking course with the new professor as well though. I had some space in my schedule and I thought why not? That sounds so interesting, doesn't it?"

"Oh, well, there you go Alistair," Thomas said, nudging him forward a little. "He's taking all the classes Professor Winterbourne is offering, there. You'll know someone."

Alistair tried to smile, but he felt awkward and put on the

spot, and judging from Zeta's reaction, it came out as a strained grimace. She didn't flinch, but a confused sort of horror flitted across her features.

Alistair cleared his throat, tried to relax his features. He needed to try harder to be polite and nice, to fit into society, and now was a great opportunity for it. "Yes, I'll look forward to seeing you there, Zeta."

"You too...?" Zeta peered at him, as if he was the puzzle that needed solving and then her features relaxed a little.

"Sorry," Alistair blurted. "Please forgive me. I'm very new to having friends and I'm terrible at it. You seem very nice, and I will be happy to get to know you more."

Martha giggled once, and Alistair's cheeks flushed.

Zeta smiled wider and nodded. "I understand. I look forward to our classes together."

"Right, well, thank you. See you soon. Now, Sam, shall we look at some of the other tables?" He yanked on Samal's arm and made his escape.

CHAPTER 11

*A*listair's first class was the next day. Curse Breaking with Catherine Winterbourne. He made his way up to the room which had been assigned, one in a whole hallway of rooms dedicated to classes. It was smaller than any other Alistair had been in. He sat down in the front row of chairs.

Professor Winterbourne stood at the front of the class, eyeing the chalkboard with something remarkably like distrust. Alistair understood. The chalkboard was a horrible piece of equipment, creating dust and awful screeching noises, and the content written on them was temporary, and often hard to read.

He pulled out a fresh, blank notebook and busied himself readying a fountain pen. He inhaled the sweet smell of the unused pages and tried not to give in to nervousness over the class and the new teacher.

Professor Winterbourne turned to look over the students. Including Alistair there were only five of them, all seated in seats spaced a few apart as if none of them trusted any of the others enough to sit close to them. He recognised Zeta from the student association, but she was looking down at her bag, so it seemed imprudent to wave at her.

"Hm, there ought to be six of you," Professor Winterbourne said. "I suppose we shall have to wait."

The door to the small classroom opened and in walked the girl who had been in the front of the line for registration on the day Alistair had arrived. The one with the small pointy hat, which was was wearing again today. She grinned at the professor and then at the class.

"Sorry, I got a little lost."

"It's no trouble," Professor Winterbourne said. "Please take a seat and I'll begin, Miss....?"

"Wood. Kimber Wood," the student said. She bustled into the front row and sat beside Alistair. He had to suppress the urge to edge away from her. Clearly she hadn't understood that those in this class sat at a distance.

Kimber had a small patchwork bag from which she pulled large books and supplies which didn't appear as if they ought to fit inside. Finally she produced a tiny furry animal, which scurried up her sleeve to perch on her shoulder. It was a long, thin animal, four legged with a sweet face.

"Is that a weasel?" Alistair asked. He'd startled a little from the movement of it, and he was concentrating very hard on keeping his breathing controlled.

"A stoat," Kimber said. "He's my familiar."

"Right," Professor Winterbourne said, her dry voice cutting across the room. "Let us begin with a quick discussion. I should like to know if any of you have any experience with curses, or the breaking of them."

Alistair froze. He hadn't *technically* broken the curse on William, and his own curse had been broken by the wellspring and the magic of Melusine's fountain, but he had surely done some curse-breaking as a toddler. His hand started to rise, but then he realised there was little use in claiming that as experience since he couldn't remember it at all. But Ambrose had reassured him that was their gift, and that curse breaking was in his blood.

He half raised his hand, feeling a little like a coward. He glanced around the room to see only two other students had their hands up, one was Zeta and the other Kimber, sitting beside him.

"Miss Wood, why don't you tell us a little about your experiences," Professor Winterbourne said.

Kimber cleared her throat and lowered her hand to fold it with the other on the desk. On her shoulder, the stoat sat up to attention.

"Of course, Professor. I admit, I don't know too much, but I managed to break a small curse which had plagued my family's home for some time. A previous suitor of my eldest sister had cursed the stove so that any bacon we attempted to cook would burn."

"Very good," Professor Winterbourne nodded, and her gaze slid to Alistair. "And you, mister...?"

"Lennox." Alistair said. He was about to continue when Professor Winterbourne clapped her hands and grinned in a rather alarmingly enthusiastic fashion.

"Professor Barlow has told me all about you, Mister Lennox. I'm glad to have you here in my class. I knew your parents, and I believe we may have even met before although you would have been far too young to remember. For those of you unaware, Alistair here broke curses as a toddler." There was an interested murmur around the small class. Professor Winterbourne's eyes roamed and settled on Zeta. "Miss Blake, what has your experience been of curses?"

Alistair felt his cheeks warm, rather embarrassed that although he had never actually broken a curse on his own, he apparently had some sort of reputation for it. Plus the Professor declaring in front of everyone that she knew his parents? That he was gifted? It was practically the same as calling him her favourite pupil, and in the first couple of minutes of the first class? He felt put on the spot and obvious in the worst way.

Then dread flooded him as he remembered that most of the magical world had resented his parents, even hated them, and rather than singling him out for a good reason, she may have been more or less warning him. Not for the first time, he fervently wished that people would simply say what they meant, instead of playing at politeness and confusing matters.

He hadn't been paying attention and now Professor Winterbourne was drawing their attention back to the front of the room.

"To be truly successful at curse breaking requires a great deal of study and a logical approach. Many have likened the breaking of curses to the removal of any sort of magic, but this isn't entirely a useful parallel. I think it's much more apt to compare curse breaking to the solving of puzzles. With that in mind, my first challenge for you as a class is to research, examine and do your best to unravel the curse on the ancient tomb of Tutankhamen."

The Professor turned, waved her wand, and from thin air, a large scroll of canvas unfurled itself and fastened itself to the wall. The canvas was covered in lines of hieroglyphs, and there was a murmur of soft voices through the class.

"Have any of you read hieroglyphs before? No?" No one spoke up. "They're not so different from runes, but you do need to learn the basic forms. So, let's read them together one by one, make sure you're ready to take notes."

Alistair picked up his pen and started to make notes. The class passed in record time, Professor Winterbourne moved quickly, which suited Alistair, but was clear in her explanations and was very willing to answer any questions that came up. Zeta asked several, and although Alistair himself had one about the particular direction a glyph faced, he bit his tongue, shy to ask it.

He managed to relax about Kimber sitting next to him at

least. At one point her stoat even moved to curl up on the bench between the two of them and went to sleep. It was rather cute, he decided.

Professor Winterbourne wrapped up the class by assigning them a chapter of reading on the various rumours and stories the mundane world shared about the curse on Tutankamen's tomb. They were to make notes on which made sense as actual parts of the curse and which the student thought might just be speculation and invented stories. Then, she swept out of the classroom, her canvas of hieroglyphs rolling itself up and vanishing as she did.

"Gosh, that was really fun, wasn't it?" Kimber said. She grinned at Alistair as they both stowed their notebooks and writing implements away.

"Uh, yes, it was," Alistair said. His instinct was to leave it there, but again he wanted to be making friends. After the things Professor Winterbourne had said at the start of the class especially, and he was grateful Kimber hadn't brought it up. He plunged on, trying his best to make eye contact. "I'm looking forward to the chapter, it's fascinating to me to see what parts of the magical world filter through to the mundane."

"Oh, absolutely," Kimber said. "Weird of the Prof to say those things about you as a kid." Kimber smiled sympathetically. "I expect after all that happened you don't wish to remember it all?"

Alistair was flooded with relief and warmth towards Kimber at these words. "Yes," he said. "I really wish she hadn't said all that. I felt very exposed."

"It's all right," Kimber said. She shrugged one shoulder. "I don't think people will remember it after a few days. I'm sure they'll want to get to know you, not the stories of your folks."

"I hope so." Alistair said. He finished packing his things up. He really was grateful for her words, warming to her, so he pushed himself to express it. "Thank you. That's reassuring."

"No worries. Well, see you around." She scooped up her stoat, stuffed him into the pocket of her tartan skirt and bustled off.

The class had taken up most of the morning, and Alistair's stomach was starting to rumble, so he shouldered his satchel and made his way to the dining hall.

He ran into Thomas who was coming from another direction.

"Morning, Allie. I was thinking, since it's such a lovely day, why don't we take our lunch outside, make it a picnic?"

Alistair nodded. He longed to be back in the garden, even if it wasn't the secret one. Misselthwaite was so gloomy, because of Lord Carlisle's condition, and sometimes one just needed fresh air and light.

"Wonderful. Let's collect up the best picnic things from the dining hall and sit somewhere the others can find us."

CHAPTER 12

*A*listair was grateful that Thomas had suggested the picnic. He probably wouldn't have thought of it on his own but it was exactly what he needed. They spread a woollen blanket Thomas had brought on the grass near the entranceway to the university, where there were some trees for shade. The trees were lovely, young oaks with an abundance of green leaves. Alistair got a pleasant feeling from them as they set up underneath their branches.

"This is perfect," Alistair said. Thomas beamed at him.

Martha and Samal appeared first, seemingly having had the same idea, judging from the blanket under Martha's arm and the small basket of muffins Samal carried.

"Come join us!" Thomas said.

Martha spread the blanket out beside Thomas's.

"Where is everyone getting these blankets from?" Alistair wondered.

"There's a basket of them just inside the door," Martha said, cheerfully. She flopped down onto the blanket without grace and gave him a smile. "You've never noticed it?"

Alistair shook his head. He wondered how he could have missed it all the times he'd gone in and out of those doors.

"Have you noticed the chandelier in the entrance hall?" Martha asked. She raised an eyebrow and smirked. "Or do you only notice handsome men?"

Alistair flushed and Samal nudged her shoulder. "Don't tease him like that, he doesn't ever know how to react."

"Which is exactly why it's so fun to tease him." Martha winked at Alistair, and he flushed business himself setting out the scones and jam brought from the dining hall.

William found them next, and he sank gracefully into the deepest bit of shade next to Alistair, crossing his legs and looking elegant all the while.

"How did everyone enjoy their morning classes?" he asked, helping himself to a bottle of lemonade.

"Really interesting," Alistair said. "Professor Winterbourne is a very good teacher, and I think like her approach to curse breaking."

"I'm glad to hear it," William said. "Father has been rather profuse in his excitement at securing her for a term. It's good to know he's pleased for a valid reason."

"Shape Shifting was interesting," Thomas said. He was halfway through a sandwich already. "Some of us are going to try and attempt bird forms this term. It's notoriously difficult on account of size and bone density and all that, so we have to do a lot of research first, but having others try at the same time makes it feel like a group project."

"Bone density?" Martha asked.

Thomas went into a diatribe about the lightness of bird's bones, and Alistair started to eat, only paying partial attention. He loved Thomas, but he had heard about bone density before, and it didn't terribly interest him.

He looked around, at the verdant green of the summer grass to the bright blue of the sky, then to the various students going in and out of the school. Two were heading their way, and he realised with a start that he recognised them. Alexander and Kimber.

Alexander spotted him and waved, and the two angled their walking to approach Alistair and his group.

"Hello Alistair!" Kimber said, brightly. "Do you mind if we join you?"

"You can tell us if we're intruding," Alexander said quickly. "We don't want to be a nuisance."

Alistair felt glad to see them, if they were approaching him that must mean that he hadn't made a bad impression on either of them. His campaign to make friends might in fact, be working.

"No, of course, it's fine," Thomas said. "The more the merrier."

"Please, sit," Alistair added. He introduced everyone around with a minimum of fumbling. He finished with Thomas. "Thomas is a shapeshifter," he said, not able to keep the pride out of his voice. He wanted to show off his lover to Kimber, he wanted to impress her, perhaps. "Maybe you'd like to show him your familiar, Kimber?"

Kimber giggled. "Sure." She dug into her pocket and produced the stoat and he sniffed the air and looked right at Thomas.

"Oh, he's lovely," Thomas leaned forward and offered a hand for the stoat to sniff.

"Alistair, you're really not supposed to ask people to whip out their familiars," William said dryly. "It's a little impolite."

Alistair's mouth went dry. "It is? I'm sorry." He looked at Kimber, hoping she would see how stricken he was. "I had no idea."

"It's fine," she said. "I really don't mind." Alistair breathed out, relieved that he hadn't upset her, but mentally berating himself for once again not knowing enough about magical society.

She giggled again as her stoat sniffed Thomas's hand and then swarmed fluidly up his arm to nuzzle under his ear. Thomas laughed.

"What's his name?" he asked. "He's trying to tell me but my mustelid is very basic."

"Horatio," Kimber said. "And he's a sweetheart, although he will eat all your hard boiled eggs if you're not vigilant."

"Sweet," William said, although he didn't sound like he meant it.

"How do you know Alexander?" Alistair asked Kimber. He'd met them both separately after all, but they'd walked up together looking quite friendly.

"Our rooms are over the hall from each other," Kimber said. "We just got to talking and hit it off, didn't we, Alex?"

He beamed back at her, eyes crinkling. "We did! And we have the same preferences at breakfast. Pastries over eggs."

Kimber giggled. "That's right, pastries all the way." Alistair liked the way she laughed with her entire body, leaning towards Alexander as if she couldn't hold herself up.

"I wholeheartedly agree," Alistair said. He turned his attention to Alexander. "And how were your morning courses, Alexander?"

"Oh, they were fine," Alexander said. "My magical talent is towards potion making, but since it's first day back we were mostly doing stock inventory and the professor made sure all our equipment was up to snuff."

"Potions?" William nodded. "There's a specialisation you don't often hear about."

Alexander flushed and once again Alistair felt he'd missed something.

"You don't? Why is that?"

Kimber sniffed, levelling a glare at William. "Some people seem to think that because anyone with magic is capable of following a potion recipe, that there's no skill in it at all. Of course, they're wrong."

William's back stiffened and he raised an eyebrow. "I'm sure Alexander's talent aids him greatly."

"It does, and his potions are the best quality you'll ever see," Kimber snapped.

Martha grinned and patted Kimber on the knee. "Don't mind William," she said. "He's very much of the old school, but he can't help it, his father's the principal and you know how he is. William only really means about a third of what he says."

"Don't speak for me, Martha," William said. He flicked a dry leaf towards her, and it drifted halfway across the blanket and settled on a scone. "I mean everything I say."

"Yeah, but that doesn't mean you can't be wrong about things." Samal moved closer to William and elbowed him gently, smiling. "These people are our new friends, and the stars know we could all use some more of those."

Horatio was nosing around the plate of egg salad sandwiches, so Kimber scooped him up.

"Sorry if I flew off the handle there," she said. "I just hate it when people look down on other people's magic. It's all magic, it's all wonderful and no one's talent is any lesser than anyone else's."

William sat up straighter and shook his head. His expression softened as he looked at Kimber. "I'm sorry, I do actually agree with you. I didn't mean to be rude, sometimes these things just slip out. I'm realising, since meeting Alistair, that I have a few lessons and assumptions from childhood that I need to unlearn."

"It's all right," Alexander said. He shrugged a shoulder. "I'm sure I don't have it anywhere near as bad as Thomas. People can say some awful things about shapeshifters, which is so silly because shapeshifting is amazing."

"Still, it doesn't make it all right to say," William said. "I am sorry."

"It's all right, you'll get there," Alistair said. "I barely know anything about the magical world at all! I didn't know magic even existed last Summer." He had meant it to be a sort of joke, but the others just sort of blinked at him in confusion.

"The point is," William went on. "Please don't be scared off by my words."

"Oh, not a chance of that," Kimber said. "Alistair is such an oddity, I'm so interested in him and what he'll do next."

"You should have seen him in his first classes last year," William said. He smiled affectionately at Alistair.

Alistair looked between them all as they made tentative amends, and scowls were replaced with smiles. Were these really his new friends?

Kimber was forthright, but he liked her, and Alexander, well, he was a little awkward, but something about him made Alistair feel comfortable. Maybe their awkwardness matched up?

He would very much like the two of them to be his friends, and friends with his boyfriends and Martha as well. He pulled the fabric napkin off the raspberry slice he'd brought from the dining hall.

"Right then, who'd like some of this?" he asked. He smiled as everyone agreed they'd like to try a piece.

CHAPTER 13

The day after the picnic, Alistair and Thomas went down to the greenhouse together for their first Botany class of the term.

It was entirely possible that Zeta Blake had been in the previous term's Botany class with Alistair, but he had no recollection of her.

The only students he had noticed in the previous class were Thomas, of course, and the irritating and ultimately dangerous Birch cousins. There had been other students, he thought, he could dimly remember other bodies in the greenhouse, but now that he knew who Zeta was, he noticed her setting up on the other side of the greenhouse.

Zeta caught Alistair staring at her, and gave him a little wave. He startled, realised that he had been staring, and waved back with an awkward smile, before focusing his attention back on the tray in front of him.

Professor Weatherstaff had left a notice up on the board, instructing them to prepare a tray for seedlings. The Professor himself could be heard bustling in the store room, and occasionally grumbling.

Thomas and Alistair were working side by side, filling the

seed trays with a mixture of soil and compost that Weatherstaff had provided in large barrels at the front of the class.

"Oh, there's Zeta!" Thomas said, he waved at her as well. "Should we ask her to sit with us? I had quite a nice talk with her about the student association."

"Uh, yes, if you like?" Alistair said. He was perfectly happy to work with just Thomas, but it didn't seem as if Zeta had anyone to work with.

"Hey Zeta! Do you want to share our table?" Thomas called out.

Zeta's face broke into a wide smile and she nodded, gathering up the seed tray she had already filled and carrying it over to sit opposite Thomas at their table.

"Thanks," she said, brightly. "Nice having someone to talk to, isn't it?"

"Who did you pair with last term?" Alistair asked. It was foremost in his mind. Zeta blinked at him and then her cheeks warmed.

"Oh, uh, I was paired with Eulalia Birch. If you don't feel comfortable with me sitting here, knowing that, I will absolutely understand." She looked down at her seed tray and waited for their response.

Thomas and Alistair were both silent. Alistair could hardly forget that Eulalia Birch had tried to kill him on more than one occasion, but Zeta had never been involved. Had she?

"Well, I mean, as long as you don't act the way she did," Alistair said. "And if you have any issue with me personally, you could well, talk to me about it rather than trying to curse me to death."

"I don't have any issues with you at all," Zeta said quickly. "And of course, I'd only ever talk. Curses are so..." she wrinkled her nose with distaste. "Unsavoury, don't you think?"

Alistair leaned back on the stool he was perched on and folded his arms. Her answer had been totally perfect, reassuring and warm. But then, if she was trying to gain his trust for a dark and nefarious reason, she would hardly say anything else.

How could he possibly trust what she said?

But by the same token, he wanted to make friends, and he had no real reason to believe she'd be lying about this. If she truly had a problem with him she could have refused Thomas's invite to join them.

Thomas glanced between them. "I'm sure we all agree that curses aren't good," he ventured.

"They aren't good at all," Alistair said. "One might even say that curses and the people who use them are evil."

Zeta blinked at him and nodded slowly. "Yes, we are one hundred percent on the same page."

Kimber hurried in, out of breath, her stoat familiar clinging to her sleeve. She caught sight of their table and made her way straight over to them.

"Don't mind if I join you, do you?" She asked.

"Of course not," Thomas said.

Alistair relaxed as Kimber settled beside Zeta. Somehow, she added balance to the group, and Alistair's suspicions about Zeta seemed unreasonable.

Professor Weatherstaff stumped in then with an introductory and rather gruff clearing of his throat. "Welcome back, first day, all of that." He waved his hand, as if he was dismissing the ordinary class pleasantries of starting out. "Today you'll be planting lettuce. It's entirely the wrong time of year for this particular strain, they prefer a cold ground and a hard frost to really thrive, but that's the challenge of it."

He set a stack of paper envelopes of seeds on the front table. "Come take a packet of seeds per table, get the seeds into your tray and we'll get started on microclimate spells."

"I'll go," Thomas said. He hopped off his stool and went to get the packet of seeds before anyone could say anything.

Zeta turned immediately to Alistair with an intense look.

"I know what they tried to do to you," Zeta said. "I had no idea. Eulalia wasn't anything but polite to me, and I certainly had no idea what she was capable of."

"None of us did," Alistair said. He waved his hand and shook his head. "Please don't worry too much. It was certainly nothing like any of the pranks I'd read about in books."

Zeta blinked as if she didn't follow. "Books?"

"Never mind." Alistair looked her in the eyes and saw that she needed him to acknowledge that she wasn't involved. He sighed. "I believe you. I just... I'm honestly not very good at any of this, making friends, getting to know people and the like. The Birches..." he shrugged. "It seemed to come from nowhere, so I am a little suspicious just at first, but I feel fine about you now."

"I understand." She gave him a shy smile.

Kimber looked between them with interest, and Alistair imagined that her expression meant she wanted to ask more but was too polite to.

Thomas returned with a packet of seeds and shook some into each of their hands for planting. Alistair closed his fingers around the tiny specks and let the familiar tingle of his magic wash over him. He didn't want to talk to the seeds, exactly, but he wanted to see what he could feel.

The magic teased around the seeds in his hand and he felt them respond, very slowly, tired. He had woken them from hibernation. He silently apologised and let his magic ebb away again. He opened his eyes and set about planting the seeds in his seed tray, giving each an inch or so space from the others.

"Now, who among you knows what the word climate means?" Weatherstaff asked.

Zeta's hand shot up.

"Yes, Blake?"

"It refers to the weather," Zeta said. "Specifically the prevailing sort of weather in a particular area."

"That's right enough. So when I say 'microclimate' what might that mean?"

There was silence in the room, and then Alistair tentatively put his hand up. "Micro means small, doesn't it? Like in the word microscope, so does it mean... small weather?"

"Nail on the head," Weatherstaff said and nodded. "The greenhouse we're standing in is a microclimate, it keeps things warm and humid whatever horrible storms are going on outside. What we're going to do now is learn about crafting something even smaller. A weather system confined to just your trays. We will make it winter for these seeds, to make them sprout and grow against the season."

Alistair felt a flutter of excitement in his chest. This was truly interesting magic with a practical use. Perhaps there were things in the Secret Garden which could benefit from such a spell?

Maybe he could take some of the summer flowers and keep them alive through winter?

"We start with focusing on the weather we want to create," Weatherstaff said. He proceeded to instruct them, taking things one step at a time and ensuring everyone in the class had completed the step before moving onto the next.

Alistair was sweating after an hour, the magic was precise, and delicate in a way he hadn't encountered before with spell crafting. The sketching of the new runes and the singular focus required was difficult to manage, more difficult as the spell progressed. However Professor Weatherstaff was surprisingly patient and happy to repeat instructions.

By the end of the scheduled class, each tray had a small crystalline dome of magic placed on top of it.

"Remember to use labels to name your work," Professor Weatherstaff said.

There was a general bustle as people wrote their names, either with grease pencil or with magic on their seed tray labels.

"There's a shelf set aside for these, on the East side of the greenhouse," Weatherstaff gestured. "Be careful shifting them, you don't want a crack in the dome. And if I see anyone deliberately interfering with someone else's project it will be an automatic fail and report to Barlow. This school, as I'm sure you all remember, has a zero-tolerance approach to bullies, and we are being extra vigilant about it this term, following recent events."

Alistair's shoulders rounded as all the eyes in the room turned to him.

After a moment, people started to get up and carefully move their trays to the designated shelf. It seemed an unspoken rule to leave a few inches in between trays, which seemed sensible to avoid jostling and possibly brackages, Alistair thought.

He was the last to put his tray on the shelf, feeling rather humiliated at more or less being the well-known victim of terrible acts, and therefore the cause of added precautions.

Thomas met him at the door with a smile and slipped his arm through his. "Come along, it's not that bad."

"Everyone just stared at me," Alistair said. "I hated it. It made me feel like I was weak, or something."

"You're not weak for being picked on." Thomas leaned in and kissed his cheek, and he felt a little better. "In fact, extra caution is a very good thing. This way we'll keep everyone safe. Your case was extreme, but I'm sure there's smaller acts of bullying happening where perhaps people have looked the other way before, but now they can't be ignored."

Alistair nodded. "That does make a certain amount of sense."

"So there, you've improved things for everyone."

Alistair leaned against Thomas's shoulder. "Thank you, you always have the best way of seeing things."

CHAPTER 14

The next day no one had any classes scheduled. The four of them sat around the breakfast table with Martha. Alistair felt half asleep still, as he munched on his morning toast and jam.

"Why do none of us have classes on a Thursday?" He asked.

"It's so that we focus on homework and extra study," Samal said. "We'll be grateful for it later in the term when our essays and things start to come due."

"So, what shall we do today?" Thomas looked between them.

"I was thinking of visiting the..." Alistair trailed off when he remembered Martha was at the table with them. He swallowed and added. "Garden, just a walk around the garden maybe?"

"Maybe," Martha said. She wrinkled her nose. "I sort of want to do something more fun than that though."

"How about a visit to Misselthwaite village?" Thomas said. "It's pleasant enough, and we could get lunch at the tea shop there."

Alistair nodded. "I've never actually visited it, that might be fun."

"I could use some extra notebooks," Samal said. "I thought

I'd packed plenty but I don't seem to have enough with all the extra things Madame Waxleaf is suggesting."

"Sounds grand," William said. "I'll come along. I'm sure a walk would do me good."

An hour later they were walking down the hill away from Misselthwaite Manor and into the small, sleepy village of Misselthwaite proper.

Alistair thought back to the shopping trip they'd been on in London and smiled, linking arms with Thomas. The air was clear, the sky was blue and all around him the breeze whispered through the fine oaks that lined the carriageway.

Martha and Samal were leading the way, walking side by side and talking about spellwork.

William fell in beside Alistair. "You look cheerful," he remarked.

Alistair shrugged. "Why shouldn't I be?"

"Oh you should be, it's just unusual for you," William said. "I like it, though. It looks good on you. It's good to see you relaxed and making friends."

Alistair felt his cheeks warm and wondered if he would ever get used to how flirting made him feel, especially when it came from one of his beloved boyfriends. Probably not. He was doomed to blushes and embarrassment for the foreseeable future.

They turned the last corner of the carriageway and the village of Misselthwaite unfolded before them. The main road housed all of the shops, many of them with apartments on top of them. There was a butcher, a fishmonger, a green grocer and a general store. On the other side of the road, a florist, a clothier, a pub and a tea shop. The shop that drew Alistair's eye immediately was a combination bookstore and stationery vendor.

He must have tensed because Thomas exclaimed and patted his hand. "Try not to squash my arm, Allie."

"Sorry," Alistair said. "But there's a bookstore here! I mean, I have access to plenty of books at the library of course, but it's not quite the same…"

Samal turned back, alerted by the slightly raised voices and smiled fondly. "I suppose we'll be visiting the bookstore, then?"

"Yes, please," Alistair said. "I'm happy to look at all of the shops, though I don't know that we'll have a particular use for the butcher or the fishmonger."

"Hmm," William said. "It might be pleasant to have a bonfire some night, as the summer winds up. We could get some fish to roast on the embers?"

"Or sausages to toast?" Samal asked.

"Mmm," Thomas nodded. "That does sound lovely. We could get to know your new friends a bit better, Allie."

"Perhaps." Alistair wasn't nearly as excited about this idea as he was about perusing the bookshop though.

Their first stop was at the general store, since it was the first they came across. Inside was a wealth of gardening supplies as well as the usual household necessaries; balls of twine, jars of nails, tools, soaps and the like. Thomas and Alistair went to examine the seed packets and paper bags of bulbs ready for sowing.

"I wonder if we need anything like this for the garden," Thomas said, his voice hushed. "You've been very good at finding the old things in the earth, but perhaps something new would be good to add as well?"

"I think so too." Alistair ran his eyes over the handwritten labels and read out the ones he was interested in.

"Anemones? I thought those were things that lived in the ocean." William said, looking over Alistair's shoulder.

"Well, apparently they are also plants." Alistair said. "I don't think we have any in the garden, but I've seen them in books, and they look pretty though." He picked up the bag and once again remembered he didn't have disposable income. He swallowed and looked at William pleadingly. He nodded.

"Pick what you like, I don't mind paying."

"Dangerous words," Samal said. He was teasing, Alistair knew he was, but he hated to think he was taking advantage of William's kindness and his wealth. He tightened his grip on the bag, looked briefly at the other bags of bulbs and then shook his head slightly.

"Just these are fine," he said. "Thank you William."

"If you're sure," William said. "Thomas?"

"King sundew? I haven't heard of this one," Thomas said. He picked up a packet of seeds. The shopkeeper, a ruddy faced woman who had apparently been listening, spoke up.

"Those are new, in from a trader who'd just been to South Africa, he said they're a carnivorous plant, and they flower with bright purple. Sounded pretty to me."

Thomas's eyes started to shine. "I want to try them."

William took their chosen purchases to the shopkeeper. "Thank you Mrs Owen. Do you have any more of that wonderful tea you used to make?"

"Of course, lad," Mrs Owen said. She turned to the shelf behind the counter and pulled down a sizable glass jar filled with dried flowers and herbs. "How much would you like?"

"Oh a pound for now, please," William said. "You know how much Father appreciates it. I'll probably return for more in a few weeks."

Mrs Owen smiled and used a scoop to measure out the tea into a bag which she popped into a carrier along with the seeds and bulbs. "You give my regards to Lord Carlisle, if you please," she said, as William paid.

"Of course I will," William said. "Thank you."

They left the general store and Alistair wondered why he felt surprised that William might be on good terms with a shopkeeper. It made complete sense, William had lived here his whole life, and his life had spanned many years, even if a lot of them were spent in a kind of magical torpor.

But something about the exchange tugged at him as they walked out into the light. Mrs Owen knew the family, knew Lord Carlisle. But how much did she know about what ailed him, or why William probably hadn't really aged in the time she'd known him? It wasn't really a conversation to have now though.

"What sort of tea is it?" Samal asked. He leaned over to peer in the carrier bag, which William promptly handed to him to carry.

"A medicinal blend, chamomile is the chief ingredient, but she puts a lot of other things in there, it's very soothing although not at all magical."

"Does she know about magic?" Alistair asked, his voice low.

"No," William said. "But she's what once might have been called a village wise woman or hedgewitch. Knows a lot about herbs and natural remedies, and there's plenty of natural magic in the things she puts together."

Alistair smiled a little at that, and glanced back at the general store. "That's sort of wonderful."

"Mam uses lots of Mrs Owen's teas and things," Thomas said. "Best general store in all of England, she likes to say."

Alistair and William chuckled at that.

The bookshop didn't look large from the outside, but the wealth of books inside was impressive, and Alistair was drawn to it like a magnet. He gave the window display a cursory glance, and went in to browse, starting with the display table in the front.

After a little time, the others grew bored.

"Alistair, are you nearly done?" Thomas asked. Alistair looked up, he had no idea how much time had passed, he'd been so busy reading blurbs and examining covers.

Samal was leaning against the wall near the door and William was walking towards Alistair.

"Oh, uh, well, not really," Alistair said. "But if you want to leave, we can?"

"How about this?" William said. "You take your time, we'll go find a table at the tearooms and you can join us there when you're done."

Alistair nodded, but the thought of money dried out his mouth. "No, it's fine, I can't really afford any of the..."

William silenced him with a raised finger. "The bookstore can bill me at the manor, just pick what you like, and they'll write it all down. Just remember you have to carry it back up the hill afterwards."

"Or get Sam to carry it for you." Thomas grinned. "That seems to be William's approach."

"Are you sure that's all right?" Alistair said. He felt it was an imposition but there were so many interesting looking books he'd already seen. "I won't be much longer."

William squeezed his shoulder. "Allie, you can spend all you like. I wouldn't say it if I didn't mean it."

Well, Alistair knew that was true. William wouldn't offer anything at all if he didn't care to, and Alistair was grateful for that. He knew he would be honest.

The others left Alistair to it, and he delightedly went back to examining the books on the shelves.

CHAPTER 15

A full hour later Alistair was having book titles written into the ledger for billing. The bookstore had no books of magic of course, but there were plenty of volumes on gardening, plants and the like. On top of that there were novels he hadn't seen, and a new one from one of his favourite authors. The pile of books was eight high.

Although he had meant to try and be restrained in the number he collected, he justified the stack by telling himself he would pay William back, when he came into his own fortune.

The clerk was an avuncular sort, and he was cheerful enough about the arduous task.

"Would you like a bag for all of these?" He asked. "We have some good sturdy canvas bags , and I can add it to the bill easily enough."

He gestured to the wall behind him where in between bookshelves was a blue canvas tote bag with the store's logo printed on the side.

"That looks perfect, yes, thank you," Alistair said.

With the books safely bundled into the bag, Alistair made his way out of the shop and blinked in the sudden harshness of daylight. Just up the road was the tea shop, and he made his way towards it and his friends, feeling slightly sheepish about the amount of time it had taken him to rejoin them.

The street was a little busier than before, with clusters of students here and there. He saw Zeta, unmistakable in her brown trousers and well-fitted waistcoat, she was in a group of five or six, leading the way and laughing with them. He thought he recognised a few of them, but they were across the road and busy, so he didn't try to say hello.

He let himself into the small tea shop and spotted William immediately, he sat straight-backed, gesturing and saying something that had Samal and Thomas laughing. He looked like a young Gothic prince holding court. Alistair felt his heart thump a little faster as he wended his way through the chairs and tables to join them. They were all so handsome, and it sometimes took him by surprise.

"There you are! We were about to send Samal in to rescue you," William said, his eyes laughing. "Tear you away from the stacks of books that threaten to eat you alive."

Alistair ducked his head. "Sorry, I sort of lost track of time."

"It's fine," Samal stood up and pulled out a chair for Alistair. "I mean, I knew you liked books, I just hadn't quite understood quite how much."

"Did Martha leave?" Alistair asked.

"Yes, she had some transformation homework that needed attention," Samal said.

"We've already had a round of scones," Thomas said. "But we agreed they were so good we'd just have another round when you joined us."

Alistair felt his cheeks warm. Next time he wanted to peruse the bookshop perhaps he'd just come down on his own, then he wouldn't be inconveniencing anyone.

William signalled to the waiter and soon their table had a large plate of steaming scones, homemade raspberry jam and fresh whipped cream on it.

Alistair's stomach rumbled, and he helped himself. Thomas poured him a cup of tea from the pot in the centre of the table.

"So, what's the plan for the rest of the day?" William asked, after they'd polished off all the scones.

"Perhaps some time in the garden?" Alistair suggested.

Samal nodded. "It's a very good day for it, weather-wise."

"Agreed," Thomas said. "I feel like I want to run and jump and roll in the grass."

The walk back up to Misselthwaite Manor was a little on the difficult side as Alistair's book bag got more and more heavy the longer they walked. Finally Samal noticed, and took it off him.

"You really don't have to," Alistair said. Samal winked at him, and Alistair smiled in relief. "But thank you."

Back in the university proper things weren't as quiet and serene as they'd been earlier.

There was a lot of chatter, and the cause was obvious; there was a huge green creeping vine, which seemed to have erupted out of the ground, and was rapidly climbing the East wall of the hallway.

It looked like some strain of ivy, common enough, except the leaves were the size of dinner plates and Alistair had never seen a strain of ivy that grew this quickly.

The vines grew as they watched, climbing towards the ceiling and threatening to overtake the chandelier. It put Alistair in mind of the incredibly large and fast growing flowers which had come from his magic in the Secret Garden when the four of them had done the ritual together.

Professor Barlow and Mrs Medlock were standing in a clear spot in the entranceway, and there were groups of students gathered, watching from a respectful distance.

"Someone needs to get Professor Weatherstaff," William said. Thomas turned to go, but Professor Weatherstaff was already stomping in, his expression thunderous.

"What do you think it is, Ben?" Barlow asked, as the students parted to allow Weatherstaff through. "Some kind of new strain?"

"No. Some idiot student pulling a prank." Weatherstaff's tone was gruff and impatient. Alistair moved closer, wanting to see how Weatherstaff countered the growth spell, for that was surely what it was.

There was a sudden crash as a vine grew under a picture frame, forcing it from the wall.

Barlow winced visibly.

"It'll just take a moment to slow the growth, then I should be able to reverse it," Weatherstaff said. He raised his hands and spoke a couple of runes Alistair thought he'd be able to replicate if needed. The ivy's growth slowed down.

Medlock waved her wand and rescued the damaged picture, magically restoring the glass and holding it in the air until the vines had receded.

It didn't take long at all, perhaps a half minute for the ivy's growth to stop entirely. Then Weatherstaff spoke another word and the ivy withered and died, shrivelling into withered, dried leaves and falling to the floor.

At this point Alistair saw that the vines hadn't sprung out of the floor, or pushed through from below; they had emerged from an ordinary seed tray. Just the same as the ones they used in botany all the time.

A dark foreboding came over him as Weatherstaff bent to pick up the tray and read the label on it. "Lennox and Sowersby."

Alistair had the unpleasant experience of everyone in the room turning to look at him all at the same time. He felt horribly naked, and misunderstood. He flushed red, and shook his head.

"It wasn't us!"

Thomas stepped up beside him, looked down at the floor, and said nothing.

Weatherstaff made a grumbling 'hmmm' noise and looked

away, waving his hand to sweep up the dead plant matter and send it out the door. Presumably to the compost. The silence in the entranceway was so complete that Weatherstaff's grumble no doubt carried to the ears of everyone present.

Barlow approached Alistair and Thomas. "You knew nothing about this?"

"No Professor Barlow," Thomas said. "We've been in the village, having tea."

Barlow nodded. "I see, and I expect if we asked the owners they'd be able to vouch that you were there the entire time?"

"Yes, sir."

"I was in the bookshop for a time," Alistair said. He had a sinking feeling. He hadn't been with his friends the entire time, would they suspect him of anything? No, that was preposterous. "But the shopkeeper was there too, he'd be able to tell you. See? There's the bag." He pointed at Samal, who held the tote bag over his arm.

There was a soft murmuring among some of the students, and Alistair felt himself flush more. He felt horribly guilty, even though he knew he had done absolutely nothing.

"Professor, if Alistair were to do a prank like this," William stepped forward and put his hand on Alistair's shoulder. Possessive, almost. "I think we can agree that he'd at least have the forethought to not use a seed tray with his name recorded on it."

Barlow seemed to relent then, and Alistair wondered if it was because of William's reasoning or simply his presence. William was the son of the principal, and perhaps that came with a certain advantage, such as less questions being asked.

"Right," Barlow said. He looked around and waved off the gathered students. "Out of the way, please, Medlock and I will finish the tidying up. Please go back to whatever you were doing!"

Thomas slipped his arm through Alistair's. "Do you still want to go to the Garden?"

Alistair nodded, but he felt at a loss. He wasn't sure who had done this, or why they had wanted to bring him into it, but it all felt a little dangerous, portentous perhaps.

"Come on, let's go straight there," William said. He turned to usher them all back to the main door. "The less people associate us with what just happened, the better."

The Garden was at least a comfort, he could plant the new bulbs for anemones - the bulbs themselves looked almost nothing like plants, they looked like strange small, misshapen rocks, but when he held them in his fingers he could feel the faintest pulse of promise within them.

There was something deeply satisfying about clearing a flower bed of old, dead growth, turning the soil to make it fluffy and burying little clusters of bulbs together.

As he covered them back over with soil, he let a little magic flow from his fingers and into them, encouraging them to wake up a little quicker than they usually would. Each of the bulbs responded with a tiny spark of a reply, which made him smile.

While Alistair worked on that, Thomas had shapeshifted into dog form to run about the meadow and roll on his back, the picture of doggy joy.

William was seated at the fountain, looking up at, and possibly silently conversing with the spirit of his long dead mother. He had a serene expression every time Alistair looked over.

Samal had made it his personal mission to tend a wall of old roses. They had been overgrown and neglected for so long, and it suited his talent for healing to spend time gently pruning back what needed pruning, finding just the right blend of fertiliser and compost, and talking to the roses to ensure he was doing what they needed.

It would have been very easy to be distracted watching any

one of his boyfriends enjoying themselves in gentle ways in the Garden, and a few times Alistair did allow himself to watch just for a time, but he wanted to ensure the anemones were in the ground and ready for the next rainfall.

So much of the Garden was improved from when they'd discovered it, but Alistair felt a certain reluctance to make it too perfect. It was right that some of it should run wild, he thought. He should probably make sure the others agreed with him on that.

Finally, the afternoon started to wane and Alistair stopped removing overgrown grass from a plant bed. His work had taken him slowly closer to where Samal was nursing roses, and as he sat up and stretched the crick out of his neck, Samal smiled down at him, then pointed over his shoulder.

He looked around to see William seated on the tiles, his back to the retaining wall of the fountain, and his legs stretched out in front of him. He had one of Alistair's new books in his hand, and was apparently several chapters into it already. Thomas in golden retriever form flopped across his lap, snoozing. William's other hand was in Thomas's fur, petting him softly.

"Rather a picture, aren't they?" Samal asked softly.

Alistair's heart responded to the fondness in Samal's tone, matching it with Alistair's own fondness for all three of them. "Yes, they are."

"Don't be too loud," William stage-whispered. "You'll wake him up."

"We should probably be getting back," Alistair said. Although he felt horribly reluctant to disturb Thomas, his stomach had begun to rumble.

Thomas wuffed and looked up, blinking sleepily at all three of them. They packed up their tools and stowed them away in the usual place.

"Mind if I keep reading this?" William asked, showing Alistair the cover. It was a romantic novel which had promised all sorts of lurid excitement, and Alistair grinned, pleased William was enjoying it.

"You finish it," Alistair said. "Just don't tell me what happens in the end before I get a chance to read it myself."

"Thanks," William said. "I didn't think I'd enjoy it, but the writing is quite compelling."

They made their way back up to the Manor slowly. Thomas changed back into human form, but couldn't seem to stop yawning, slinging his arm around Samal's shoulder and leaning on him as they walked. Samal was characteristically quiet, and William had his nose in the book.

They were almost out of the maze of walled gardens when they overheard some students talking. Alistair would normally have ignored other people's conversations, but he heard his name, and that caught his ear. He stopped, listening hard, the other students must have been just on the other side of the wall.

"I don't know that Lennox is capable of such a thing," one said.

"Barlow stopped asking questions as soon as William Carlisle stepped forward," someone whispered. "And everyone knows William and Alistair are thick as thieves."

"Well, he's hardly going to tell the principal's son that he's wrong."

"Alistair is so new, he barely seems to understand what to do in classes," another voice said. "I wouldn't put it past him to use his own seed tray and not think anything of it."

"And that's the thing, he's bloody talented at some magic, so it's not like he *couldn't* have done the spell that made it happen."

William frowned, looked up and took Alistair's arm. "Come on, there's no good can come of eavesdropping."

"But... I... they..." Alistair sputtered. Thomas and Samal hadn't stopped walking, they were further up the path by now.

"It doesn't matter what they think," William said. "Come on." He started to walk, half dragging Alistair with him.

"But they're wrong!" Alistair protested. "I had nothing to do with it, and they think I'm... I don't know, simple or something."

"All they said was that you're not that *au fait* with school, and to be perfectly honest that's true. You barely had anything do with society more than a few months ago, and it's perfectly natural that it will take you some time to understand the unwritten rules of things."

"So you agree? You think I'm hopeless?" Alistair asked, stung.

"That is not what I said," William said. His tone was an uncomfortable balance of exasperated and reassurance. "Don't take it personally, Allie, it's just idle gossip. They probably don't even really believe what they're saying, they just want something to natter about."

Alistair folded his arms and breathed out heavily through his nose. He didn't like being the focus of people he didn't know, and he didn't know how to process it at all. William was right, it was just idle gossip, but if people were so willing to believe something so wrong about him, that felt even worse. That night he took some time to write in his journal.

I suppose it was inevitable that people would start to talk about me. I don't like it one bit though. The incident with the rogue plant and the seed tray certainly seemed intentional. Someone must have taken the seed tray from the greenhouse and then done the spell to make me look bad.

I do wish they hadn't also made Thomas look bad in the doing of it. He doesn't deserve to be looked down on in any way.

Then those people - implying that I got away with something simply because Will is my boyfriend, and he has sway over the teachers. It's infuriating.

But I can see how it could look that way from the outside. Why, the first time I saw him at Misselthwaite he seemed to use his influence to get an extension off Barlow... although I think he didn't actually get away with that in the end.

Social politics are fun to read about in novels but when you're embroiled in them, they're no fun at all.

I shall have to try even harder to be kind and make more friends. That way people will be able to see I'm not the kind of person to do a silly prank like that. And perhaps they can see that I'm trying my hardest to fit in as well.

Kimber, Alexander and Zeta all seem to be becoming friends. I shall try to ensure I don't scare them off in any way.

Must remember to think before I speak.

CHAPTER 16

*A*listair's first meeting with April Quinn had been rather delayed, with the confusion of the start of term and various other commitments her life as a postgraduate student seemed to dictate. When Alistair knocked on the door of the office she'd been assigned, it was Monday morning.

"Come in!" The cheery voice from inside was encouraging, breathy and pleasantly deep. Her accent was broad, perhaps from the colonies somewhere?

Alistair let himself in to see a woman with long purple hair twisted into two long plaits down her back. She wore a full skirt which was midnight blue with silver stars on it here and there, and a pale blue blouse. She turned to greet him, smiling wide behind small silver framed glasses.

"Miss Quinn, I presume?" Alistair said, moving into the already cluttered office. It was a small space, barely larger than a storage room, with the desk taking up one wall. He felt too tall, as if he had too many elbows and was liable to knock into something at any moment.

"Please, just call me April," she said. She pointed at the second chair in the room, which had a stack of books on it. "You can sit there, just put the books..." she hesitated, looking around, seeing no obvious place for the books she held her hands out. "Hand them to me, I'll deal with them."

Alistair picked up the stack of books - library books from the looks of the titles, including one he'd borrowed twice last term - and handed them to her. Then he sat on the chair and put his hands between his knees.

"I'm Alistair Lennox, Professor Barlow said you might be interested in chatting with me."

"Yes." April shoved the books on top of the stack of notes she had on her desk and turned back to Alistair with an expression which was intimidatingly enthusiastic. Her eyes fixed on him and he felt unable to look away. "I don't know the details, but I have heard that you made a major step forward on the William Carlisle curse."

Alistair sat very straight and still. He was somehow sure that if he moved too quickly she'd pounce on him. "That is correct."

"How did you do it?" She asked. She leaned further forward. "Because my direction of study is very particular in regards to curses, and I know that I'm sorta going against the normal way of things, but I've found my methods very effective indeed."

Alistair was heartened by her insistence that she was doing something unusual. He was so far from understanding society, and here was a woman deliberately going against it. She was less likely to judge him than others, he hoped.

"I, well, it was a peculiar spell, a ward really," Alistair said. "It involved the power of a wellspring, and since I'm so new to all of this, I leaned on the magic of my... my friends as well. Some healing magic, some shapeshifting, that made a huge difference, really."

"A wellspring!" April sat back, breaking eye contact, and Alistair let himself breathe again. "That would be handy, but I suppose it's not just something you can carry around with you, ready to use at any moment."

"No." Alistair said. April spun in her chair, shoved the stack of books aside and tugged out a piece of paper which she started to write on. Alistair wasn't sure if he should keep speaking, or if he should perhaps leave altogether, but then April tapped her fingers on the desk and spun back to face him.

"So, I'm here doing my doctorate. It's about using blood magic to break curses, and as I said, it's sort of against the accepted normal. Most magic users look at blood magic as sort of... well, forbidden. Taboo. But I've discovered that I can use it to absolutely obliterate curses. It's a different method to unpicking them, all that fiddly code-breaker work, but it's effective, no one can say it's not."

Alistair swallowed. She'd spoken so fast he felt like he needed a couple of seconds to process her words.

"I see," he said, which was purely politeness. He had no idea at all what blood magic was, let alone how one could use it to destroy a curse.

"So if you're interested," she continued. "I'll be carrying out some experiments, and teaching some very casual classes. If you'd like to be involved, and just so we're crystal clear, I *really* would like it if you were involved. I think we could learn a whole lot from each other, Alistair, you can sign up right now."

Alistair swallowed. He didn't think too hard about the taboo aspect of what she'd said. Perhaps there were branches of magic which were more dangerous, but he had seen first hand that discrimination based on what society thought was incorrect was wrong and unjust.

Thomas was at University purely because Lord Carlisle believed in including everyone.

He decided to read up on it, and ask William. They'd spoken briefly of blood magic on the train, but not very deeply about what it meant.

But for the moment he was willing to take a chance on this.

"I, yes, I'd like that very much," he said. "I want to destroy the curse on William, what I did was really a stopgap, a ward between the curse and his soul. The curse is still there, it's just not able to affect him to the same degree."

April's eyes went wider still and her mouth fell open. "Amazing. I'd never have thought of even trying something like that." She turned to write on her piece of paper again, her voice had dropped a little deeper and her accent had gotten stronger at the same moment.

"Your voice," Alistair started. He stopped, realising he'd meant to say something quite different, he'd meant to ask about her accent, but April was already answering.

"When I was born the doctors thought I was a boy," she said, waving her hand. "They were obviously wrong, but the tone of a person's voice doesn't change as easily as their hair."

Alistair swallowed, feeling like he'd crossed a line of politeness purely by accident. April was looking at her desk, writing something more under her note about the wellspring.

"I beg your pardon," Alistair said. "I really didn't mean to pry, I simply meant to enquire as to your accent, where are you from?"

April's expression softened. "I'm from the United States of America, New York City to be precise."

"Did you study there as well?" Alistair asked.

"No, I went to Harvard," April said. "Well, the magical school part of it anyway. It's in Massachusetts."

"This is the first school I've ever been to," Alistair blurted. "I didn't know magic was real at all, and then my parents died and I had to come here. I don't know anything about anything."

April smiled softly at him and tilted her head. "That's okay. I've never been to a British school before. Maybe we can help each other out a little."

· · ·

*a*listair allowed a smile in return. "That would be nice. Thank you. Right, well. Welcome to Misselthwaite, I suppose."

"Thanks." She beamed at him, and handed him a fresh piece of notepaper. "Put your name up at top with your room number and I'll send an imp when I know what time classes are and where."

"An imp?"

"Oh, yeah, it's a family thing," she said. "Old contracts and the like. I'll tell you about it another time, yeah?"

Alistair wrote his name and the number on William's suites on the paper and handed it back. "I didn't even know imps were real," he said. "There's so much I don't know."

April grinned and patted his shoulder. "You're going to do great things, I reckon."

"Thank you."

"Now, off you go, I have to finish these notes and find out if there are any other students interested in my methods."

Alistair nodded and saw himself out, feeling butterflies of promise and new possibilities.

CHAPTER 17

Over the next week the new schedule settled in.

Samal was often busy with extra work, due to his talents for healing, Madame Waxleaf had given him something like an assistant teaching role, and began calling on him to help with grading papers as well as practical work as and when it came up in the infirmary.

This meant that Samal could be called away at any hour, and Alistair grew used to not having him around at dinner or in the evenings several times a week.

Samal also had a semi-regular 4am class which inevitably disturbed the others when he got up for it.

Thomas was more busy than the previous term as well, in addition to the hard work in shapeshifting class, he was often supporting Zeta with the student association. The opening meeting had been pleasant enough, but Alistair declined to assist with the running of it. It seemed to involve an awful amount of planning and paperwork, which Thomas didn't seem to mind.

He often came back from his meetings with Zeta flushed and smiling, and when Alistair asked what could possibly be so pleasing about paperwork Thomas said he found Zeta's attitudes to class and privilege refreshing.

William, for his part, was also working harder. He seemed to be top in all his classes, and determined to prove himself. Although as Alistair pointed out, he didn't *need* to prove anything to anyone, William would wave him off and mutter something about family honour.

Many an evening in their shared suite passed with Alistair working at his desk, and William at his, neither of them speaking to the other.

Alistair had plenty of homework from his own classes. The basics of wand work and spell casting were easy enough to keep up with but Winterbourne's homework was time -consuming and needed a lot of concentration. He also had plenty of reading for Botany, and keeping track of what needed to be done in the Secret Garden.

He took comfort in his journal.

There is nothing in the world wrong, but something feels somehow not right.

I've spoken with Ambrose every day since I got back to school, and I'm living harmoniously with my boyfriends, but I feel at a loss. Lonely.

I expect I'm being needy because they are all rather busy with various courses of study and so on. But I don't know why I feel this way. I knew they wouldn't be spending every waking moment paying attention to me, and the very thought of that is off-putting. I don't want constant affection. I do feel sad though, so I suppose I need more affection than I'm getting?

How much attention and affection is normal? I have books to compare to but those are fiction.

I think I just need to relax and try not to worry about how much attention I'm getting. And perhaps make sure I'm also giving attention and affection to the others. Perhaps they are feeling similarly, with all this rushing around.

he first lesson with April Quinn was unexpected.

The imp as promised, had delivered a note with a time and location in the second week of term. It was a small, slim being with red skin and generous horns curling out from its head. It asked politely for Alistair at the door to the suite, handed him the note, bowed and vanished in a puff of smoke.

William sniffed dismissively but Thomas and Alistair talked a while about how interesting imps were.

There were only a handful of students, so the class was in one of the smallest rooms. It was right in the back of the ground floor's West wing, practically next to the kitchen.

There was a chalkboard on a stand and a half dozen chairs arranged around two tables. Alistair took the chair in the middle of the room, and set out a blank notebook on the table in front of him. The other students filed in soon after.

Zeta sat down with Alistair.

"Rather exciting isn't it?" Zeta asked, her eyes were bright with anticipation.

"I suppose so. I have no idea what to expect, which is certainly... making me feel apprehensive." He gave her a smile which was more nervous than anything else.

Zeta let loose a gale of laughter and shook her head. "You have nothing to feel apprehensive about, it's just school."

"Hmm," Alistair said. "School has been rather... well. Horrible at times to me."

Zeta's eyes widened and all traces of mirth fled from her face. "Right, that business with the Birches. I'm sorry."

"Well. Hopefully that's behind me now," Alistair said.

"Morning you two." Alexander sat down on Alistair's other side and gave them both a friendly smile.

"I didn't expect to see you here," Alistair said. He realised he might once again have come off as unfriendly so quickly added. "But it's good to see you. Good morning, Alexander."

April strode into the classroom, a stack of books under one arm, a pair of spectacles on her head. Her hair was down in one thick braid which hung down her back. Behind her trotted an imp holding an untidy sheaf of papers in its arms.

"I hope you're all ready to learn something unbelievably strange," she said. She set the books down on the table in front of Alistair and the imp distributed the papers between all the students. "I'm April, and you have all met me so you know to call me April and not any of that professor nonsense. I'm barely older than you. Got it?"

Alistair nodded and Zeta smiled. "Yes, April."

"Right, good. Prof Barlow is supervising me this term, so if you see him in the back of class please be on your best behaviour and only ask questions that you know the answer to already. Then we'll all look smart." She winked to show she was joking, and there was a murmur of laughter from the students. "Now. The papers I've given you are a sort of plan for what we'll be covering, but expect me to throw that out the window after a few weeks because I've never run a class in my life so I don't know how to plan for it."

Alistair had to admit that April's honesty was refreshing, he felt himself warming to her even more.

"Right, let's get right into it, shall we?" She reached into the folds of her burgundy velvet jacket and withdrew a long, thin blade. It looked to Alistair like an extra long envelope opener, but judging from the runes engraved on the handle, it was purposely made for magic. The students in the room went very, very quiet.

April didn't seem to notice anything out of the ordinary. "Right, with blood magic, the basic component is of course, blood, so the first thing I'll need you all to do is get comfortable with the drawing of it. Any old blood will do, but it's safest and most ethical to use your own." April tilted her head to the side. "I don't suppose any of you thought to bring any kind of blade, did you? I know I didn't remind you."

"Uh, I did." Alexander rifled through his bag and produced a roll of heavy canvas tied with a string. He undid the string to reveal a series of different sized knives, all in pristine condition. "Essential for cutting up ingredients for potions," he said, when Alistair gave him a quizzical look.

"Splendid," April said, looking over his collection. "If you don't mind loaning them to your classmates, I have a very good cleansing spell that will have them ready to use again right after."

"Of course," Alexander said. "I sterilise them after every use so they'll be safe enough."

He pushed the unrolled knife holder towards Alistair who chose one at random and set it on the table before him. Somehow he hadn't expected this. He had thought they'd start with theory and build up to the actual blood.

Alistair looked down at his hands and frowned. He had never intentionally cut himself in his life.

"Of course, you can also use a slicing spell," April said, as the students each took a blade and looked at each other uncertainly. "But the level of control required for a spell of that nature is rather more than if you use the tool itself."

Slicing spells. Alistair had, of course, first hand experience with the wickedness one could do with magic, but slicing spells put an extra thrill of fear through him.

"Now, the position of the slice matters, of course. You mustn't cut anywhere that will endanger your life, and I *strongly* suggest you don't cut your palm. Lots seem to think it's terribly romantic or something, but it hurts like the dickens and it takes longer to heal. The back of the forearm on your non-dominant hand is the preferable place, in my experience. Now, everyone give it a go, and I'll show you the power you all hold within your blood."

For a few long seconds, nobody moved.

Wildly, Alistair imagined what might have happened if Lord Carlisle was in the room. He wondered if William had any of the same hungers as his vampiric father, he had certainly inherited some of his nature, after all... but the ward was holding it back.

He heard a faint hiss, and he turned to see that Zeta had rolled up her sleeve and made a small straight cut on the back of her left arm.

Alistair picked up his own knife and steeled himself. He didn't want to do it. It was so counterintuitive to hurt oneself. But he did want to know what blood magic was about, especially if there were practical uses in curse breaking.

Alexander stared at his arm with a fierce determination and sliced himself with a quick movement.

"Barely hurts," he said, noticing Alistair watching, "they're good sharp knives. No need to fear."

Alistair swallowed, and rolled his sleeve, copying the placement Zeta had chosen on his own arm and drew the knife swiftly over his skin. Alexander had been right, the cut itself didn't hurt really at all, but the aftermath stung. He watched unhappily as blood bubbled out.

"Great work everyone," April said. "You really just went ahead and cut yourselves just because I said so!"

"Well, you are the teacher," Zeta mumbled.

"In the future, I'd really like you all to consider the commands and directions you're given," April said. Her expression had turned serious. "You shouldn't just cut yourselves without question, just because I said so. Feel free to ask questions and challenge me. It's the best way to learn."

Alistair swallowed. He hadn't even considered challenging a teacher, and he wondered if any of the others had either.

"Right, now, focus on your magic. What we're going to do is any basic spell that you feel comfortable with. Something that you've cast so many times it feels like you could do it in your sleep. You'll be familiar with how it feels to cast, and you'll see the difference. Everyone got something in mind? Good, now before you cast it, draw some power from the blood. Use your wind, point it or dip it in and use the pure force of life in your spell."

She gestured behind her as she spoke and the chalk wrote the salient points on the blackboard unaided.

Cut self - get blood
Think up familiar spell
Focus on blood
Cast spell

"Everyone ready?" April asked, brightly.

Alistair pointed his willow wand at the drops of blood on his forearm, careful not to touch it, and thought of the simplest spell he knew. Probably the basic mud-removal one he'd had to learn for his trousers, although it never got quite everything out, he'd used it plenty of times.

"Yes," he said. The others in the class also gave their affirmation.

"Cast!" April waved her hands like she was conducting an orchestra, and around the room words of power and runes were spoken. Alistair swallowed, focused his magic on the blood and spoke the simple combination of runes that made up the cleaning spell.

Immediately he could feel the difference.

Usually the spell wasn't a hardship to cast, it was fine. But this time it happened instantly. He had pointed his wand at the knee of his trousers, since there was still a faint stain of dirt there.

The stain was gone, and the spell had felt as simple to cast as speaking. He tugged on the fabric, bending forward to examine it closer, and found that there was no evidence of dirt in any of the fibres.

He straightened back up, impressed.

Around the room there were soft exclamations.

Beside him, Zeta showed him a mending spell, tearing a seam of her shirt sleeve and then fixing it up again and Alexander showed off a spell that sorted his pens and pencils from a muddled pile into ordered rows, sorted by length and colour.

April was positively beaming, all her teeth on display. "How was that?" she asked, as if she didn't already know.

"Incredible," Alexander said. "It's a simple spell but it felt like nothing at all."

This sentiment was echoed several times over. One student who had introduced himself as Lewis Trudgeon, was exulting loudly. "I've always had trouble with this kind of spell, but this made it positively easy!"

Alistair glanced back at him and saw he'd cut his arm rather deeper than everyone else had. Lewis caught his eye and seemed confused, Alistair tried to school his expression as he was sure he had curled his lip and looked repulsed by the amount of blood Lewis had clearly used.

April nodded. "I'm glad you understand," she said. "Now, present your arms for healing and we can dive into some theory. I simply wanted to show you the power available to you so you'd really understand where my study is coming from, and some of the discoveries I've been able to make. And I also want to emphasise that because something is easier, doesn't mean it's safer."

She flitted around the room, healing up all their wounds and magically cleaning Alexander's knives.

She started in on the theory with everyone in the class listening devotedly.

By contrast the more regular lessons with Professor Winterbourne continued to be largely theory and deep technical problems, which required a lot of decoding and intense concentration. Alistair often felt exhausted after her lessons and somewhat headachey, as if he was using parts of his brain which had never been used before.

He was also somewhat muddled by her command that they cut themselves and then insisting that they should question things like that.

On the days he had a Professor Winterbourne class he inevitably went straight down to the Secret Garden to unwind after it. Reconnecting with the earth and the power of the wellspring eased his aching head, and allowed him to focus on the world outside of curse breaking again.

It was on one such visit, a couple of weeks after the start of term, that Alistair first noticed the wildlife in the garden was getting a bit unusual.

There were the usual insects, lots of butterflies, and birds singing in the trees. There were often rabbits here and there, and little lizards and things in the undergrowth - heard more than seen. But he caught sight of something new. It scuttled near Alistair's hand as he was working on clearing space around the base of an old forgotten climbing rose, and it startled him so badly he sat up with a cry.

It was about the size of his hand, strangely flat and spade shaped. Like a sort of crab, but it had green skin instead of a hard shell. It looked to have six legs like an insect, but it wasn't any sort of insect Alistair had seen documented before. It moved fluidly over the soil and fallen leaves and then scuttled up the brick wall, where Alistair watched it join another of the same species. Both reached the top of the wall, and turned, looking back down at him with beady black eyes which slightly protruded from the front of them.

"What on Earth...?"

He stood and examined them closely, so he'd be able to describe them to the others later on. He'd never quite considered the possibility of magical creatures here in his garden, but on reflection it did stand to reason there would be something of the sort. The wellspring was a magical force, it made sense it would attract magical things. Perhaps Alistair and the other's frequent use of the wellspring had stirred these things up?

That night he tried to describe the things to the others, but none of them seemed to recognise the creature from his words. He tried to draw them, but had some trouble getting the proportions to make sense.

"I'll go down to the garden with you tomorrow," Samal said. "Maybe we'll see them then."

CHAPTER 18

*A*listair had half expected Samal would need to cancel their planned walk in the garden. It had happened so often lately, and Alistair had never been the optimistic sort. But to his delight Samal met him in the dining hall at lunch and after they'd eaten they walked down together. Alistair was so pleased that he was getting some alone time with his busy boyfriend that he even was bold enough to link his arm with Samal's.

Samal smiled when he did that, and tugged him a little closer. "I know we haven't had too much time together since we came back to university," Samal said. "But I'm learning so much all the time, it feels as if the time has flown by."

Alistair nodded. "I am too. Between Professor Winterbourne and April's classes, I feel as if I hardly have the energy to speak at the end of the day."

Alistair felt excited, he wanted very much to show Samal the weird creatures, but part of him was just thrilled to have this time together, just the two of them. Samal's presence in itself was soothing, Alistair knew he would be protected, even if there was nothing he needed to be protected from, but he also got an incredible sense of calm from Samal. He theorised it was something about his angelic nature that exuded peace. Whatever it was, Alistair enjoyed it greatly. But besides that, he also enjoyed talking with Samal.

He let them both into the Secret Garden with the brass key, and Samal closed the door behind them.

The day was a perfect example of Yorkshire Summer, bright and warm with the hint of a breeze to keep it from getting too stifling. Alistair had changed into his gardening overalls, and although perhaps there had been some odd looks his way at lunch, he found he didn't care in the least. He was dressed for what he loved, and he was in the garden now with one of the men he loved.

"Right, I uh, I saw the things down by the uncleared bit of rose garden," Alistair said, and started down the path in that direction. Samal followed behind, humming to himself.

"It's not terribly surprising," he said. "The wellspring attracts more than just people like us, magical folk. It would be attractive to all sorts of magical creatures as well. I'm mostly surprised we haven't seen any before now, when I consider it."

"I didn't consider it at all until I saw them," Alistair said. "I'll have to ask Kincade if there's a book or two on magical garden fauna. I didn't enjoy being surprised like that."

Samal rubbed his back in a consoling way, and Alistair smiled. There was an old bench that they'd managed to unearth near the spot he'd found the things, so he sat down on that and tugged Samal down beside him.

"I'm sorry you were here alone," Samal said. He slipped his arm around his shoulder. "Want to tell me about it?"

"There's not that much more to tell, really," Alistair said. "I was just weeding and they scuttled out and peered at me. They can climb walls."

Samal leaned back and smiled. "This is nice."

Alistair leaned against him. "I was thinking that too, on the walk down. It's been a while since it's just been the two of us alone."

"How are you holding up?" Samal said. "This term is so much busier."

"I'm all right, I think," Alistair said. "It's been an adjustment for sure, but I'm learning so much. Especially with April, I think I might really be able to get somewhere with William's curse."

Samal tensed a little beside him. "I've heard rumours that she's teaching blood magic," he said. "Is that true?"

"Yes," Alistair said. He felt a sinking sensation in his stomach. "I know it's not exactly a common type of magic."

"It's not common because it's usually used for evil," Samal said.

Alistair turned to look at him.

"Not that I think what you're doing is evil," Samal said. "But blood magic. Blood is in everyone. In the past there have been mages who use it to control others, to make them do terrible things. Sometimes to get more power, blood mages have made sacrifices. Human sacrifices, unwilling, obviously."

Alistair pulled a face. "April isn't like that, she's taught us to always use our own blood, because it's the most ethical."

Samal licked his lips. "I'm sure she isn't like the stories, or she wouldn't be in residence here, let alone teaching. But the stories all say that the use of blood magic can corrupt. It can make people more and more power hungry, and then they stop caring about things like ethics. Perhaps it takes years, or decades, but the more you do it, the more likely..."

He trailed off, apparently unwilling to say more. Alistair's stomach swooped and he cleared his throat. Was Samal implying he thought Alistair could be corrupted easily?

"I don't understand," Alistair said. He folded his arms. "Yes, blood magic has a certain power to it that simply focusing on my own magic doesn't but so does the wellspring. I've never heard you worry that I'll get addicted to the power of the wellspring and start doing nefarious things."

"I didn't mean-"

Alistair's temper flared and he cut him off. "Are you saying I shouldn't take April's classes? That I shouldn't investigate every possible avenue of magic? I shouldn't try to do my best to break William's curse, and after that, the curses of others?"

"No, of course I'm not saying that." Samal put a hand on Alistair's knee and rubbed his thigh. "I'm... listen, the fact of the matter is, I'm worried about you. I didn't mean to imply that April is evil or that she's leading you down a dangerous path. I'm just expressing my concern."

"But you did imply those things," Alistair said. He dropped his hand to his lap and sighed. "I don't like feeling like I'm scaring you, but the magic she's showing me is powerful and useful. I am constantly feeling behind in everything else, you and William and Thomas all have these basic understandings of magic and how it works that I can never hope to catch up to. The spell my parents did saw to that. But I want so badly to be good at this, to help William and show his father that his faith wasn't misguided."

Alistair stopped, and swallowed twice around a lump he hadn't known was building in his throat. He had hardly known he felt that passionately about it until he started speaking, and he hadn't been consciously aware of his desire to prove himself to Lord Carlisle. But now that he'd said it out loud it felt self-evident. That *of course* it was motivating him. He had been tasked with an important job, practically handed a quest by the lord of the manor, and just like the heroes of so many books he'd read, he wanted to succeed. He wanted others to see him as a hero, not just a sour young man with the bare minimum of magical education.

He blinked back sudden dampness in his eyes and looked up from his hands to see Samal watching him with a soft expression. There was so much affection and compassion in his expression that Alistair's tears welled over and he hastily swiped them away with his sleeve.

"Alistair..." Samal said, his voice soft. "You don't have to prove yourself to Lord Carlisle."

"I want to, I think," Alistair said. "After all the stuff with my folks..."

Samal took one of his hands and squeezed it softly.

"I've never really told you about my parents, did I?"

Alistair tried to remember what he knew. "You told me that your mother was doing magic and he noticed her, and I think you said something like angels don't have genders. Oh, and he didn't stay with her?"

Samal nodded. "Angels don't think about gender the way we do, but he adopted masculine ways of dress. He fulfilled the role of father as far as getting my mother pregnant."

Alistair nodded.

"The worst thing was we'd hear about him," Samal said, sighing. "Mother raised me alone, and it was hard on her. I was a needy baby, the angel blood mixing with the human, it takes some time to settle, and Mother was run off her feet. She had some family money, thank goodness, and her brother was good enough to give her his townhouse for us to live in. But she still needed to manage so much. Things a husband would have done, she had to do. When I started flying I imagine it got even worse."

"How young were you when you started to fly?" Alistair asked. He rubbed his thumb over the back of Samal's hand.

"I don't think I was five yet, pretty small. Of course, I thought it was a wonderful lark, but mother... she saw her child vanishing into the sky. Thankfully she had magic to pull me back in, but it can't have been good for her nerves."

"And you said you'd hear from your father?"

"No." Samal shook his head. "We'd hear *of* him. For a time

at least, he was travelling around England, performing miracles and doing great healings. His picture would be in the newspaper, mundane as well as magical, and mother would clip it out and save it in a book. I used to look over the clippings and hope one day I'd be as grand and impressive as him."

"But you don't have to be," Alistair said quickly.

"Exactly what I realised," Samal said. "But it took some time. Eventually I stopped trying to compare myself to him and just decided to be who I am. And that includes things like deciding to be a nurse, which is a far smaller career than my father."

Alistair nodded, letting Samal's words sink in. He felt a pang in his chest and sighed.

"The problem is that I don't know who I am, not in the magical world." He wrung his hands together. "I felt so at home with the plants, and here in the garden, and then I found out that I have this big important gift. I want to use it to help people, I truly do."

"Of course you do, and you will. But you don't have to do it all at once, or exactly right on the first try."

Alistair took both of Samal's hands in his and looked into his eyes. "Thank you."

Samal blinked back, looking baffled. "Thank you for what?"

"For telling me about your parents. I know you better now, and I'm grateful for that. And you helped me with my own problems."

"I hope so," Samal said. He smiled, leaned in and gently brushed his lips against Alistair's. "You are so adorable, Alistair. However you end up finding who you're supposed to be, I hope you don't change too much."

Alistair flushed. He had no idea how to respond to such sweet words, but a flicker of movement caught his eye and he exclaimed, dropping one of Samal's hands to point. "There!"

One of the strange little green creatures had emerged from

the underbrush and was trundling along the edge of the flower bed.

"What's that?"

Samal frowned, watching it. "Well, it's definitely something that wasn't here last term," he said. "Perhaps our big magic ritual in proximity to the wellspring attracted it?"

"That's a good theory," Alistair said. They both watched as the thing was joined by several smaller versions of it - its offspring? They looked like little green bread and butter plates, following after their parents. "I'll see what I can find about them in the library. Hopefully they're not dangerous in any way."

"If they are, we'll deal with it," Samal said. He pulled Alistair against his side and they spent a little longer in the sun, enjoying each other's company and the quiet noises of nature.

CHAPTER 19

The classes with both April Quinn and Professor
Winterbourne continued to occupy much of Alistair's
time and mind. He paid the barest amount of attention in his
history of magic and spellwork classes, doing the minimum of
what he needed to get by. Botany classes were twice a week, and
Professor Weatherstaff wouldn't put up with any of them being
distracted. So even if he was still trying to untangle a new
puzzle, he had to set it aside. Those classes felt like a holiday in
some ways, a chance to stop puzzling over the conflicting
approaches and how best to handle them and just focus on his
hands and the plants and the soil.

Alistair ran the risk of being overwhelmed by the work. But
the fact that he could see he was improving with his magic use
and his confidence in being able to tackle harder problems, and
bigger spells gave him energy to push through.

One night however, six weeks after the start of term, Alistair
hit a wall with his homework assignment.

April hadn't been assigning a great deal of homework to
them, so when she did it usually meant they really had to
complete it to be able to understand the next lesson. Alistair had

read and re-read the instructions she'd dictated but still couldn't see exactly how the spell was meant to work.

He was in their shared suite, when William interrupted him by slamming his palm on Alistair's desk, making him startle. William could move entirely silently when he chose to, and Alistair had no idea that he had even moved from his own desk until that moment. One hand went to his chest where his heart was thundering.

"Will! Please!"

"You have been sighing for at least thirty minutes," William said. "What is the problem? I can't stand listening to you suffer any longer. You sound like a lovesick poet." He rolled his eyes expressively.

"It's this homework from April," Alistair said. He picked up the piece of paper and flapped it.

"The blood mage?" William asked, his tone dry.

"Yes, her," Alistair said. He hadn't talked it over with Thomas and William the same way he had with Samal, but they all knew the nature of the class he was taking. "I'm meant to truly understand the particles in the blood, pull them apart and then use them as elements in a powerful spell that will make a soothing sleep charm. I've gone over and over the theory and the diagrams but I can't work it out. And Ambrose is no help, he never had any experience with blood magic, and the others in the class are all busy trying to work it out as well."

"Perhaps a practical attempt at it would be elucidating," William said. He leaned over the back of Alistair's chair and read the notes he was poring over. "I could try and help if you like, make sure nothing untoward happens."

"Are you sure?" Alistair twisted in the chair to look up at him. "That would actually be the best help, yes, good."

"Of course," William said. "If it stops you sighing incessantly then I'll do anything."

Alistair grabbed his wand from the side of his desk, the

ritual knife he had ordered for spellwork, the sheet of draft instructions he had come up with (although he was certain it wasn't right yet) and got to his feet.

"Thank you," Alistair said. "Now, I'll need to start by cutting myself..."

William took two steps back and nodded, taking a quick breath. "Yes, fine. Go ahead."

Alistair made a cut and started to talk through the steps he had come up with.

"There's nothing immediately different about the start of the spell, I'll do a quick rune casting using the blood, to give it form." Alistair realised he was talking through what he was doing because he was nervous. He hadn't ever done blood magic in front of the others. He took a steadying breath, then spoke the basic runes for a sleep charm. "It's this next bit, really getting into the particles."

William's voice was strained when he spoke again. "Perhaps it requires a meditative state, shutting out the rest of the world and its distractions and giving the blood the entirety of your attention?"

"Good thought," Alistair said. He wasn't by any chance an expert at meditation, but it did seem like the correct direction to take. "I'll try it. Would you be able to hold the runes?"

"Of course," he said. Alistair glanced up to see why William sounded so peculiar and saw he was staring with intensity at the blood drops on Alistair's arm.

"There's nothing to worry about," Alistair said. Although he had no idea if that was true at all. William had something of the vampire curse on him, and although a lot of the side effects were gone, he certainly wasn't completely human. Perhaps this hadn't been the best idea, but Alistair reasoned that they had started, so they might as well keep going.

"I have the runes secure," William said. His neck had corded and there was a twitch in his jaw, as if he were working very hard on the spell, although Alistair knew it wasn't the spell that was taxing him.

"I'll try and do this quickly." Alistair turned his gaze to his arm, and put all his attention into the red drops of blood. He let the world fall away, breathing deeply and slowly. After a minute or so, he felt he could see deeper and he let himself follow that sensation. The blood was slowly showing him its secrets, and he followed the secrets, trying to see what the answers were.

After a time he straightened his back, using his wand to spread miniscule droplets of blood into the air, spreading them out so he could see it easier. This made sense, he thought, he could see what April meant. He simply had to draw power from the blood *there* and a little from over *here* and use only the parts which were fit for this particular purpose.

William made a low noise that was part growl, part whine, and Alistair hurried to work the spell, drawing the pieces he'd found in the blood into the runes and sealing them with a binding word.

It was close to being done, Alistair needed to wait for the runes to form into a physical charm, and that would take time. He examined the suspended drops of his own blood with interest.

The door to the suite swung open, banging hard against the wall as Thomas walked in.

"What in the world is going on here?"

Concentration dissolved, the blood droplets fell to the floor, and Alistair lunged forward to catch the half-formed charm.

"William was helping me with a homework assignment," he said. He examined the charm, hoping that it would finish solidifying into something he could show April.

"It looked like you were tormenting him with blood," Thomas said. "Will, are you all right?"

Thomas hurried across the room and Alistair looked up to see William had turned away, one hand covering the lower half of his face, the other clutched to his stomach as he hunched over.

A wave of concern flooded Alistair. "What happened?"

Thomas put a hand on William's back and William flinched away from him, flattening himself against the cold stone wall. "Stay back! I think I have it under control but ... I need time..." his voice sounded thick as if he had something in his mouth he was talking around.

Fear chilled Alistair's blood. Perhaps he really had been tormenting William. Hastily he set the charm down on his desk, healed the cut in his arm and did a cleaning spell to collect up every drop that had been used.

Thomas turned back to Alistair, fury in his eyes like nothing Alistair had ever seen before from him.

"What were you thinking? Bringing him into your weird blood rituals?"

"He... he offered," Alistair said. He could hear how pathetic it sounded, how weak. He should have known better than to accept the offer of help. He should have gone to ask Alexander for help, or Zeta, they understood magic and were in his class. Instead, he'd jumped at William's kind offer and done the stupidest possible thing. "I'm sorry," he said.

"I...you just..." Thomas sputtered, gesturing at the room. "You didn't think!"

"No, I didn't," Alistair said. He nodded, hoping Thomas would see how sorry he was from the forcefulness of his nodding.

"And this blood magic thing," Thomas took a breath, his chest heaving. "I don't like it. I'm going to sleep somewhere else tonight. Don't do anything more stupid than this."

He turned, picked up his bag and stormed back out again.

Alistair felt like he'd been slapped across the face. Sweet, kind Thomas was furious with him, and had told him off, and he was entirely correct to do it.

Alistair swallowed down a sob, and walked slowly towards William. He didn't seem to be in as much distress now. His breathing had slowed and his posture was a lot more relaxed. He leaned his back on the wall, and his face was tipped up, looking at the ceiling.

"Will, I truly am sorry," Alistair said, slowly. His voice cracked with shame. "I didn't think. Thomas was right, and I've caused you distress. I..."

William tipped his head forward, his pointy chin highlighting the gauntness of his features. His eyes seemed to burn with dark fire.

"I'm all right now," he said. "It's passed. I feel it's as much my fault as it is yours. I have been suffering so much less since the ward was put in. I suppose I thought all the symptoms were somehow behind me."

He held a hand out to Alistair, who closed the distance between them to take it, squeezing it tightly. William tugged him close, wrapping him in a tight hug which felt a little less comforting and a little more like getting caught by a predator.

"If, if there's anything I can do to make it up to you," Alistair said. He inhaled the scent of William and pressed his cheek to his chest. "I'm used to the blood thing now, if you ever think it would help to drink, I can let you do that... from me..."

William swallowed so heavily that Alistair felt it in his chest. "One hopes it will not ever have to come to that. But I appreciate the offer."

They pulled apart and made their toilet to prepare for bed. Samal joined them just as they were putting the lights out, and he didn't ask about Thomas, which had Alistair wondering if they'd already spoken.

He was too shy, or too ashamed to ask.

They went to bed, and regardless of being sandwiched between William and Samal all night, Alistair didn't feel nearly as warm and safe as he usually did.

CHAPTER 20

*A*listair had slept fitfully, and there had been a heavy stone in his stomach as he washed and dressed and gathered his things for the day.

William and Samal were quieter than usual, moving around the room and not saying much. Alistair realised it was usually Thomas carrying the conversation in the mornings, he was always cheerful first thing, where William needed time to wake up, and to an extent so did Samal.

Thomas was waiting at their ordinary breakfast table.

At the sight of Thomas eating his bacon and eggs, the stone in Alistair's stomach seemed to lift and he felt a smile tug at the corners of his mouth. He sat down opposite Thomas and tried to think of what to say. There were so many things in his mind, but the first and most important one popped out of his mouth without much thought.

"I'm sorry," he said. "I really didn't mean to scare you."

Thomas chewed on his mouthful thoughtfully, then swallowed. "I know you didn't. But it did seem very careless to do that kind of magic with William."

Alistair nodded quickly. William and Samal were at the

buffet, filling their plates, and Alistair glanced over his shoulder. "I know, you're right."

"I don't..." Thomas sighed a little and rubbed the bridge of his nose. "I'm pretty angry with you, to be honest. Blood magic, well, everyone knows how dangerous it is, and that's even without taking into account William's... condition. You didn't know what magic was six months ago, and now this is what you're experimenting with? You can't blame me for being concerned."

Alistair nodded. "I don't blame you."

"And I wish you'd listen to people who have more of a background in magic when we tell you there's danger here." Thomas's eyes were blazing, and the intensity of it caught in Alistair's throat.

"I understand, and I'll be cautious. But I want you to understand that I can feel the power of it, and it's not hurting anyone, not the way April is teaching us. She's very concerned about the ethics of blood magic, and she's talked on numerous occasions about how misunderstood it is as an art."

Thomas sighed more heavily. "I understand. And well, I'm never going to be entirely comfortable with it, but I do understand that you're doing your best. Please, just, if something starts to feel wrong with it will you promise to come to me or Sam about it?"

"Yes, I can agree to that," Alistair said. He thought of someone else Thomas might like to know was involved. "Zeta's in April's class, and she seems to have a fairly firm handle on right and wrong, as well. Does that help?"

Thomas's eyes widened. "Oh? Yes, that does help. I like Zeta. I think she has her head screwed on right"

Alistair reached over the table and took Thomas's hand. "I'm truly sorry. Will you at least forgive me enough to sleep in our suite tonight? I really missed you."

Thomas threaded their fingers together and squeezed. "I

forgive you, Allie. But I'm still a little angry and upset. Give me the day, I'll have a think about it. I want to sleep in there, but if it's going to make me more upset then there's no point."

Alistair swallowed. It hadn't been the answer he wanted. But he had to accept it. "Yes, of course."

Samal and William set their plates down at the table, and Sam slid another plate over to Alistair. It was heaped with fresh currant buns and a small bowl of porridge, with a cut orange on the side.

"Thanks, Sam, this is perfect," Alistair said. His heart warmed a little, knowing that even if Thomas wasn't entirely happy with him, he had been forgiven. Samal cared enough to bring him breakfast, and William, well, William was a steady companion. He was pouring tea for them all and asking Thomas quietly how he was.

Breakfast was made a little less awkward when Kimber asked to join them.

"Of course," Alistair said. Pleased that she might alleviate some of the tension. "Please sit."

Kimber shared her eggs with her familiar, Horatio, and asked them all how their term was going so far. It was pleasant, idle chatter, and it did seem to relax Thomas somewhat.

They were polishing off the last of the tea and starting to think about their morning classes when there was a commotion at the door to the entrance hall. Several students were pointing and shouting.

"What in Merlin's name is that!?"

"Stun it!"

"Stars, there's more of them!"

"Lookout!"

Then the sounds of clattering and spells being cast.

William got to his feet swiftly, the others followed suit as he strode towards the source of the ruckus. Zeta, Alexander, and a couple of other students Alistair didn't know by name were crowding the door, the source of all the trouble was evident once they were closer.

Several of the strange, spade-shaped green animals Alistair had noticed in the Secret Garden were swarming the entrance way.

Thomas pushed through the throng of people. "Don't hurt them!" he cried. "They're just innocent animals."

A girl screamed as one scuttled over her foot and tried to climb her leg, she kicked it away. Thomas cried out and tried to gather the thing in his hands, although it didn't seem inclined to let him, falling to the ground and heading for the wall.

Alistair dithered, confused and shocked to see the things inside, and at a loss for what to do - everyone shouting and making a fuss seemed to fill his brain with fluff so that he couldn't think at all.

There was a firmly spoken word of magic and Zeta waved her wand in a wide circle. Her wand summoned up a wind, which whisked the animals into it with quick precision.

"Where did they come from?" Alexander asked, hurrying to Alistair's side. "I've never seen anything like them."

"The Se... the garden. I've seen them in the gardens," Alistair said. He stuttered over his words, he'd been about to say the Secret Garden, even though they had determined to keep it a secret. He looked helpless at the miniature tornado with the green animals caught up in it, their spindly legs waving in the air.

"Please, just... Can you bring them outside?" He begged Zeta.

Zeta nodded, and directed the magical wind to the front door, the other students parting before her quickly and silently.

Alistair hurried alongside her and looked out the door. What did he know about them? They liked the garden, the walls... What was close to the school and hospitable for them? The front garden had mostly trees and low walls, but perhaps that would do.

"Down here," he said, pointing the way to the most sheltered of the small walls. "This would be good."

Thomas was at his side, breathing heavily, and he nodded. "Yes, that will shelter them."

Zeta made quick work of transporting them down where Alistair pointed and the wind eased off. The animals immediately all made for the shelter of the wall, and some even disappeared into the fallen leaves at the base of it. All up, Alistair counted perhaps a dozen of them.

"Weird thing to have happen," Zeta said. She replaced her wand in its holder, dusted off her hands and made her way back up to the Manor.

Alistair lingered a little longer, watching them and trying to understand how they had got inside. To get from the garden to inside the Manor they would surely have had to march up the path and in through the door, but they seemed like timid creatures who preferred the quiet garden. He didn't think they'd have come out into a busy area on their own.

Which meant someone had found them and brought them inside.

But for what purpose?

When he turned to Thomas his expression seemed to be just as perplexed as Alistair felt.

"What are they? It seemed like you'd seen them before," Thomas said.

"Yeah, I did, I told Sam about them, and made some drawings, I didn't ... I've never seen them outside of the Secret Garden."

"Why would you bring them into the Manor?" He asked, his voice hushed. "I don't get it."

Alistair blinked, unable for a moment to parse exactly what Thomas was asking. Then it hit him. "You think I did this."

Thomas huffed a breath out of his nose and dragged a hand through his floppy hair, pulling it back from his face. "I don't know, you are the only one who's ever talked about creatures like this. You saw them in the garden and you showed Sam."

Alistair felt as if Thomas had slapped him. "Why would I bring them in and scare them in such a way? Thomas, it's not. I'm not that kind of person."

"I don't know why you'd do it." Thomas spread his arms wide. "What I do know is that you endangered William with your blood magic, you are the first to admit you don't really know how to behave around so many people all the time. Just at the moment, I'm finding it hard to know what kind of person you are."

Alistair's blood ran cold and he shook his head, tears springing to his eyes at the unfairness of it all. "No, Thomas, no. I wouldn't. I didn't. I know I'm not very good at social things, but I know better than to do something like this."

Thomas looked him up and down, searching for something. He met Alistair's gaze then seemed to relent a little as Alistair's tears welled over.

"All right. I'm sorry for accusing you," he said.

Alistair launched himself at Thomas and hugged him tight. "I don't want us to be fighting, Tom. I missed you and I love you and I hate it."

Thomas wrapped his arms around him. "I didn't like thinking you could have done something like this."

They held each other and Alistair desperately tried to gather in his emotions. "I don't know who would have done this. As far as I know no one else knows about these things, I'd never seen them outside the Garden."

"Maybe they're more common than you thought," Thomas said. He sighed and pulled back from Alistair, reaching up to wipe his cheeks with his thumb. A tender gesture that warmed

Alistair's heart. "Perhaps they moved into the grounds over the break and soon we'll be seeing them all over."

"Perhaps," Alistair said. They linked arms and walked slowly towards the greenhouse for Botany. "I'm really trying to do the right thing, you know that don't you?"

Thomas squeezed his arm and rested his head on Alistair's shoulder. "Yes, Allie. I know."

CHAPTER 21

Thomas seemed to have forgiven Alistair, and over the next day and night things mostly got back to normal, although Alistair still felt a little on edge, worried that he would make another misstep and Thomas would find evidence that Alistair was a terrible person and leave him.

Things were relatively normal until Alistair made his way to the school library on Wednesday afternoon - the day after the creatures had disrupted the end of breakfast.

Kincade was standing behind their desk, looking uncharacteristically annoyed. They had a stack of books in front of them, some open and some shut. When Alistair walked in, Kincade scowled at him.

"Mister Lennox, I hope you're prepared to pay for the damage you did to these books."

Alistair swallowed hard. "What? Damage? I didn't-"

Kincade held up a brown leather bound book with a familiar title *Advanced Curses and How to Unravel Them.* The cover had a nasty looking slash mark across the front, something which looked like it had been done with a sharp knife.

"You were the last to check this out, Alistair, and it wasn't damaged before then."

"When I returned it the other day it was fine. Kincade, please..." Alistair had an uncomfortable recollection of trying to convince Thomas he hadn't brought the creatures inside the Manor yesterday. The same thing was happening now, he was being blamed for something he hadn't done. It was so unfair, but he liked Kincade, and he wanted to convince them that he was innocent of this as well. "I love books, I'd never damage one on purpose. I'll pay to replace it, or uh, I suppose I'll get William to pay for it, there's some complications with my own personal finances, but they will be replaced."

Kincade sighed and set the book back down. "It's not always a simple matter of paying for a replacement, some of these books are incredibly hard to find. I'm sure you didn't *mean* to damage the books, but honestly, you should have just brought them to me right away. I could have done some spells."

Alistair chewed his lip. "But Kincade, I didn't damage them at all. When I brought them back last night they were fine."

Kincade picked up a book on gardening, which Alistair had borrowed several times. It had a large brown stain. It had pasted the pages together and stained the cover.

"Tea," Kincade said. "I can reverse damage like this but only while the beverage which stained it is still hot. Book magic is incredibly precise and finicky. Now I don't know what I'll do with it."

Alistair thought hard, trying to remember if there was any chance he might have spilled his tea on the book. He was sure he hadn't. He'd have remembered something like that.

"Can I... can I help with the repairs?" He asked, his voice very small.

"No. I'm furious. I will bill your student account." Kincade's voice was low and relatively quiet, but that just made the admission of their anger even more frightening.

"I'm sure I could be of some help," Alistair said. He felt desperate. The library was his favourite place in the whole college, and the thought that he had upset its guardian, who he respected, was repellent. "I'm so sorry. I just don't understand how it could have happened. Please, let me help."

"It would just irritate me further to have to explain it all, and try and teach a student ... no. Just, please leave. I'll talk to Lord Carlisle about increasing the book insurance fund. Perhaps he will be able to find some suitable replacements to these volumes on his travels."

Alistair felt a lump in his throat again but unlike Thomas, Kincade wasn't someone he could beg for forgiveness. They were angry and rightfully so, their precious books had been damaged. There were scorch marks on one of the others in the stack, a red covered book of runes Alistair had used for translations, recently. Every title was familiar, and most of them had been in the collection he had pushed through the returns slot the night before.

"I'm deeply sorry, Kincade," Alistair said. He bowed and backed away. He felt like an intruder, but he remembered that he wanted to check the family records, see if the youngest Birch child, Elmer, had indeed died of his curse. The one that Alistair's parents had done nothing about. The letter that had never been answered.

He fancied he could feel the weight of Kincade's glare on his back as he made his way to the Magical History section and pulled down the same book that had once revealed the existence of his own dead brother. He laid the book carefully on a table and with utmost delicacy, flipped to the Birch family tree.

There. Elmer Birch. Decreased. With a date of passing only a few weeks after the date that Ambrose Lennox died and the Lennoxes went into mourning. A sour taste in his mouth, Alistair replaced the book on the shelf and hurried out of the library.

His mind raced as he made his way through the corridors and up the stairs to his suite. He set aside the confirmation of

Elmer's death to think about the more pressing problem of the damaged library books.

Those books had been in fine form when he'd returned them, but when Kincade had opened the library and cleared the returned books they were damaged. That meant someone had gained access to the library and sabotaged them.

But why?

And why just the books Alistair had borrowed?

Was it possible someone was trying to frame him? To make him look like a disruptive student, a bad sort who caused trouble for no reason?

Who would do such a thing?

He stopped in his tracks, halfway up the stairs. A student behind him made an annoyed noise and gave him a dirty look as they went around him. He paid them no mind. He didn't want to be in his suite, he realised. He wanted to go to the wellspring, to the Secret Garden, and try and think things through there. Hopefully with Ambrose's help.

He made his way back down the stairs and out the back door of the Manor, taking the paths down to the Secret Garden at a brisk walk, his hand in his pocket, warming the brass key which at that moment felt like the key to all the solutions he needed for his various problems.

The weather was changeable, sunny one moment then dark and cloudy the next, seeming to reflect Alistair's own conflicted state of mind.

He was in such a hurry to enter the Secret Garden that he paid no attention to whether or not there was anyone else on the path or waiting to see if the coast was clear. Instead he pulled aside the ivy, unlocked the gate and let himself in with single-minded focus.

Once inside the garden it felt like he could freely breathe for the first time since he went into the library. He leaned back against the door, and closed his eyes. The air was sweeter within these walls, and his mind cleared somewhat as he breathed it in.

Sighing out a bit more of his tension, he made his way down the path not towards Melusine's fountain, but to a different part of the garden, one he didn't visit as often. The effects of the wellspring could be felt throughout the garden, after all. He passed under the arch, now blooming with pretty climbing roses thanks to Samal's care of them, and into the corner of the garden where they had unearthed lots of fragrant herbs and flowers that bees seemed to love.

With care and time they had tamed some of that part of the garden, but there was still a lot to do. Alistair thought longingly of the tweed trousers he had bought in London, longing to get down on his knees and dig his fingers into the earth, to tend to the garden, remove the weeds and forget himself for a little bit.

"Not what you need..." Alistair felt the familiar chill and relief that came every time he heard Ambrose's voice, soft as a breeze through the fallen leaves.

He looked around, although he wasn't likely to actually see his dead twin. He spoke aloud. "No? Then what do I need?"

There was a moment when Alistair heard nothing and he wondered if Ambrose had forgotten what he was doing and vanished again, it happened sometimes. A ghost twin was nothing like reliable, but Alistair hoped that he would keep talking with him all the same. What did Alistair need? He needed his twin to answer his questions. He needed to understand more about what had happened in the past so he could plan effectively for his future.

He needed Ambrose back, and to speak plainly of what he could see, what he knew. Alistair often got the feeling that Ambrose had insight from beyond the veil, far beyond what Alistair could hope to access from his plain of being.

Still no sound or reply.

He bit his tongue before he said something impatient.

He counted his breaths. One, two, three.

"Look inside...there's..." Ambrose's voice waned and Alistair reached inside to draw up some of his own magic, hoping it would give Ambrose an anchor. "You are learning that which will help."

Alistair sighed. The use of his magic had seemed to help Ambrose, but he couldn't seem to speak in a straightforward manner.

"Which things? I'm learning a lot. In Botany we're examining the imported bulbs from the Americas, we have sundew plants. Then there's Professor Winterbourne's theories and logic puzzles, and April's blood. Which is it that will help me?"

Ambrose seemed to laugh directly in Alistair's ear. "All of it. But your talent is in your blood, it stands to reason that your blood would unlock your talent."

Alistair licked his lips. He thought of Thomas's misgivings about blood magic. But he was basing his beliefs on outdated thinking and superstitions, wasn't he? Ambrose was right. He had the wellspring beneath his feet and blood in his veins, he could access whatever power he needed.

But for what purpose, exactly?

He had already withdrawn his willow wand from its pocket on the inside of his jacket, and he felt the power of his magic thrumming. He had to cast something, something to understand what it was he was missing.

Was there truly dark power to be accessed through April's teachings? He didn't think so. But perhaps he could understand more about his potential, and then he'd understand what his path should be. What step should he take next?

It would also be beneficial, he thought, if he could get better at shields.

He pulled out the small silver knife he used for bloodwork and was briefly distracted by the reflection of his own eyes. They stared back at him, looking slightly wild, as if he had the answers. The usually muddy brown of them seemed flecked with something more interesting in the sunlight - gold or the illusion of it. Perhaps he could cast some sort of divination, use his own blood, something of Ambrose's presence, and see if the universe would answer him. A kind of wild call out into the unknown to seek answers to his own tangled mind, his history and his possible future.

He had read, briefly, of that kind of spell. It had been early on in his time at Misselthwaite, and he didn't remember the details, just that it was the kind of thing a magic user could do.

"Right then," Alistair said. He cleared his throat, thinking of the runes which might help with such a question. He came up with a handful that felt correct. Something to cast his call far and something that broadened his intention to the universe, to get the most broad answers possible.

He took a seat on the grass and set his tools down, shrugged off his jacket and rolled up his sleeves. Then he drew blood and began the spell, pointing his wand at the welling blood and focusing his intention on the power within it.

Ambrose was in his ear, suggesting runes, so he added those into the ones he had already decided to speak, and closed his eyes, chanting each three times for maximum potency. The spell was a strange one, since it had no planned physical outcome, but Alistair felt the effect of it almost immediately. The power of the wellspring was behind him, a reassuring rock face he could press his back to. Ambrose felt like an owl on his shoulder, facing the same way, an ally.

Before him, Alistair could feel the vastness of the universe.

It was utterly terrifying. For the duration of a breath he felt the infinite unwinding of time, the world and everything in it, living and dead, the vast consciousness of humanity and the incredibly smallness of his own body.

His heart thrummed in his chest, entirely too fast and frail. He could feel his body dying around him, every moment another concession to entropy, which would inevitably end him and everything he knew.

On the verge of madness, his mind raced, trying to take it all in and make sense of it. But Ambrose's voice in his ear reminded him it was impossible, and to focus.

He spoke a quick rune of protection, and the infinite ebbed enough that he could face it without panicking or giving into despair.

The spell held, and Alistair knew he had only moments of it left. The spell he had done was too powerful to hold for long.

"Please," Alistair said, his voice strained. "I need direction. I need protection. How do I know which path is mine?"

The universe didn't respond with words, although it did respond. Alistair's mind was flooded with images and his body overcome with sensations.

He saw himself, breaking the curse on William. Triumphant, breaking other curses. Standing on a beach and fighting off a vast sea creature of some sort. He felt the power he had in those images, searing through his veins.

The wellspring at his back, fueling more adventures. Alistair climbing a mountain covered in snow, heading in the direction of some sort of low roofed building, nestled in between craggy peaks. A new garden, one even larger than this, and Thomas, Samal and William beside him, tending it and creating new strains of magical plants.

Vines from the earth reaching up and entangling his limbs. The hiss of a vampire in the dead of night, Alistair could sense his hunger but didn't feel afraid.

His arm twitched and itched, and he realised the sensations he was feeling was the ghost of more cuts. The power of blood magic allowing all these fantastical feats. Giving him what he needed.

That was his answer then.

The spell ended abruptly and Alistair was once more on the

grass, feeling wrung out, tender as if he'd been in a physical fight, but elated. He had an answer, and that was to embrace the blood magic and use that as his path.

He fell backwards on the grass, laughing, and stared up at the swirling clouds. He knew then that he was doing the right thing.

Ambrose seemed to be gone, although he could still feel the wellspring. Mostly he was enjoying the relief of the answer. Sure, there had been some frightening images as a result of the spell, the vines and the vampires, but he could hardly expect his future to be only good things. Rosy happiness and perfect contentment, those didn't seem realistic for the human condition, and Alistair didn't expect them.

Whatever happened, he would handle it. He had the power, and he was well on the way to getting all the knowledge he needed.

With a whispered word of thanks, he sealed up the cut on his arm with a basic healing spell and threw his arm over his eyes, allowing himself a brief nap after the exertions of the casting.

CHAPTER 22

The next morning Thomas and Alistair went to Botany class and found a disaster.

Most of the lettuces and cabbages that had been carefully growing in their delicate microclimate spells were ruined. The shimmering spell domes were shattered, and the lettuces and cabbages wilted and browned. It was weeks worth of work, and all gone in an instant.

All except one tray, which still had an intact microclimate dome and thriving lettuce seedlings inside it.

Alistair's heart sank as they walked in. So much that time and effort had been wasted maintaining the spells which were now destroyed. Now practically the whole class would have to start over. The one remaining pair was lucky, Alistair thought.

Then he saw the name label, and realised whose it was which was still intact. His and Thomas's.

Professor Weatherstaff was at the head of the class, his arms folded and a thunderous look on his face.

Kimber and Zeta were looking sadly at their forlorn trays. Kimber prodded at the dried out soil and sighed audibly.

"This is the work of a vandal," Professor Weatherstaff said. His voice vibrated with fury and Alistair felt himself shrink back from it. "I locked the greenhouse after my last class yesterday and some time yesterday afternoon or overnight someone broke in and did this. I don't know who it was, although I suspect it was one of you, since the only work attacked was the projects from this class. The first year's seedlings were untouched, as were the far more delicate post-graduate projects."

He scowled deep, furrows forming on his face, arching down from the corners of his nose to his chin. His forehead similarly ridged and his eyebrows so far down over his eyes that the piercing black stare was almost hidden. But Alistair could feel it plain as a sunbeam when Weatherstaff turned it on him.

"You'll remember that I said that if I found anyone interfering with another's work it would be an automatic fail and report to Barlow?"

Alistair swallowed and nodded. "Yes, professor."

"Well. I didn't see who did this." He said. "But it is mighty suspicious to me that there are only two projects untouched, wouldn't you agree Mister Lennox? Mister Sowersby?"

Alistair felt his cheeks flame and he cleared his throat. "I agree it's suspicious but I didn't-"

"I can't prove anything," Weatherstaff said. "And I won't go to Barlow without proof. But I am watching you, Lennox. And you, Sowersby."

Alistair nodded, not at all sure how else to respond.

Thomas's shoulders were rounded and his head was down. Alistair hated to see him that way, as if he'd already been punished.

Alistair opened his mouth but closed it again. It didn't seem like arguing was going to achieve anything at all. As with the ivy prank in the entranceway, he hoped that people thought he wouldn't be foolish enough to include his name in a prank like this. However, the dark looks he received from the other students didn't give him much hope in that regard.

The class proceeded miserably after that. Thomas became

sullen and quiet, his responses to Alistair monosyllabic at best. The other students had to start their projects over, of course, and although it pained Alistair to see it, he couldn't see any way to help.

He did offer, with the students at the next table over, but they gave him distrustful looks and refused with an icy sort of politeness.

Alistair and Thomas finished their work far sooner than the rest of the class, and Professor Weatherstaff was busy helping the others, too busy to assign further work. In the end Alistair and Thomas just sat and read through their textbooks. They could probably have left, but something told Alistair that would be an even worse look. He did also consider offering to help Zeta and Kimber with their project but he was afraid that would give them the message he didn't have faith in their skills.

Thomas hurried away as soon as the class was done, and Alistair walked slowly behind him, feeling hopeless. He hadn't done anything wrong, but there was no way to prove it. Thomas was furious with him. He was getting the brunt of their classmate's scorn all over again, and it appeared to be Alistair's fault as well.

He found his feet making their way to the garden, but he didn't want to go there while he felt like this. He had the dreadful suspicion that if he went there in too sullen a mood, he might contaminate the magic of the wellspring. He redirected his path and made his way up the stairs and to his old room.

Miraculously, it hadn't been assigned to a new student, and the door stood slightly ajar.

Alistair pushed his way inside, settled on his old mattress (now back to a sensible one person size) and curled into a ball.

🖋

Some hours later, he felt a hand on his shoulder, and startled awake, heart pounding. He had been dreaming of... he wasn't sure now, it all faded as he tried to get his bearings. William had woken him, and then immediately stepped back as if afraid Alistair would lash out. Alistair could barely see him. He had cast a small witch light which he held in one hand, but that was the only illumination in the room. The curtains were open to show a pitch black world outside. The small hours of the morning, Alistair guessed.

"Are you feeling all right?" William asked, after a moment.

Alistair rubbed his palm over his forehead and sat up. "Yes, I suppose so. Although I didn't mean to fall asleep in here."

"I should say not," William said. "There's no pillow or blanket."

"Alistair sighed deeply and looked up at William. "You came to find me?"

"Thomas told us about what happened in the greenhouse," he said. "Samal thought you might need some time to yourself, and Thomas is still doing his kicked-puppy routine, but I wanted to be sure you hadn't got into any trouble."

"I didn't, well, not any more than I was already." Alistair swung his legs over the edge of the bed, as if he were going to get up. Then he realised that William hadn't exactly asked him to return to their shared bedroom, so he looked at his hands and sighed again.

"Do you want to talk about it?"

Alistair looked up at William, surprised. "I didn't think you would want to hear me whining."

"I don't want to hear you whining, that's true," William said. "But if it would help things between you and Thomas to talk them through with me, then I'm happy to listen."

"I don't even know," Alistair said. "It's like someone set me up to appear to have done something. The same with the green insect things in the front hall. It's like someone wants everyone to hate me. They shouldn't bother going to all this trouble, it's not like people liked me in the first place."

William sat down beside him, tossing the witch light so that it hung suspended in the centre of the room.

"That's not true, you have lots of people who like you," William said. "Besides me, Sam and Thomas."

"Thomas doesn't like me right now." Alistair frowned at his hands.

"Thomas loves you, and he'll get over it." William slipped his arm around Alistair's shoulder. "And you've made lots of new friends this term. Zeta, Alexander, Kimber. Kincade likes you, and Professor Weatherstaff from what I've heard. As much as he likes anyone at all. Even that new grad student, you like her classes, you said she'd been congratulating you on your work there."

Alistair huffed and leaned against William. "Professor Weatherstaff thinks that I sabotaged the other students' projects. He thinks I'm a villain."

"The truth will out, one way or another." William said. "I don't believe such a thing about you, besides, when were you supposed to have sneaked away to do that?"

"I don't know. There's also, the other thing. Thomas and Samal think I shouldn't be doing blood magic with April."

William didn't respond for a moment. "I know where they're coming from," he said, finally. "There are so many horror stories about blood magic."

"Do you think I should stop? I did almost... trigger something bad in you."

William picked up Alistair's hand with his outside one and threaded their fingers together. "The way I've come to see things is like this. Everyone has some darkness within them. For some of us it's rather obvious. Rather closer to the surface than." Alistair straightened up to turn and meet his eye. William shrugged. "And for some of us it's more hidden. But all of us have it, none are truly pure and good."

"Samal might be," Alistair said. "He's half an angel."

"I saw Samal steal a bite of your French toast the other morning," William said. "He's not as perfect as he acts."

Alistair chuckled. "I didn't know he'd done that."

"My point is, that there is a darkness in us, and we can't deny it, not safely, what matters is how you use it, and how you let it change you."

"Am I changing?" Alistair squeezed William's hand. He wasn't sure he liked the idea of changing in ways his lovers would notice. What if he changed into someone they didn't like as much?

"Of course you are," William said. His tone was unconcerned and light, and it eased a tiny amount of Alistair's anxiety. "Everyone changes."

Alistair frowned deeper as he considered this.

William took a breath and continued. "But what I've learned over the years is, if you keep in mind the kind of person you want to be, and don't let yourself get wrapped up in the darkness inside, or whatever might be tempting you, then you'll be fine. Remember that your actions impact others, whether you intend them to or not. So, you have a responsibility to think of others, to think of whatever is around you, when you take actions."

Alistair hummed softly, thinking that over. "That sounded very wise, Mister Carlisle."

William chuckled. "Well, if anyone has a close and intimate relationship with inner darkness, it's the Carlisles, after all."

"I'm sure you're right."

William let go of Alistair's hand and wrapped both arms tight around him. "You know you can talk about this sort of thing with all of us," he said. "You don't have to storm off on your own and brood."

Alistair squirmed, the hug was a strange angle and he could

feel his shoulder digging into William's sternum. "I'm not sure I do know that. It's all so new to me still. Having friends. I'd been alone in that house for so long, I find I'm still uncertain of how to act."

"We're all of us outsiders in some way," William said softly. Alistair considered that. Thomas because his family didn't have the same money and privilege as those in the upper classes. William because of his curse. Samal because of his parentage … they were all outsiders. He didn't know enough about Zeta, Kimber and Alexander yet, but perhaps they, too, had something about them that made them feel outside the normal.

"Maybe so. The problem is, when it feels like everyone hates me, hiding where no one can find me feels like I'm doing the world a favour."

William hummed. "That doesn't sound like you, Allie."

"It doesn't?"

"The Alistair I know wouldn't care what the world thinks of him, he'd just keep on doing whatever he wanted to do and if it upsets the world, well so be it. It's one of the things I truly admire about you. How sure of yourself and your convictions you are."

That straightened Alistair's backbone and he pulled away from William's grasp, feeling energised. "You're right. Why should I care what others think?"

"Exactly."

"I know I'm not responsible for what happened in the greenhouse, and I can investigate, find out who it really was. That's what they always did in the school adventure books I used to read. They'd find the culprit and expose them."

"That's the spirit."

"And from the spells I've cast, I know how to use blood magic, and it's powerful, but it's not any more harmful than other magic. Of course it could be used to harm, but so can all of it, so what's to fear?"

William nodded. "Exactly, and if you use it with your full attention, you will notice if anything untoward happens. Just like using the power of the wellspring."

"Change isn't something to be feared..." Alistair finally said, his voice softer and more slow. He wished for his pen and journal so he could capture this idea. "But it's something to be aware of, and to I suppose... aim in the direction you wish for it."

"Well said." William stood up and offered Alistair his hand. "Come on, let's go to bed."

Alistair took his hand and allowed him to help him up. "All right."

They walked the deserted halls in silence, William opening the door to the suite and ushering Alistair in. They undressed and climbed into bed with the others. Alistair did glance briefly at his journal, wishing to record all that he and William had talked about, but reconciling with Thomas was more important at that moment.

CHAPTER 23

Alistair had a scheduled private tutorial with Professor Winterbourne at nine in the morning, so he was first to breakfast and first to finish. Thomas was acting cordial towards him, if not as warm as normal.

Alistair made his way to the room Professor Winterbourne used as a study and knocked on the door.

"Come in, Lennox I presume?"

"Yes, Professor." Alistair entered the room and sat down in the chair Winterbourne indicated. She shuffled some papers, found the one she wanted and pulled it out.

"I was very pleased with your work on the latest assignment, Lennox," Winterbourne said. "You have a sharp mind, and I can see the evidence of the research you've done. Please don't forget to include all your references in the bibliography at the end though."

She handed him the paper, which was graded with red ink and marked with a "92%" up the top. "You show excellent potential, and I'm pleased to see you embracing your talent in such a way. You have a bright future ahead of you, young man, assuming you don't..."

She cut herself off abruptly and Alistair looked up from the paper. Professor Winterbourne was a woman of surety and conviction and it wasn't like her to falter in any way.

"I beg your pardon, Professor," Alistair said. "But assuming I don't do what exactly?"

Professor Winterbourne's mouth formed a tight line and she rearranged her skirts. "I'm aware of your studies with Miss Quinn," she said. Alistair's chest tightened, feeling his back stiffen as he readied himself to defend the study of blood magic once more. "I trust you're a sensible sort, and you won't intentionally do anything dangerous to yourself or others, but I also know that you're new to the world of magic."

Alistair took a deep breath and let it out slowly. "I know that blood magic is poorly regarded and that there are historical accounts of it being used for horrible things. I can assure you, I am being very careful." His jaw was tense, and he could hear it in his voice.

"As I understand it she is advocating for a sort of brute force approach with the breaking of curses. I can't say I approve of that one bit. The art of curse breaking has always been to go softly, to treat it as you might a wild animal, and to unravel the working of it little by little. As you well know from my teachings and assigned readings." She took a quick breath. "One might also use the example from your own family's history, although..." she shook her head. "That was unkind and insensitive of me to bring up. I simply urge you to be cautious. Curses are a uniquely unpredictable sort of magic, and they can respond in unexpected ways to the things we attempt."

Alistair's hand was white knuckled on his bag strap, and he consciously unclenched his hand, taking a deep breath before he responded to her.

"Thank you for your concern, but you don't need to worry about me in that regard."

Professor Winterbourne straightened her back and fixed him with a squint. "Very well. I simply ask that if you start to doubt the teachings, or feel that you are being pushed into something untoward that you report to me. Are you comfortable with doing that?

Alistair hesitated. "Yes, Professor. I would maybe, perhaps, approach Professor Barlow first though, as I believe he is April's supervising professor."

Professor Winterbourne nodded and gave the ghost of a smile. "That would be fine. As long as you know there are structures and procedures in place should anything go wrong. Now, we have some time left if you wish to use it. Was there anything in particular you would like assistance with in my course?"

Alistair pulled out his notes and flipped to the notes from the recent courses and asked some follow up questions. His questions and ideas, as always, focused on the curse within William and the ways that Winterbourne's teachings might be applied to that puzzle.

When his session with Professor Winterbourne was up, Alistair's head felt stuffed full of possibilities now that he fully understood the things which had been nagging at him.

He was halfway through the hallways back to the suite he shared with his lovers before he realised he didn't really want to go there. He stopped, turned on his heel and made his way down towards the library. Perhaps he could try and make amends with Kincade, and spend a pleasant hour perusing whatever new novels they'd got in.

However he was intercepted at the bottom of the grand staircase by Alexander and Kimber.

"Alistair! How are you?" Kimber's glasses slipped down her nose and she pushed them back up with one hand. "I feel like I haven't properly spoken to you in an age. Want to join us? We were going to go to Alex's room, have some cups of tea and pretend to study."

Alistair wavered. He felt overwhelmed after the tutorial with Winterbourne, feeling first defensive of blood magic, and then utterly engrossed in her teachings. The idea of just sitting somewhere quiet with some gentle company who wasn't in the midst of judging him or asking him to justify his studies was in fact, very attractive.

The library and his attempt to make peace with Kincade could wait. He nodded.

"Yes, fine. I'll do that."

"Come on then." Kimber slipped her arm through Alistair's, much in the way that he was accustomed to Thomas doing. There was a sudden queasiness as he tried to remember if Thomas had done it lately, or if there was something inherently wrong about Kimber taking his arm, but there was nothing harmful in her intention, it was simply a gesture of friendship. He squeezed her arm with his in what he hoped was an equally friendly manner and the three of them made their way to Alexander's room.

The room was the same standard student apartment that Alistair had used the previous term, but Alexander had made it uniquely his. The bed was shoved against the wall in the corner, and sat unmade with rumpled sheets.

"I beg your pardon for the mess," Alexander said. He immediately hurried over to straighten the bedclothes. "I wasn't expecting to have people to visit."

His desk was surrounded by shelves which Alexander must have had installed. It took a while to take it all in, because every shelf was packed with jars and bottles and beakers. Each jar contained a different substance, Alistair recognised some bay leaves and sprigs of dried thyme, next to them, a jar full of what appeared to be the root of another plant. There was a bottle with something moving inside it, a strange barely glowing spectre of some sort. One entire shelf held powders of different colours and textures, some rough as gravel and some finer than flour. Alistair looked around, amazed.

"These are incredible." Alistair turned back to smile at Alexander. "I had no idea that you'd need so many things for potion making."

"Well, you don't really," Alexander said. He rubbed his hand over the back of his neck. "I just like to collect things, and have it all on hand in case I happen to need it."

"Alex likes the look of it all, I'm sure he's going to open an apothecary and then refuse to sell anything." Kimber teased, laughing, and Alexander laughed as well.

Alisatir nodded, their laughter making him feel more at ease. "I think I'm sort of the same but with books. I love bookshops, and it would be fine to own one. But parting with the books would be horrible."

Kimber busied herself with the copper kettle that Alexander had on a hook over the fire, filling it and setting it to boil.

"Please, sit down Alistair," Alexander said. He had three large, comfy looking cushions near the fire. As with every room in Misselthwaite, although it was hot outside the room held a certain chill. Alistair set his satchel down against the wall and sank into one of the cushions. It was even more comfortable than it had appeared.

"So, how are you finding this term?" Kimber asked.

"I don't know," Alistair said. He sighed. "I had thought things were going well, and I was making steps towards what I need to do, but now everything feels like it's going wrong." He picked at the fringe of one of the cushions morosely.

"It does?" Alexander frowned, and sat down on the next cushion pile over and offered Alistair a sweet from a round tin. Alistair looked at the sweets, they were hard boiled, in the shapes of various fruits with corresponding colours. He picked out one which looked like a raspberry.

"Thank you. Yes, it feels as if everyone is warning me against something terrible, but blood magic, the way April teaches it, doesn't seem that bad. But Samal and Thomas don't see it that way, especially since... well, some homework went wrong with William." Alistair sighed heavily again, popped the sweet in his mouth and immediately crunched it up.

"The four of you are so cute together," Kimber said. She brought over cups of tea and handed them to Alistair and Alexander. "I hope you can all work it out."

"Thank you?" Alistair wasn't entirely sure he liked being thought of as cute, but he thought he understood that Kimber was only trying to be nice. He accepted the tea cup and gratefully inhaled the smell of it. The steam smelled of vanilla, and something a little less familiar. In the cup the tea was a warm red colour. "What kind of tea is this?"

"It's a rooibos, or uh, redbush. It's from the South of Africa. It's good. This one is blended with vanilla." Kimber said said. "We're addicted to it."

Kimber settled cross legged on a yellow cushion, facing both of the boys.

Alistair sniffed the tea again and chanced a sip. The flavour was earthy, warming somehow. "That is good, thank you."

Kimber smiled and flicked her hair behind her shoulder. "I got a taste for it when my aunt brought it back from her travels, now I have to get it imported."

Alistair relaxed a little, leaning back against the shelves and stretching his legs out in front of him. It felt good to be with his friends, these two weren't judging him for anything.

"How did you go on your potions quiz?" Kimber asked, turning to Alexander.

"I think all right," Alexander said. "Professor took the papers to mark overnight, but there were no questions that surprised me so I think I'll have done fine. The real challenge will be the final assessment."

"What do you have to do for your final assessment?" Alistair asked. He regarded Alexander in the warm afternoon sunlight, the way it picked out highlights in his hair. Alistair was beginning to feel quite sleepy.

"I have to come up with a new variation on a sleeping potion," Alexander said. "It's cursed hard work, because we have to test what we come up with, and I always end up dropping off."

Alistair chuckled. "That does sound rather -" he broke off to yawn.

"Are you sleeping all right, Allie?" Kimber asked. Her forehead crinkled with concern. "You look quite tired all of a sudden."

"No, not really." Alistair finished his tea and set the cup aside, folding his hands over his stomach. "All the things that have been going on, I just..."

"Your boyfriends aren't always right, you know." Kimber pointed a teaspoon at Alistair. "You shouldn't take all their judgements to heart."

"But they know so much more about... About the whole magical world,.About how people are supposed to act and what kinds of magic are appropriate," Alistair said. His words were running together a little, almost as if he had drunk too much wine.

"You know plenty now," Alexander said. "Kimber's right. You're an adult, you have the knowledge you need to make your own choices."

"And no one should be dictating what kinds of magic you do," Kimber said.

"Kimber's right," Alexander said. He smiled broadly at Kimber and then Alistair.

"I'm a terrible adult," Alistair replied. He laughed a little. "I have no idea about how anything works. How did I even become your friends? How did I do that?"

"Oh, Allie," Kimber said, her voice all sugar and sympathy. "You're a kind person, and we wanted to get to know you better."

"Do you want to lie down on my bed?" Alexander asked. He looked concerned, and his eyes were wide, caring. Alistair liked him very much. "I don't mind, truly."

"I'll be all right," Alistair said. "Just need to rest my eyes for a moment."

He let himself slide sideways and snuggle down into the softness of the cushions.

CHAPTER 24

Alistair strolled through the Secret Garden side by side with Ambrose. Ambrose was dressed in a cheery buttercup yellow waistcoat and cream linen suit. Alistair's suit was his customary charcoal grey.

"The thing you have to remember about rabbits is that they will always run away," Ambrose said. Alistair was struck by how warm Ambrose's voice was, how it lightened his heart to listen to him.

"I suppose that's true," Alistair said.

"But perhaps they needn't be such a pest, if we simply make a separate patch of lettuces, a little further from the kitchen garden, something to feed them so that they don't get at the supply we need." Ambrose slipped his arm through Alistair's. Everyone had been doing that lately, he thought. He quite liked it. The touch of another human.

The garden walls stretched higher than Alistair remembered, several stories high, arching towards a bright blue sky. "How do the rabbits even get into the garden?"

"They use the ladders of course," Ambrose said.

"Of course." Alistair felt foolish for having to ask, when the answer was so patently clear.

Melusine turned the corner and approached them from the other direction on the white seashell path. Alistair had never seen her in person before, he had only seen her rendered in cream coloured marble. In life her skin glowed a warm umber, her eyes a bright, flashing grey. She smiled at Alistair and he felt the magic emanating out from her - cool and sparkling as a rainshower. Her dress was an elegant, if dated style.

"Alistair, Ambrose, my darling boys," Melusine said. "Every time I look at the two of you, it's like seeing mirrors."

Alistair and Ambrose stopped walking, turned to look into each other's eyes and laughed. He supposed it was strange, having someone who looked just like him. But even as he thought that, he could see the differences. Ambrose had no scar on his chin from falling out of a carriage at age eight. He had been dead by then...

The day shifted, Ambrose clutched his hand as the world shifted around him. All around him Alistair could see his face repeated, or was it Ambrose?

Were there dozens of him?

Dozens of both of them?

Each face the same, as if Melusine had conjured a horrible mirror curse and the world was all Alistair, all Alistair's grey eyes, repeated in the face of his twin. Laughing and laughing, in how many voices?

Things came back together with a hiss of air and it was just the two of them once more. Ambrose and Alistair side by side, no noise at all. The Secret Garden's sundew seedlings and pitcher plants had grown so large, so huge that Alistair was in danger of slipping inside one of the flowers. The pitcher plants long, jug-like flowers had sweet nectar inside, for tempting in insects and then killing them slowly. The sundew grew in strange curled vines laced with pricks of silvery liquid, to trap and poison. Both were dangerous to small insects normally, but now they were large enough to ensnare unwary humans. Alistair didn't want *these* plants to thrive quite so well in the Secret Garden.

He squeezed Ambrose's hand.

"I don't recognise this part of the garden," Ambrose said.

Alistair was consumed with fear then. He didn't recognise any of the trees or plants either, and the path beneath their feet was of an unfamiliar black flagstone.

Could they be lost? Lost in Alistair's Secret Garden? It didn't at all seem possible.

"How can this be?" he asked.

Ambrose shook his head, his hair came loose from the yellow ribbon holding it back and fell around his shoulders. "We must have taken the wrong path."

"I don't see how." Alistair dropped Ambrose's hand to turn on the spot.

Behind him stood William, his eyes unnaturally sunken, his cheeks gaunt and his skin an unnerving shade of grey. His hair was slicked back and his hands curled, as if he had claws.

When he opened his mouth his teeth were long and pointed, and there were too many of them, rows upon rows of long teeth. Alistair was in no doubt that he wanted to bite Alistair, to feed on his blood, and tear his throat.

"William, listen, it's not you, it's just the curse," he said. William didn't seem to hear him, and started to reach for Alistair. "Let me help you, I know I can help you if you just let me-"

William closed his hand around Alistair's wrist and drew it towards his mouth, sinking fangs in. The pain flared through Alistair's arm and he cried out, tugging uselessly against William's grip.

"Please William, there's a process, a way these things are done!"

Where had Ambrose gone? Alistair called his name, desperately searching within himself for the magic which would bring his ghost twin back to him, but nothing responded.

William pulled back from his feast, and Alistair yanked his hand away. "Please, Will, let me help you!"

William lunged, growling, more monster than man. Alistair flinched back and his heel skidded, setting him off balance.

The flagstone beneath his feet yawned open, revealing the belly of a pitcher plant's deadly flower, just the right size to swallow him whole. His feet slipped on what was left of the flags and he began slowly, inexorably, to fall into the flower. All around him, the fleshy, lush petals that promised to make a fine resting place. At the bottom he could see the yellow liquid, he could smell the cloying sweetness of the nectar, ready to take him in and consume him slowly, bit by bit until there was nothing left but bones.

"Ambrose! Please help!" Alistair screamed, hands clutching at the slippery path as he fell, but fingers finding no purchase. William loomed closer, his clawed hand reaching for Alistair's wrist, but would being killed by William be any better than death in the flower?

Alistair thrashed, trying in vain to find a way to escape death. There had to be a solution, didn't there?

He woke up overly warm. His face was buried in a silky cushion which he'd made a small wet patch in by drooling.

He sat up, feeling a crick in his neck as he did, and tried to shake off the adrenaline of the dream. It had all felt so real, his heart was pounding. The room was too warm... he looked around and saw that the fire had been stoked up high, high as if it were mid-winter.

Kimber and Alexander were gone and he was alone in a sweltering room.

Alistair got up and banked the fire and opened a window. He leaned out to take a breath of fresh air and felt his head clear a little. He still felt quite dopey from the sleep, and unsettled by the dream.

The image of William, lost to vampirism and trying to feed on him felt seared into his mind's eye, and he hoped that it was only a nightmare, that he would never have to contend with that in the waking world.

He felt queasy about the way in the dream, he'd been pleading with William, practically begging to help him even as he was approaching with dread intent. It had felt...Alistair sighed, took another deep breath of fresh air and tried to think of the word. Weak, pathetic perhaps. No self-preservation, only this craven need to save him.

He wasn't sure that he was at all like that in the real world. Was he?

It wasn't like he didn't have good reasons for helping William, and William had been so good, so human, since the big collaborative spell in the Garden. Alistair had been spending a lot of time researching and learning new techniques, but that wasn't the same as sacrificing himself.

Was it?

He leaned his head on the windowpane and closed his eyes. He hadn't been getting enough sleep. He'd distanced himself from Samal and Thomas, because they didn't like the course his studies were taking him on. True, they were busy themselves, but Alistair hadn't sought them out for alone time, or to check in on them.

He'd spent time with his new friends instead of trying to smooth things over with Kincade. That showed a certain selfishness that Alistair wasn't sure he liked the feel of.

He could be better than this, couldn't he?

His hand twitched, a need to write it all down, commit it to his journal and puzzle out what to do next. Only this wasn't his room, and his journal was on his desk in the suite he shared.

He tugged the black ribbon out of his hair. Looked at it for a moment and wondered about buying a yellow one, to honour Ambrose. He dragged both hands through his hair, trying to comb it until it sat flatter, and then tied it back again.

Alistair looked around, picked up his satchel and let himself out of Alexander's room.

He walked up the hallway, settling the strap of the satchel on his shoulder. He trudged towards his own suite, which necessitated crossing the landing of the grand staircase. As he approached it, he became aware of a gathering of people, most of them talking in hushed voices and looking at something on the ground, towards the top of the stairs.

"Healer coming through!" Samal alighted, wings folding into his back, as the crowd parted for him. Alistair's footsteps stuttered as he saw what the crowd had been staring at.

Lewis Trudgeon, whom Alistair knew from April's blood magic class, lay prone, his limbs slack, over the top three stairs. His feet were at the topmost point, and his arms spread wide. Great pools of blood spilled from wounds on his arms and chest, and his face was pale. He didn't seem to be breathing.

Samal crouched on the steps, his hands extended and a softly glowing golden web already forming in the air as he spoke softly. The crowd went silent, watching him work.

The silence was broken by the sound of rapidly approaching footsteps. Alistair looked up to see Medlock and Madame Waxleaf running towards the scene from the entranceway, hurrying up the stairs.

Medlock glared, waving her hand at the gathered students. "All right, you've seen enough, go back to your rooms and your classes and stop gawking!"

Alistair drew closer to Samal as the others started to

disperse. He saw Zeta muttering to a friend, both of them stealing glances at him.

The others were talking in hushed voices, glancing over their shoulders at Samal and Luis, and then pointedly at Alistair.

Reaching his side, Madame Waxleaf took up the spell Samal had started and together they pooled their magics. Luis coughed once.

"There, he's breathing," Samal said.

"He's not at all stable," Madame Waxleaf said. "Hold the spell, I'll try and replenish what he's lost."

Alistair's stomach sank as Medlock picked up something from the floor. It was a familiar object. Long, thin and pale. His wand, hand crafted from a willow tree in the Secret Garden.

"Mister Lennox, you'd better come with me," she said, in a tone that brooked no arguments.

Samal spared the barest of looks to Alistair as he walked after Medlock. His expression was plain to read; he looked terrified.

Terrified of what had happened, or of Alistair?

Alistair's stomach knotted and he hurried after Medlock, not wanting to see that expression on Samal's face for a moment longer.

"Please, Medlock, it wasn't me," he said. She held up a hand to silence him. They were climbing a back set of stairs, Alistair recognised the route to Headmaster Carlisle's study.

"Save your breath, Lennox," she said. "The most important thing to do right now is to get you somewhere secure."

Secure, Alistair thought. Not safe. Secure. Like I'm a danger to all around me and need to be locked up. She held his wand firmly in her hand, and Alistair wondered briefly what would happen if he tried to snatch it back.

He decided it would make him look more guilty than anything else, so he clasped his hands behind his back and followed.

Medlock stopped part way up the hallway and unlocked a room. It was much like the student apartments on the floor below, although clearly unused. There were some extra heavy chairs stacked in one corner, and the bed had an old looking mattress on it and no bedclothes. She gestured for him to go in and he did so.

She had half closed the door before she spoke. "Lennox. I am not at all sure what has happened, but an attack of this nature has to be taken seriously. You know that from last term. I expect authorities will be called. You will remain here until some sort of resolution is made."

Alistair took a steadying breath and said softly, trying to sound utterly reasonable and sincere.

"I had nothing to do with it, I was asleep. Someone's tried to make it look like I did, same as the plants and the creatures, and the projects in botany."

"Someone will be by as soon as possible to get your side of events," Medlock said. She searched his face, her eyes cold, but searching. Alistair thought that perhaps she didn't want to believe that he had been responsible for this. It was cold comfort when she shut the door, locked it from outside and then sealed it with a magic spell though.

Alistair sat down on the dusty mattress and stared at his hands.

CHAPTER 25

It was perhaps an hour, perhaps longer, before the door unlocked and Medlock came back in with Professor Barlow and William tagging along behind. Medlock's customary stern expression was unchanged, and Barlow looked a lot less friendly than usual as well. William was paler than ever, and his eyes were wide with concern.

"Lennox, we need to hear your side of things," Barlow said. He magicked a chair down from the stack in the corner and sat down on it, knees spread, one elbow resting on one knee, and leaned in to look Alistair directly in the eye.

It was intimidating, and Alistair twisted his hands together. He swallowed, glanced over at William. William nodded once, and Alistair knew whatever happened next he had William's support.

"I have no idea what happened," Alistair said. "I was asleep in Alexander's room."

"Alexander Destefano?" Barlow cut in.

"That's right. Alex and Kimber and I were having tea, the room was warm, and I fell asleep. When I woke up they'd both left, and I guess my wand was missing but I didn't realise that until I saw it on the stairs."

Medlock folded her arms. He could feel the weight of her stare, but kept his gaze steady on Professor Barlow's, willing him to understand and to believe him.

"We have spoken to Destefano, and he said that they had left about a half hour before the attack happened."

Alistair swallowed. Alexander and Kimber were the only alibi he had. It was the creatures and the seedlings all over again, someone was trying to make him look bad.

"Isn't it possible someone stole my wand and did this to frame me?" Alistair said. His voice sounded whiny and he hated that. "It's just, there have been other incidents..."

"We have an eye witness who said they saw you shouting at Luis, and then cursing him with a cutting spell. The same one April Quinn has taught all of you using blood magic."

"I wasn't there! Luis is in that class too," Alistair blurted. Feeling suddenly like there was no way to save himself. "I'm not the only one using that spell!"

"Noted, but we hardly think that Luis did this to himself."

Alistair looked down at his hands again. "I don't understand. If I was there, and someone saw me, why didn't they do something then? I was asleep in the room the entire time."

"It does seem rather out of character for Alistair," William put in from near the door. Barlow looked over at him with a bemused expression.

"It was just last term that you and Lennox got into a screaming match in the hallway that led to blows, was it not?"

Alistair's cheeks warmed. He had forgotten about that. "I'm not a violent person," he said, instead. "I have nothing at all against Luis, and there's no reason for me to have attacked him. Please believe me, Professor, someone is doing this to make me look bad. Maybe to get me thrown out of Misselthwaite altogether." Something occurred to him as he spoke. "The Birches! It will be them! Trying to get me thrown out so that they can get their revenge."

Barlow breathed out heavily through his nose. "Eulalia, Eleanor and Everett Birch are banned from school grounds with magic spells that know the very cells in their bodies. It couldn't have been any of them."

Alistair rubbed his forehead. "I believe it is, somehow."

"Is there anything else you can tell us?" Barlow asked. "Anything you want me to know?"

"I don't know what else to tell you. Someone made it look like I sabotaged the other students' work in Botany, and now this. I don't know who it is if it's not the Birches."

Barlow ran a hand through his hair and nodded once before he stood up. "Very well. I'm afraid for the moment we will have to keep you confined to this room, while we get to the bottom of this whole incident. William will bring you your meals."

"Is Luis all right?" Alistair asked. Something about the way Barlow had stood alarmed him, as if the end of this conversation was the end of Alistair's options.

"He's not out of the woods," Medlock said. "Waxleaf and her assistants are finding the wounds curiously resistant to their healing, there was some extra complication on the spell, perhaps a warding." She fixed Alistair with a gimlet gaze and he shrank back a little.

"I do hope he pulls through," he said.

William cleared his throat. "Is it alright if I stay and talk to Alistair a while longer?" he asked. Barlow nodded, ushered Medlock out and shut the door behind them.

William sat beside Alistair and for a moment the two of them said nothing. Alistair huffed and spoke finally.

"I didn't do it."

"I know you didn't," William said.

Alistair hadn't realised how much he needed to hear those words. The fear, the sadness and the horror of it all welled up in him and he barely suppressed a whimper.

William put his arms around him immediately and Alistair wept a little. "Thank you," he managed, his voice cracking.

"I don't know who Zeta saw, but I know it wasn't you," William said.

"Zeta was the eyewitness?" Alistair blinked, surprised. He had thought Zeta was one of the people who would be on his side in this. She knew him well enough, surely?

"That's right. The way she tells it, she and Luis were walking up the stairs, and you appeared in a rage, called him names and cursed him with the cutting spell. Only the cutting spell you use doesn't resist healing, which is another weird part of this."

"I've never used magic that resists healing, I didn't even know that was possible." Alistair straightened up, looked William in the eyes. "Tell me, what do Sam and Tom think?"

William looked away, his mouth drawing into a frown. Alistair's heart sank and he let go of William, shuffling back on the bed with horror. How could his boyfriends not know that he wasn't responsible for this?

William shook his head. "Thomas doesn't know what to think. I know he doesn't really believe that you did it, but he needs to know more, he needs to know who is responsible. Sam's been busy trying to heal Luis, I don't know what he thinks. Luis lost a lot of blood, too much perhaps, and all the people who showed up first either had no idea how to do a first aid spell or just didn't bother trying."

William sounded harsh, and bitter, and Alistair felt much the same in that moment. "If I could just see Tom, maybe I could convince him," he said.

"Maybe. I'll see if he wants to come up with me when I bring your dinner," William said. He rubbed his hand over Alistair's leg, the only bit of him he could reach without moving. "I'm sorry. We'll get to the bottom of this, I promise."

Alistair nodded and swallowed a lump in his throat. "I hope they'll let me out of here soon, I want to investigate."

"Father has called in Councillor Rutherford." He said, his voice a little softer, as if he didn't want to be delivering this news.

"Who's Councillor Rutherford?"

"He's sort of like the magical police chief," William said. "He'll get to the bottom of what happened and clear your name, I'm sure of it."

Alistair's stomach sank further. He'd known his situation was serious, of course he had, but the idea that the constabulary were involved... it just brought it all home.

"What if he can't? What if I get expelled, banned from Misselthwaite?" Alistair wrung his hands. "I can't be separated from the Secret Garden, Will. I couldn't stand it. How could I talk to Ambrose? And you, and Sam and Tom. I couldn't bear to be sitting alone at home after knowing how wonderful it is to be with you all. To have companions, friends."

All at once his strange nightmare came back to him. The twisted garden, William, the monster, wanting to devour him.

"We'll make sure that doesn't happen," William said. He frowned, leaning in to examine Alistair's face. "What is it?"

"I had the strangest dream, it must have been while whoever it was attacked Luis. Your curse had overtaken you, and I was lost, the garden tried to devour me and Ambrose... he said we'd got on the wrong path."

William frowned a little. "Your dreams, I don't think you've ever talked about your dreams before."

"I don't usually remember them," Alistair said. He shrugged. "This one still feels clear as day, though. Do you think it means something? It couldn't be prophetic could it?"

"Let's hope not." William hummed. "I'll go and get your dinner, and some blankets and things."

It dawned on Alistair that he would have to sleep in that room, all alone, and he felt another wave of despair threaten him. At least he had some books in his satchel to keep him occupied.

"Thanks, Will. If it's not too much trouble, when you return would you please bring my journal as well?"

"Of course." Will planted a kiss on Alistair's forehead. "I'll be back soon."

He left and as the door fastened itself magically Alistair became aware of how desperately alone he was. Determined not to sit and feel sorry for himself, Alistair pulled out one of his course notebooks, flipped to the back and started a list.

By the time William returned Alistair had a list of suspects and was part way through trying to think up possible motives. William entered the room with an armful of supplies and a plate of hot food balanced on top of it. It smelled wonderful and Alistair's stomach rumbled, reminding him he'd missed out on his usual afternoon snack.

"Eat up," William said. "Councillor Rutherford is on a special express from London and should be here within an hour. I don't know how he manages it, sometimes."

Alistair set his notebook aside and accepted the plate, gratefully. It held slices of roast pork, apple sauce, roasted potatoes and parsnip and a heap of green salad. Alistair picked up his fork and started eating, pushing the notebook towards William with the other hand.

"This is how far I've gotten."

William read through the list and raised an eyebrow. "Do you really think Zeta would frame you because her lettuce wilted?"

"She does take her grades very seriously," Alistair said through a mouthful of potato. He swallowed before continuing. "And she doesn't much like people from families like yours and mine. That could have something to do with it."

"I don't think socialism necessarily leads to making it look like another student killed someone," William said, dryly.

"She's still a suspect, she said it was me doing the attack and if she's the only witness, and she has another motive..."

"Luis is the other witness," William said. "If they can get him to wake up again."

Alistair finished his dinner in record time and was about to start explaining the rest of his list when the door to the room opened, admitting an impressive looking man in a wheelchair. He was broad shouldered, bearded and his expression stern.

William was immediately on his feet. "Councillor Rutherford, this is Alistair Lennox," William said.

Alistair was immediately intimidated. Councillor Rutherford had an aura of authority, a no-nonsense aspect to him and he would have filled up the room entirely simply with his presence. When he fixed his eyes on Alistair it was as if every mistake Alistair had ever made was obvious. He felt guilty of a thousand things, from stealing extra bread rolls and missing dinner parties to the mysterious circumstances of his parents' death. He felt as if there was no need to confess because Councillor Rutherford could already see it all. He intuitively saw all of Alistair's crimes and he was here to judge them. The councillor was attended by a man in a blue suit who appeared to be an attending officer, from what Alstair could guess.

Professor Barlow walked in behind the Councillor's chair and his attendant and shut the door, his expression blank.

"Good evening, Lennox," he said. His voice, which Alistair had expected to be deep, booming and final as a coffin lid closing, was actually rather normal. "I understand you were asleep during the events of this afternoon?"

Alistair cleared his throat and nodded. "That's right, sir. I was having tea with some friends, and I fell asleep. When I woke up and left the room the attack had already happened."

"These friends of yours, what were their names?"

Once Alistair had answered, Rutherford sent his officer to talk to them and search their rooms. Alistair reddened. It felt as if he was accusing them of something.

"I have men doing a check over the site of the attack," Rutherford said. "Sometimes there are clues which others miss. I intend to speak with all your teachers to get an idea of the kind of person you are, and if you have any enemies who may have been involved."

A wave of relief hit Alistair and he felt his shoulders sag from it. It didn't sound like Rutherford doubted his story at all. But then, perhaps he just wanted to check all available avenues before making an arrest.

"Take heart, there's more than one type of magic which can make it seem like someone was there when they weren't. Unlike in the mundane world, where eyewitnesses are the best source of evidence, it's not always true for our investigations."

Alistair let himself hope just a little bit. He hadn't considered that there might be other explanations for why Zeta had said she'd seen him. Magic could do so many things, and he often forgot about it, even after all the things he'd learned. "Everett could change shape, look like other people," Alistair said. "But he's blocked..."

"I knew your parents, Lennox," Rutherford said. He pinned Alistair in place with his stare.

Alistair's heart sank all over again. No one who knew his parents had anything nice to say about them since their withdrawal from magical society. His hope that Rutherford was on his side dimmed considerably.

"I'm sorry," Alistair said, his voice soft.

"What happened was a shame," Rutherford said. "They did their best to help where they could. Neither of them had the greatest of gifts, but even before your birth they had a good line in combining their gifts to grow above what they were capable of. It was a terrible shame what happened. And then the circumstances around their death, very tragic."

"Thank you sir," Alistair said. He felt even more horribly on the spot that he had previously. Rutherford seemed to know a lot about Alistair's family and history, and Alistair hoped it didn't somehow count against him. Rutherford seemed sympathetic, but he had no idea if he was being sincere, or if it was some sort of ploy to get Alistair to open up and reveal something, confess even. Alistair pressed his lips firmly together.

"It's best for the school if you stay out of sight for the night," Barlow said. "You'll remain locked in here for your own safety as much as that of the other students. Hopefully by the morning Luis will have woken up and we can get his side of things, if not, and we believe you to be innocent, we may let you out and see if that draws out whoever it was."

Alistair nodded, then tore the page of his notebook where he'd made his list and offered it to Rutherford. "If this helps, this is what I was thinking through since it happened. It's a list of possible culprits and any reason I can think of that they might have done it."

Rutherford raised an eyebrow at the piece of paper, and Alistair felt he'd made a terrible mistake, but the man at least took the paper. He scanned it, nodded and folded it into his pocket.

"It's a start at least."

He turned his chair around, Barlow held the door open and they exited. The tension in the room eased, but Alistair's stomach turned over unpleasantly. His dinner was set inside him like a wet lump of mud.

"What's wrong, Allie?" William asked, looking at him closely.

"Have I just accused everyone I know at Misselthwaite of

framing me for attempted murder?" Alistair wrapped his arms around his stomach. "I did, didn't I?"

"No." William tried for a smile. "You didn't accuse me, or Tom or Sam?"

"Oh god." Alistair leaned forward until his forehead touched his knees. "I'm a horrible person. Deep down I'm disgusting and hideous. I bet if it was Kimber in my place she wouldn't have done something like this. You wouldn't either. No one would. I'm the worst."

"You're not." William put his hand on Alistair's back and sort of patted it. "You're in a horrible position, that's all."

Alistair reflected that Thomas would have been more comfortable dealing with him while he was upset like this, but Thomas probably thought he had tried to kill Luis, so he wouldn't be seeing him any time soon. He groaned softly.

"How about I make you some tea?" William offered. "Just, sit back on the pillows and try to relax."

"That's all very well for you to say," Alistair said. He lifted his head and scowled. "I am a terrible horrible person who trusts absolutely no one and I don't deserve friends or a boyfriend, let alone three."

"Now you're just being ridiculous." William kissed him on the forehead. "I'll be back with tea, and scones if I can con the cook into letting me have them."

"Thanks," Alistair said. He sounded even more sullen than he felt.

CHAPTER 26

When Alistair woke up the next day, he felt even more out of sorts than he'd been before he slept. He found it hard to wake up, his head fogged up as if he were getting sick, although he didn't have a sore throat or any sniffles or symptoms. He forced himself to sit up and eat one of the leftover scones and jam through sheer stubbornness. William had kindly brought him some of Kimber's rooibos tea the night before, he'd said she'd insisted, that she felt terrible about leaving him alone so he didn't have an alibi. The tea had helped soothe him to sleep, and now he had some more of it with the cold scone.

He looked at the time, annoyed that he would be missing his classes due to this whole debacle. He pulled his notebooks out from his satchel and read over his most recent notes, but none of the words meant anything to him. He couldn't seem to make any sense of them, when his head was full of the unfairness of it all.

Then he felt another wave of guilt at giving Rutherford the list of people he knew. They'd all know how terrible a friend he was now, how little he trusted them when it came down to it.

He flipped to a fresh page and started writing his journal.

I have no idea who could be behind this blasted scheme to make me look like a villain. It's obvious that the Birches would want to do something like that, but I am assured they cannot be on the grounds of the Manor. Is someone working for them, as an agent?

I feel strongly

Alistair paused. He looked down at the paper, and tried to remember what his sentence had been meant to say. He couldn't recall. What did he feel strongly? A sense of injustice, surely. He continued to write.

I feel strongly that this injustice is to sully my name, and to further ruin the family name of Lennox. The Birches have a link there too. And... Why has it never occurred to me to think of my parents' death as suspicious?

Didn't I feel a certain something, watching them drive off that night? Didn't I hate them at that moment? They were off party without any cares in the world. Some stupid party amd not me

Is it... could it be possible that I am capable of doing more than I am aware of?

Have I done things without knowing? Was the dream I had my mind distracting me from the unknowing motions of my body? Is that possible?

His head started to ache, gently at first, just behind his right eyebrow. Frustrated, he set the pen down, and looked at the strange way his writing had gone, the sentences didn't read quite right but he thought he'd hit something important. He needed to examine how his parents had died. Another thing to investigate. But first he needed to get out of this room.

He flipped a page in his notebook and wrote a to-do list, as his head felt fluffy and full and he didn't trust that he'd remember otherwise.

1. *Get out of this room*
2. *Say sorry to Tom and Sammy*
3. *Find out who framed me*

4. *Find out how my parents died but really*
5. *Go to Garden*
6. *Take*

He was interrupted from point six when the door opened and Rutherford wheeled in. His expression was bright. Barlow followed behind him and gave Alistair a brief smile.

"There's nothing more than circumstantial evidence," Rutherford said.

"I thought Zeta saw me do it?" Alistair said.

"It appears there was magic involved," Rutherford said. "Madame Waxleaf was able to trace a little of it from one of Zeta's tears."

"Zeta was crying?"

"No, it's a simple procedure that Waxleaf invented, extracting it. It wouldn't have shown anything if there had been no magic involved, and it would have been absent in another day, but as with everything else in this world, magic leaves traces."

Alistair blinked at him. Looked down at his letter and then up at him again. "How long do traces last?"

"Mm?" Councillor Rutherford looked perplexed. "You're free to go lad, for the moment the investigation is ongoing. Have your wits about you, as it's possible the actual culprit might target you."

"Just, before I go," Alistair said, heistatting. "Is Luis well? Is he going to make it?"

Rutherford's expression went carefully blank. "They're doing everything they can. He is holding on, but we're not entirely sure how long he will last."

"I'm very sorry to hear that." Alistair looked at his feet. Then something about what Rutherford had said about traces niggled at his brain. "Right, and thank you for telling me, but I need to know. If something happened months ago, a spell or a curse, would there still be any magical trace of it?"

Rutherford, although still looking confused, considered this. "Yes, although it would depend on the kind of magic as to how much evidence remained. Some magic requires runes to be carved or drawn onto a surface, those would certainly leave a physical record. Some magic is large enough in terms of ritual that there are what we might call magical echoes. Other things would require a very powerful and specialised spell to detect the evidence at all."

Alistair hastily scribbled notes under his to-do list and nodded. "Thank you Councillor, that's very useful."

"Here," Barlow said. He handed Alistair his wand back. "Just please be very careful in the next few days. I'm not at all sure what is happening in this school and I don't like not knowing that. Come to me if you find anything amiss."

"Of course," Alistair said. He slipped his wand into his jacket pocket, gathered his things into his satchel and stood. "Thank you, both of you." His head throbbed with the motion of standing and he took a deep breath, hoping it would pass.

Rutherford and Barlow were already leaving the room, so Alistair hurried after them.

His sense of urgency was somewhat dulled by the fog in his head. He briefly wondered if he shouldn't go to the infirmary to see if Madame Waxleaf had a remedy for whatever was happening to muddy his thinking. But it felt more important to talk to Thomas and Samal before he lost them forever.

He made his way through the halls to the suite he shared with them all. From the small amount of light that filtered in the windows it appeared to be mid morning.

He got to the suite door, and knocked on it, before opening it and letting himself in.

Thomas looked up from the spot he preferred to sit in on the floor of the sitting room. His expression went from hopeful and pleased to concerned.

"Alistair, there you are," he said. Which wasn't what Alistair had expected him to say.

Samal appeared in the doorway connecting the living area to the bedroom. "Allie. What happened?"

"I need to speak to both of you," Alistair said. He took a deep breath, trying to gather his thoughts but after a whole night locked in one of the dimly lit rooms, he didn't think he could think straight in this one. Even if it was filled with his things and far more familiar. "Would you both accompany me to the Secret Garden, please?"

"Of course," Samal said. He sat to pull on his boots. Thomas marked the page in the book he'd been studying from and stood as well.

They didn't talk on the way down. Alistair felt too muddled by the pain in his head, he started to experience a ringing in his ears as well. Being out in the sunlight initially felt like a mistake, it felt far too bright for his unshielded eyes. The fresh air felt good to his lungs though, and the ringing subsided from his ears as quickly as it had come up.

Finally they were inside the walls of the Garden and Alistair could feel the power of the wellspring, bolstering him.

It occurred to him then that he hadn't heard Ambrose's voice at any time since the trouble had started with Luis.

He reached out now, whispering Ambrose's name, but there was no response. In fact his own magic seemed sluggish in responding to his call. He frowned, and followed Samal and Thomas down the path towards Melusine's fountain. It was always the best place to start if they needed to have a conversation.

Samal sat down on the wall of the shallow pool surrounding the fountain and folded his hands in his lap. Thomas, who Alistair would have expected to have changed into his dog or fox form by now, stayed standing, watching Alistair, uncharacteristically sombre.

Alistair didn't know what to do with his hands, he wanted to wring them but that gesture felt too much like admitting distress. He clasped them behind his back and cleared his throat.

"I am not evil," he said. It was an odd way to start, he knew, but he wasn't thinking entirely clearly and it was what had come out of his mouth. "I know that you're both concerned about blood magic, and the corruption that might accompany it, but I assure you I am being careful, and I don't feel any different since I started using it." He paused, shook his head, winced at the pain and corrected himself. "No, that's not true. Blood magic has given me an edge, and has made me feel a little more capable of catching up to students like yourself who have been learning for years. I want to break William's curse, and this feels like an important tool in my quest to do so."

Thomas sighed and folded his arms.

"And right now, I feel very different indeed. I may be coming down with a head cold or a migraine."

Samal frowned, and got up, his hand already glowing gold. Alistair stopped him with a raised palm. "Please let me finish? I know I made a mistake with trying blood magic with William, it was a terrible error and I won't do it again. I ask you both to trust my judgement on this, but if you can't, and you really don't think you can trust me with blood magic, then I'll stop April's classes altogether. The two of you are more important to me than power." He stopped, something behind his eyes throbbing.

"Oh, Allie, I've just been so worried." Thomas crossed the distance between them in a couple of short strides and wrapped his arms around him. "I know you aren't responsible for what happened to Luis."

Alistair hugged him back, relief washing over him like a refreshing spring shower.

Samal moved closer slower. "Do you really mean that you'd give up studying blood magic if we asked you to?"

Alistair looked up and met Samal's gaze. "Yes, if you really wished me to, I would. I don't want to lose either of you, or William, and if it means I have to study longer to do so then that's fine. I'll do that. I'm willing."

Samal smiled and with it a golden glow enveloped him. He wrapped his arms around both Alistair and Thomas and Alistair's headache immediately evaporated.

Samal frowned and pulled back, looking deeply into Alistair's eyes. "There's something... might I heal you?" He pulled back from Alistair, and Thomas moved away as well.

Alistair nodded, rubbing his arm with the other hand. "Please, I've felt so muddled all day."

Samal placed his hand on Alistair's head and the fuzziness melted away, his head cleared of all confusion and sluggishness.

"What was that? I feel wonderful now," Alistair said.

"I'm not sure," Samal frowned and pulled his hand back to look at his fingers. "It felt sort of like I was healing a poison."

"Poison?" Thomas's dog ears had appeared in his hair and now they pricked up, listening for danger.

"But I've only eaten what William brought me," Alistair said. "And that was all school food."

Samal frowned. "Very odd."

"Who would've... William wouldn't...poison?" Thomas shook his head. "Maybe someone knew what he was going to bring to you and tampered with it somehow?"

Alistair rubbed his forehead and moaned softly. "There's too much happening, layers upon layers of intrigue and mystery and I don't know which to tackle first."

"Probably whoever tried to frame you for killing Luis." William's voice came from behind Alistair, who startled and turned to look at him.

"How did you get in here?"

"You left the key in the lock," William said. He tossed the key back to Alistair. "Did I hear one of you say something about poison? It must have really addled you."

"I always lock it," Alistair said, feeling forlorn. He looked at the key in his hand. "Sam just healed me, and said there was something like poison affecting me. That's why I forgot about the key in the door, and who knows how many other things."

"A slow acting magical effect perhaps," Samal frowned.

"Someone is trying to work against me," Alistair said. "Making it look like I sabotaged things, tried to... hurt Luis. It's all building and building and I don't know where it will end." Alistair closed his eyes and pressed the heels of his hands over them. "I don't know how to fight it, I don't know how to expose whoever is doing this."

He felt a warm arm slip around his shoulders and Thomas's familiar nose nuzzling under his ear. "We'll work it out together, Allie."

Alistair couldn't describe how much those words comforted him. Even if he did have to give up blood magic now, he had the support of his lovers. He was accepted, loved, and safe. He had missed this so, so much. He hated that they'd been driven apart through by the accusations and pranks. If they could be called pranks. They were escalating to a very dangerous place, and the word prank didn't seem enough.

Now, in the Garden, Alistair realised just how much he had ached for Thomas's touch, for Samal's smile, for William's wit and handsome face.

Those things had been taken from him.

"They're trying to create a rift between us," he said, softly. He dropped his hands and looked around at the three curious faces.

"Hmm?" William asked.

"They knew, if they wanted to get to me they had to do something to make the three of you distrust me, to doubt me."

Samal frowned. "Are you saying you suspect April Quinn, she's the one who's teaching you blood magic after all."

"I don't know. I suspect everyone, honestly," Alistair said. He sighed, and Thomas tugged him down to sit in the grass. The others sat as well, forming a loose ring. Alistair related all that Councillor Rutherford had said, especially the presence of magic in Zeta's tears.

"I suppose we'll just have to investigate everyone and try and narrow down the list of suspects," William said. "Whoever it is, they're inside Misselthwaite, so... it's a limited list of people to start with."

"Not that limited," Samal said. His voice was dry. "There's dozens of students, plus the professorial staff, plus all the servants and groundskeepers."

Alistair hadn't even considered the servants as possible suspects and he sighed, bending at the waist to rest his forehead on his knees which he drew up in front of him. "I should have thought of that."

"It's highly unlikely to be a servant," William said. He tapped a finger on his lips. "Medlock thoroughly checks each and every one of them, background, references and everything. I trust her judgement. I trust her absolutely and so does Father."

"Cheer up, Allie." Thomas rubbed his back until Alistair sat up again. "It sounds like a lot, but we've got all four of us to work on it together."

"I suppose," Alistair said. "The list feels very daunting though."

"Let's look at this logically," William said. "Whoever did this knows your movements, and is therefore someone you spend a fair amount of time with. We can start by looking hard at all the new people to the Manor."

Alistair picked a piece of grass and twisted it in his hands. He knew who the number one suspect would be, based on her choice of study. "April Quinn, you mean?"

"You were in Alexander's room when the attack occurred," Thomas said. "That makes him a prime suspect to my mind."

Alistair frowned. "But Alex is such a friendly person, he doesn't seem capable of subterfuge."

"It could be an act," William said. "Kimber as well. And she takes blood magic with you, doesn't she?"

"She does." Alistair sighed. "Zeta is in my blood magic class too, and we're relatively new to being friends as well."

This time it was Thomas's turn to frown. "I don't think it's Zeta, she's all about the rights of the working class and justice and all that."

"I'm not exactly from the working class," Alistair said.

"She's a socialist is what she is," William said. His voice was dry and Alistair had no idea if that meant he approved of being a socialist or not. He should probably read up on what socialism was.

"Didn't you say she'd been manipulated magically?" Samal asked. "Evidence of magic in her tears that the officers found?'

"But still, she should be on the list if Alex and Kimber are," Alistair said, obstinate. "She's not new to the university but she's new to me."

"And then, you have two new classes, two new teachers," Samal said. He caught Alistair's eye and then quickly looked at the ground as if ashamed of bringing it up. "April Quinn and Professor Winterbourne."

"Lord Carlisle invited both of them to the school," Alistair said. He looked at William, hoping for answers that would rule out April. "What kind of interview process does your father do?"

"He's usually very intuitive," William said. He leaned back on his hands. "Or he leaves it to Barlow. Between him and Medlock they would probably unearth any secret plans."

"Probably," Samal repeated. "It's not entirely reassuring if they don't do a slew of magical screening and checks."

"I think the majority of professors would object to something like that," William said, heatedly. There were two spots of pink on his cheeks. "Reputation is worth a lot in magical society."

"That's true enough." Samal frowned.

Ambrose suddenly whispered in Alistair's ear, startling him but flooding him with relieved happiness as well. "Be careful of the emotions you stir up..." Ambrose whispered.

Alistair closed his eyes and took a quick breath. He was taking this too personally, feeling protective of his new friends and being obstinate because of it. Of course William would feel the same about his own father.

"We're not accusing anyone," Alistair said. "We're just acknowledging that people might be involved, or perhaps, hiding things from us."

"That's right." Without warning Thomas flopped over Alistair's lap, dog tail wagging. It poked out a hole he'd made just under the waistband of his trousers. "We want to protect you from this happening again, or worse. We definitely don't want another Birches attacking you in the hall situation."

Alistair rubbed Thomas's hair between his ears. "I thought I was going to be expelled last night, or sent to prison or something."

"Luis is in a delicate state," Samal said. "But it seems likely he'll survive, the blood loss was extensive but Madame Waxleaf has a good potion to replenish blood, it's just slow acting."

"It does seem most likely to be a student," William said. He was sitting cross legged and had plucked a dandelion from the lawn, now he was twirling it in his fingers. "Signing up to be a professor seems like an awful lot of hard work to do just to target a student."

"It does seem rather outlandish," Samal said. "So, if we start the investigation with Alexander, Kimber and Zeta and move on to the teachers if we can't turn anything up?"

The others nodded their agreement. Alistair looked around at them all with a sense of contentment he had feared he wouldn't ever feel again. In his ear, Ambrose whispered "I missed you."

"I missed you too, Ambrose," Alistair murmured.

"Right, so how do we investigate?" William tossed aside the dandelion and dusted off his hands. "Corner Alexander and threaten him until he confesses?"

Alistair blinked slowly, trying to make sense of that as a plan, Thomas sat up and Samal shook his head.

"Not like that," Samal said. "We have to be more subtle."

Alistair thought back to the murder mystery books he'd read, most of them set in Chicago. "We have to try and search their belongings," he said. "See if they've left any clues or incriminating evidence lying about."

"I can't be seen breaking into people's rooms," William said. "It'd cause an utter uproar. Father would be furious and it would damage the reputation of the school."

"Maybe we don't need to break in. Can't we be invited?" Thomas asked.

"Or we could just confirm someone's location and break in magically while they're indisposed," Alistair said. He was warming to this idea. He enjoyed reading about detectives solving crimes, and the idea that he could take the role of one of those cool, collected types was very appealing indeed.

"I think the doors are all warded against magical unlocking," Samal said.

"Maybe there's something in Thomas's idea of being invited," William said. "Thomas has a very innocent face, he could probably ask to borrow things, or invite himself to tea and be let in easily enough."

Thomas's cheeks pinked, practically glowing under his rust-coloured freckles. "I don't know if I should thank you for that or not."

William shrugged and gave him a smirk. "I don't know either."

Samal slapped a hand to his forehead. "I might have a solution," he said. He looked up into the air.

Alistair followed his gaze and then cleared his throat as the silence stretched out. "And what might that solution be?"

Samal looked back at them and smiled softly. "My father had a truth detecting talent," he said. "I'd have to look up how he did it but I should be able to do the same thing with a bit of practice."

"I remember that," William said. "He caught that woman who was going around hamstringing men at the opera."

Thomas pulled a face. "That sounds ghastly."

"It was," William said. "But as I recall she only targeted men who had mistreated their lady companions in some way or other."

"Huh." Thomas tilted his head and considered. "They might have deserved it a little bit then."

"The point being," Samal said. "If I can get in contact with my father, I can learn the talent. I think. Or I could look at papers and reports on him, perhaps glean it from there."

"Right," Alistair said. "You do that. The rest of us will go and get some weapons."

"Weapons?" Thomas stared at Alistair as if he'd grown another head.

"If we confront someone with murderous intent we need to be able to defend ourselves."

"Quite right, Allie," William said. "Let's go back to our suite and see what I have on hand."

"We already have wands and magic," Thomas said as they all stood up. "Surely that's as deadly as we need to be?"

"Perhaps," Alistair said. He tried to give Thomas a reassuring smile but he suspected it came out as a grimace. "But all the same I'd feel more secure walking around school with something to defend myself with."

CHAPTER 27

In the end, Alistair chose a cricket bat. William, it turned out, had a chest full of possible weapons including a bottle of holy water and a few amulets that emanated horrible dark energy. William said they were cursed, and they were kept wrapped in protective muslin cloths for safe handling.

William armed himself with two wicked looking daggers which he immediately concealed about his person, almost imperceptibly, leading Alistair to wonder if he was often secretly armed.

Thomas, reluctant, picked an amulet, and shuddered as he dropped it into one of his pockets. "That feels like all sorts of bad luck."

Samal had stayed in the Garden, meditating next to the fountain as he reached out with some kind of angelic psychic power to try and contact his father. He had advised it would be a few hours.

"Is there any point in trying to investigate without Samal?" Thomas said. "If he's right and he'll be able to sense the truth we should wait for him."

"I'd like to see if we can find any evidence," Alistair said.

"Perhaps in Alexander's room? I don't think he's responsible, but maybe someone planted something, or left something..."

William nodded and checked the clock on the wall. "It's almost dinner time, let's see if we can talk to him and Kimber at dinner. We can attempt to solicit an invitation back to one of their rooms afterwards. By then hopefully Samal will have joined us."

Martha was waiting at their table. Before her was a plate stacked with all the vegetables on offer from the buffet table which she was picking at slowly, while she read from a book on cartomancy. She looked up as they sat down with her.

"Well, if it isn't the school criminal," she said. Alistair was relatively sure she was teasing, and she winked at him which reassured him. "I haven't seen any of you all day. Where's Sam?"

"He's just trying to learn something new," Thomas said. He sat beside Martha with his nicely balanced plate of meat and vegetables. "We're hoping he'll be along soon."

"Good." She smiled back at Thomas. Then turned to Alistair. "What have you been up to?"

"Trying to work out a way to clear my name," Alistair said. He didn't see any merit in lying to Martha, Samal and her were good friends and he trusted Samal's judgement. "I'm being framed."

"Makes sense," Martha said. She closed her book and leaned forward. "So who's on the suspect list?"

"It's probably best we keep that to ourselves," William said. Alistair considered for a minute and then decided to let her in on it.

"The more eyes we have over them, the better," Alistair said. "Zeta, Alexander and Kimber. And possibly April Quinn and Professor Winterbourne but also probably not, because the vetting for professors is more rigorous than for students."

"Isn't that the truth." Martha tucked into her dinner, and the others did the same. Between mouthfuls they filled her in on the names of who they were watching out for, and she nodded, not seeming at all surprised.

As he buttered his dinner roll, Alistair became slowly aware that the other students in the dining hall were giving him suspicious looks. His heart sank. Just because Councillor Rutherford had decided there wasn't enough evidence, didn't mean the student body agreed. He wasn't used to being noticed at all, let alone someone that people were eyeing suspiciously. He didn't care for it, and it strengthened his resolve to get to the bottom of it all.

Samal walked in just as Alistair was finishing his meal. He looked tired around the eyes, but his expression was bright and Alistair felt warmth spread through his chest. He met Alistair's gaze and nodded, before going to the buffet and fixing his plate for dinner.

He sat down on Martha's other side and elbowed her affectionately. "Hey Martha."

"Hi Sam," she said in a singsong manner. "I've been recruited to help spy."

"Good," Sam said. He shovelled a forkful of mashed potatoes into his mouth.

"Oh, look, there's Kimber and Alex," Will said, with a false brightness.

Alexander and Kimber strolled in and both of them lit up and waved when they spotted Alistair at the table. They hurriedly filled their plates and joined them at the table.

"I'm going to toddle off now," Martha said. "It looks like Zeta is finishing up, and I can catch up to her and ask her about the student's association, see if she lets anything slip."

Martha bussed her plate and hurried out, book under her arm, and called out to Zeta, who gave her a tight smile as they walked out of the dining hall together.

Kimber sat down beside Alistair.

"How are you, Allie? I've been so worried!" She frowned,

searching his face. Her stoat familiar, Horatio, leaned over towards him from her shoulder. Alistair moved closer so that it could cross to his shoulder and nuzzle his neck.

"It's not been fun," Alistair said. His tension over having to question his friends evaporated a little. "But Councillor Rutherford said there wasn't evidence so here I am."

"I'm so glad to hear that," Alex said. He'd taken the seat Martha had recently evacuated, opposite Alistair. "We felt so guilty, leaving you like that. I mean, when we left we didn't feel guilty, it just seemed like you needed a sleep, but once we heard what had happened." He shook his head. "I hope there are no hard feelings."

Alistair shook his head and forced a smile. "Of course not, you had no idea what was going to happen."

As he looked up at them, both Alexander and Kimber's eyes slid to the side, not quite able to meet his. Alistair looked at Samal to see if he had picked anything up, but he didn't see Alistair's eye.

Kimber's stoat hurried back to her lap and snatched scraps from her dinner plate to eat.

"I should really catch up on my homework. All this excitement over the last few days I've barely been able to concentrate," Thomas said. Kimber and Alexander were finishing up their dinners and they both nodded.

"I have an assignment that's really dragging," Alexander said.

"Have you got notes from today's class that I could look at Kimber?" Alistair asked. "Since I missed class…Perhaps we can study together for a little bit?"

Kimber's face broke into a warm smile. "Of course. I can bring them to your room if you don't mind hosting?"

Alistair found himself smiling back, the suspicion he'd felt of her earlier seemed ridiculous now. He could vaguely remember that there was some reason he had meant to go to

Kimber's room, but he couldn't recall the importance of it now. As long as they spent more time with her and Alexander the truth would come out, wouldn't it? He doubted that Kimber had anything to do with it anyway.

"That sounds fine," Thomas said. "I'll get us some biscuits for supper."

William was giving Alistair a subtle questioning look but smoothed his expression when Kimber looked over at him.

"Assuming it's all right with *all* of you," Kimber said. Her tone had gone a little less friendly and she eyed William with something like suspicion. Samal shrugged his shoulders.

"I don't mind."

"Of course," William said. "I have some reading to catch up on, and your presence is always welcome."

CHAPTER 28

So it was that within a half hour, Alexander and Kimber were settled in the living area of the suite Alistair shared with his lovers.

Alistair had Kimber's notes from the day's blood magic class with April spread out on his lap as he sat on the couch. Although he felt a little guilty about the notes, because he wasn't entirely sure if his lovers did in fact want him to drop the study entirely, but this was all in the name of investigation, so he read through and made notes all the same. April's classes were irregular, but they always contained something useful to know.

Thomas was on a cushion near the low fire, going over a book of bird anatomy, his eyes flicking up regularly to check on Kimber and Alexander.

Kimber and Alexander had taken up the rest of the couch, Kimber sitting closest to Alistair, which he was grateful for, and Alexander on the far side. He was scribbling notes in a potions notebook which looked like a handwritten recipe book with lots of the main recipes crossed out, and more notes in the margins than were contained in the main text.

Kimber was reading her notes from another class, and often looked up to meet Alistair's eyes and smile. He felt a little better every time she did, the worries easing away and the fear he'd felt becoming like a distant memory. Instead, in between making notes, he found himself thinking about just how much he liked Kimber, and how glad he was that she was his friend.

William sat in an armchair facing the sofa and watched, barely pretending to read the library book on advanced wards he had in his lap.

Alistair was feeling quite drowsy when Samal stood up from the desk in the corner and stretched his arms over his head. He walked to the small table which held the shortbread biscuits and idly trailed his hand over Alistair's shoulder.

They both froze.

Samal's hand glowed golden, and with his touch Alistair felt the distinct warmth of Samal's healing magic. His head cleared and he no longer felt tired.

Samal looked into Alistair's eyes with something like horror. Alistair shook his head, having no idea what it was that Samal had healed or how it had come about.

"Alistair... The poisoning effect..." he mumbled.

"What?" William set aside the book he'd been pretending to read and leaned forward on his hand.

"I just healed Alistair, from the same thing that was affecting his mind this morning," Samal said. "I didn't even mean to, but touching him drew it out..."

Alistair turned his gaze to Kimber. He'd been feeling so warm towards her just a few minutes before, and now ... now he was deeply suspicious.

"Kimber," he said, slowly. "I never did ask you what your magical talent is."

Alexander shook his head, his expression outraged. "What? Why are you talking about poison and healing?"

Kimber's stoat ducked into her pocket. Kimber gathered her notes up and stashed them into her satchel. "My talent? Well, I'd love to go into it, only it's getting late and I should probably-"

"Kimber." William was across the room in an instant, standing over Kimber, his face cast into frightening shadows by the flickering fire. He looked every inch the vampire heir to the magical school, and even Alistair felt a little intimidated. "Answer his question."

Samal walked around the couch and folded his arms. He didn't look as frightening as William, but when he folded his arms there was a distinct bulge to his upper arms, and his shoulders seemed broader.

Kimber took a breath, looked at the two of them and then shrugged, sitting back in her seat. "My talent is perfectly legal."

"What a soothing way to start your answer," William said dryly.

"My family has always had a certain way with a certain sort of magic," Kimber said. She had her hand in her satchel, adjusting papers and books so they all fit. "Some look down on it, but that's simply because they don't understand. You can forgive me being hesitant to talk about it when I know many would judge me based on my talent alone."

"I thought your talent was illusions?" Alexander said, his voice soft as if he were speaking from a great distance.

"No. My talent is something more than that." Kimber looked up at William and Samal and something seemed to soften around her eyes as she looked at them. William's expression slackened slightly but Samal's got angrier. "We have a certain amount of magical charisma, it draws people to us."

"Glamour?" Samal asked. His eyebrows raised but he didn't look any less irritated. "You have glamour? I actually did think that was illegal."

"The use of it against the non-magical world is absolutely illegal," Kimber said. She fluttered her eyelashes and gazed at Samal with intensity. Despite her words, Alistair found himself liking her more and more. A small part of his mind told him it was a magical effect, but it was easily ignored.

"Don't pick on Kimber like that," Alexander said. He moved forward on the couch, moving to put his body slightly between hers and William and Samal.

"Yeah," Alistair echoed. He looked up at Samal. "Why are you doing this?"

Samal sighed, rolled his eyes, and brushed past William to rest his hand on Alistair's cheek. The warm glow cleared his head once more.

Alistair, repulsed, made to get up off the couch, wishing to put as much distance between Kimber and himself as possible. However Kimber moved faster. She gripped his left arm with one hand, and the other withdrew from her bag with the silver knife she borrowed off Alexander for blood magic lessons. The shiny blade was at Alistair's throat before he could process what was going on.

"I don't know why the lot of you think dear *Allie* is so important," Kimber said. Her expression had turned hard. Alistair's breath caught. "But if you're clever you'll let me leave this room right now. I haven't used my powers against anyone non-magical and therefore I haven't broken any rules or laws."

"You are holding a knife to Alistair's throat," Samal said.

Alistair hardly dared to breathe. Kimber's fingers held him hard, her nails digging into the flesh under his shirt, and the sharp blade of the knife was scraping the skin of his throat.

"Because you two are crowding in like you're going to start something," Kimber said. "Back up, stop threatening, and let me leave in peace and nothing bad will happen."

"Want me to help?" Ambrose's voice directly in Alistair's ear. Creepy as a snake's hiss but far more welcome. Alistair swallowed, thought 'yes' as hard as he could as he didn't dare to breathe.

"Kimber, what are you talking about, what are you doing?" Alexander asked, his expression frantic. She glanced at him and something in her eyes had an effect. Alexander slumped on the sofa cushions, apparently asleep.

Samal and William both took a step back, and Thomas, whining, shapeshifted into a dog with his ears down and his tail between his legs. He was the picture of doggy uncertainty, but Alistair knew Thomas was more likely to fight in that form than his human one.

Kimber's knife moved slowly away from Alistair's throat, although she kept it close to him. She glanced down at her hand for a moment, her eyebrows knitting as she scowled.

Alistair tried to stay perfectly still as Ambrose appeared partially formed, his face showing him of an age with Alistair, his hand around Kimber's where it held the knife. Alistair could see goosebumps on her arm, and he wondered if Ambrose's ghostly touch was chilling her.

"What in the nine hells..." Kimber muttered.

William seized her moment of distraction, whipped his hand out to throw a hex at her. Kimber reacted swiftly and her eyes flashed steel as she flicked the knife up, nicking Alistair's neck enough to extract some blood which she used in a counter-curse, forcing William back against the wall with the force of it.

Alistair cried out and tried to yank away from her grip, his own magic coming to his fingertips in self-defence and sparking towards her.

Alistair's cry spurred Thomas to move as well, and he leapt at Kimber, teeth bared and growling.

Kimber drew on the power of Alistair's blood and formed a quick defensive wall which Thomas crashed into. He fell to the ground, whining, and staring balefully at the sparkling green barrier that had appeared between the sofa and the rest of the room.

Alistair abruptly lost his temper.

How dare she threaten him?

How dare she cloud his mind to make him like her?

How dare she use his own blood to hurt Thomas?

He pressed his hand to the side of her face and *shoved* his magic into her, hardly knowing what effect he was trying to achieve, just knowing that he wanted her to stop and this was the weapon he had.

Her skin turned grey under his fingers, and the effect spread from his touch like ice forming on a pond. Aghast, Alistair pulled his hand back and scrambled out of the couch, watching as the greyness slowed its spread. It appeared his magic had attempted to change Kimber into stone. He pulled his wand out and resolved to use an actual spell next time.

Kimber made a frustrated noise and stood, she said a rune and the greyness retreated from her face, shrinking back to a handprint and then vanishing altogether.

Samal had transformed into his angelic form, and the golden light from him set the whole scene into sudden bright relief.

Ambrose had been eclipsed by the brightness of the defensive wall but Alistair could sense he was still there, still trying to help. However he had no idea what use he could be to them. Wincing in anticipation, he touched his left hand pointer finger to the cut on his neck, thanking the stars that she had nicked him shallowly and not gone for the kill, and used the blood magic to bolster the hex that he wanted to throw Kimber's way.

Ambrose made the next move, letting out a keening wail. Alistair could always hear Ambrose, but from the startled reactions of everyone in the room, this sound was different. Samal went to his knees, his hands over his ears and his face a picture of pain. William seemed to be adversely affected too, shaking his head as if to clear it.

Kimber jumped, her eyes narrowing. She bolted towards the door, leaving the protective wall up where it had been cast.

Thomas dodged around it to give chase, although he was a few steps behind.

"This isn't over, Alistair!" Kimber shouted, there was a haunting touch of amusement to her words. "You were such an easy target, I'm sure it'll only be a few more days before you're missing me and resenting your boyfriends all over again. So desperate to be liked, and so completely naive and ignorant! You can't change that in a few hours!"

"Shut up!" Alistair cried, his voice cracking.

Thomas was almost on her, so she darted out into the hallway and slammed the door shut behind her. Alistair's immobility curse died on his tongue, her words striking him to the core.

Samal got to his feet and crossed to Alistair, healing the cut in an instant. "What was that noise?" he asked. "Was it something Kimber cast?"

"I think it was Ambrose," Alistair said. He felt the telltale chill near his ear.

"Sorry, I didn't think it would get *everyone* like that..."

"He says he's sorry, he thought he was just targeting Kimber."

William grabbed Alistair from behind and hugged him hard, burying his face in his shoulder. Thomas trotted back over to them and wound around their legs. Samal wrapped his wings around the two of them and they all breathed a little easier.

"You could have died," William said, his voice muffled.

"We have to move fast," Samal said. "She sounded like she was just going to keep on affecting Alistair."

Alistair realised Alexander was still on the sofa, unconscious. "Sam, can you check if Alex is all right?"

"Of course." Samal let go of them and went to Alexander, placing a hand gently on his forehead. Alexander didn't react immediately, but then he took a deep breath and woke up slowly. William seemed to be in no rush to let go of Alistair, even when Alistair moved closer to Alexander, he walked behind him, still holding on so it was a sort of awkward shuffle.

"I feel very strange," Alexander said. He looked up at Samal. "You're very beautiful."

"I get that a lot," Samal said, not sounding entirely pleased. "It's the angel glow."

"How do you feel, Alex?" Alistair asked.

Alexander sat up straighter and frowned. "Like my head is clear for the first time in a long time. And I hadn't been aware that it wasn't clear... so that's... I feel really strange."

"Kimber's talent is magical allure, charisma," Samal said. "She's probably been using it on you for some time."

"We met on the first day of term," Alexander said. "That's weeks now."

A knock on the door had all of them tensing at once.

"Who is it?" William barked.

"It's Martha," the voice said from the hallway. "If there's a code word I have to say to get in, you didn't tell me."

Samal went to let her in, touching her briefly, presumably to ensure she was really Martha.

"You all look utterly rotten," Martha said. "What happened? Where's Kimber?"

"Kimber's behind it all, it seems," Samal said. "We were just trying to form a plan for our next step."

"Oh," Martha said. She looked stunned for a moment, then shrugged. "Well, I was coming to say Zeta was a dead end, she's been studying in the library in full view of Kincade for days now, it seems. She saw the attack on Luis when she was going for a late lunch."

"Right," Alexander said. "I'm sorry but I don't understand any of this, what is Kimber behind?"

"The attack on Luis, and probably a few other things designed to make Alistair look untrustworthy and dangerous," William said.

Alistair went to sit on the sofa and William was forced to let go of him, finally. Although he immediately sat beside him and slipped his arm through his.

"I suppose she must have some kind of link to the Birches, she didn't exactly tell us her motive though." Samal led Martha to the fireside, his angelic seeming slowly fading away.

"She's been using a magical effect to make people like her," Alistair said, slowly. "To get close to me."

"It's more than just 'liking'," William said. "Allure like that, it can grow into obsession. It can make the target forget about their own needs and do whatever the person controlling them wants. We're lucky she didn't have longer with you..." he trailed off, something occurring to him. Alistair swallowed, his own mind reaching the same conclusion.

"She could have made me attack Luis? Is that what you're saying?"

"She could have," William said slowly. "But I think it's more likely that she did it with your wand and then made Zeta remember it wrong, put your face over hers in her memory with a command. Or an illusion."

Alistair crossed his hands over his stomach. "But we don't know that, it's just speculation."

Alexander put his head in his hands. "I think it was me," he said. His voice was dull. "I think *I* attacked Luis. Because she told me to."

Thomas, who had shifted back to human form, sat on the sofa's arm beside Alexander. "It's not your fault, Alex. It's hers. You weren't in control."

"I think I did the thing with the green monsters from the garden too," Alexander continued. "I have some memories of it, of going into the garden and finding them on a wall... it's blurred, like a half-remembered dream."

Alistair felt even more revolted. Using someone to do hateful things, twisting their minds against their will... Where would Kimber have stopped?

"We have to protect Luis!" Alistair stood up so suddenly the others startled. "She'll finish him off, make whoever is around think it was me, we have to get to him first."

The others flew into action, grabbing their wands and coats before hurrying out into the hallway.

CHAPTER 29

"Someone should alert Professor Barlow," Thomas said. "I'll go, I can run the fastest." He shifted into fox form before waiting for a response, and dashed off.

"Medlock too," Alistair said. He looked after Thomas. "I don't think he heard me."

"I can do that," Martha said. "Come on, Alexander, you can be my bodyguard." She took him by the hand and tugged him up the hallway, as the others moved at a jog behind them.

"I'm not sure if Father is in tonight," William muttered. "We can talk to him after, it doesn't matter. I won't leave Alistair's side."

"Fine with me," Alistair said. Samal and William were flanking him and he felt well protected, but he didn't know how he'd feel if one of them went elsewhere. He wondered where Ambrose was in all this, but as ever his phantom brother seemed to come and go as he pleased.

It wasn't far to the infirmary, but Alistair was breathing heavily when they got there. Everything was happening so fast and he couldn't keep his thoughts straight.

It was dark inside the infirmary. William went first, pushing the door open as silently as possible, and walking in soundlessly.

Alistair followed, trying not to make noise although he was panting. Samal entered behind him.

Most of the beds stood empty, but there was one with curtains drawn around it. There was the faint rustle of movement from within, and William pulled the curtain back to reveal Kimber, her hands pressed a pillow down over Luis's face.

William knocked her aside and Alistair darted in to yank the pillow away. Samal put his hands on Luis's chest and started to heal him with warm glowing magic.

"William, look at me," Kimber said. She caught hold of his shoulder and their gazes met. All the urgency in William's demeanour vanished. His expression turned from warlike to neutral. "Go stand in the hallway."

Alistair watched with utter horror as William turned and walked back into the hallway.

"William! Come back!" Alistair said.

"Come with me, Allie," Kimber said. He kept his eyes away from hers, and hoped that the healing Samal had given him less than an hour before meant any residual power she had over him was gone.

"I won't," Alistair said. He looked at Samal for help. Samal met his eyes and shook his head.

"I'm trying to keep Luis breathing, he won't do it on his own if I let go," Samal said. "I'm sorry, he's right on the edge."

Kimber smiled and closed in on Alistair. He held his wand between them and without thinking, met her eyes.

"That's it, come with me," Kimber said. He felt a wave of happiness as she smiled at him. He liked Kimber *so much*, and he wanted to go with her. Of course he did. He lowered his wand arm and nodded.

"Yes, let's go."

"Alistair don't listen to her," Samal shouted. Alistair shook his head at Samal, he was simply being foolish. Alistair could remember of course that Kimber had held a knife to his throat earlier. He knew it had happened, but it didn't matter. It had been a mere trifle. What he needed was to go with his friend now, and see what it was she had to say. And that was what he was going to do.

They walked past William who was waiting patiently in the hallway. Kimber spared him a glance, and told him to make sure Samal stayed in the infirmary. William nodded pleasantly.

Kimber and Alistair hurried down the stairs together and out the front doors of Misselthwaite Manor.

"You really are the most foolish thing I've ever seen," Kimber said. Her stoat familiar appeared on her shoulder and bared its teeth at Alistair. Kimber had firm hold of his hand and there was a flicker of fear that the stoat would run down her arm and bite him, but he couldn't hold on to the worry at all.

The summer night air was relatively cool and a part of Alistair that wasn't entirely fixated on Kimber perked up. If the nights are getting colder, he thought, that might mean that there's new things that need to be planted in the Secret Garden.

It was like a spray of mist to the face, that thought. Some of the hold Kimber's magic had on his mind loosened. His instinct was to stop and fight, but before he acted, he imagined what would happen if he did that.

If he stopped following Kimber, she'd turn and use her power on him again. He couldn't risk that. The previous healing Samal had given him seemed to have no effect at all on the intensity of her control, and he couldn't risk entirely losing himself again. Most of him was still noticeably under her thrall anyway, but perhaps he could nudge a little... suggest something to her?

Maybe the Secret Garden could help.

She had conjured a witchlight, not unlike the sort Medlock used, and it hovered in the air a few feet before her. From her direction it appeared Kimber's plan was to go to the stables and either take some horses for them or perhaps she had a carriage ready and waiting. Either way, Alistair expected that meant she intended to take him off Misselthwaite grounds, and if he was off Misselthwaite grounds he didn't have any protection from the Birches.

He cleared his throat and spoke. "Kimber?" He felt an urge to speak sweetly to her, to tell her how wonderful she was. It appeared to be part of her magical allure. He chased the urge. Leaned into it. "You're so lovely."

Kimber snorted and spared a glance over her shoulder. "Thanks."

"Before we leave the grounds..." Alistair started, his voice syrupy sweet and alien to his own ears. "I have something wonderful to show you."

That caught her attention and she slowed and then stopped, looking at him curiously. "What is it?"

He couldn't lie to her, the allure was too strong for that, so he didn't. "There's a hidden garden, a locked garden, it's beautiful and... and it's the source of a magical wellspring."

Kimber's eyes widened in the flickering light. "So the legends *are* true? However did you find it?"

Alistair shrugged and smiled as guilelessly as he could manage. "It seemed totally random, but when I got inside, and found the wellspring, it unlocked my magic. My parents had cursed me, you see, so that I couldn't do any magic at all."

Kimber's eyes narrowed at the mention of his parents and she pursed her lips. "That does sound like something they'd do. Come on then, show me where this garden is, I want to see it."

Alistair's heart swelled with happiness at being the one to give Kimber something she wanted. His entire mind flooded with joy and he led her there without any thoughts but those.

He pulled the brass key out, pushed the hanging ivy aside and opened the door to the Secret Garden. He had seldom if ever been there in the night time, and he was pleased to hear the soft hoot of an owl.

He held the door open for Kimber to enter first. She strode past and Alistair followed, not bothering to close the door behind him. There was no need, the only important thing was Kimber, after all.

She stopped at the small crossroads and sniffed the air. "Where's the wellspring then?"

"This way, at the fountain," Alistair said. He led the way down the white seashell path and felt the cool whisper of Ambrose's presence. That cleared his head better than the thought of the Secret Garden.

"Alistair..." Ambrose whispered. "Alistair..."

"I'm here," Alistair said.

Kimber was walking close behind him. "I know you're here, you dolt."

"Listen to me, Melusine says she can help," Ambrose said. Melusine's name was another moment of clarity, breaking some of the hold Kimber's allure had on him.

"It's just down here," Alistair said, trying to sound as sweet as he had before. "The wellspring is in the fountain, isn't it beautiful?"

"I can't believe it," Kimber said. "All those years and it was right here. And you found it, you of all people. The remaining child of the two greatest fools in London's magical history."

Alistair frowned. The way Kimber spoke it was almost as if she'd known his parents. He didn't think before speaking this time. "Did you know them?"

Kimber barked out a laugh. "Eleanor Birch is my goddaughter," she said. "My dear sister Alice lost a child because of the foolishness of the Lennoxes. And then they were daring to try and re-enter magical society? Ridiculous."

Alistair longed to know more, to ask questions about how Kimber could be someone's godmother when she seemed to be the same age as him, but it didn't seem like a good idea to ask right then.

"How do I activate it?" Kimber asked.

Alistair walked up to the fountain, and gazed at Melusine's likeness. "Hello Melusine," he said, as politely as he could. His hand, as ever, went to rest on the head of the small stone frog he always touched.

The effect was instant. His mind was his again, and below him the power of the wellspring bubbled to life, filling him with the essence of the earth and all the growing things within it. He thought he saw the statue of Melusine wink at him.

He turned back to Kimber and asked the questions he'd thought of earlier. "I don't understand how you can be Eulalia's godmother," he said. "Don't you have to be older than the baby for that?"

Kimber frowned at the change in the tone of his voice and stalked closer to him. "Show me the wellspring."

"Oh, you're on it already," Alistair said. "But uh, that statue up there? That's William's mother, and if she doesn't like you, she might not let you feel it the way I do."

Kimber's eyes flicked to the statue and back to him. "What?"

Alistair felt warmth at his back and knew that Melusine was agreeing with him, that she would help any way she could.

"Ambrose, is there anything you can do to keep Kimber from using her allure on me? I don't know if it would work right now anyway, with the wellspring and all, but just to be safe…"

Kimber looked around. "Is this an ambush? But you were so far under. You wanted so much to please me, even before I used my magic. You wanted to be with friends, to not be alone any more…" She spun on the spot, searching the flowerbeds and trees for others and finding nothing. "Eulalia was right about how pathetic you are."

"You wanted to take me to Eulalia?" Alistair asked. It felt important for her to admit it out loud, and he wanted the satisfaction of it. "So she could kill me?"

"Naturally." Kimber brought her wand up in one hand and

her silver knife in the other. "But I'm perfectly happy to do it myself, right here and now."

Alistair's wand was in his hand. He didn't have his own knife on him, but he had the slicing spell he could use. Although he didn't like to use magic to harm others, this counted as extraordinary circumstances. He took a deep breath, let it out through his nose, and let the magic flow through him.

Kimber made the first attack with a slashing movement of her wand, but Alistair batted it aside as if they were duelling with swords and not wands. He felt a brief-lived joy that he'd be able to win. However, Kimber was relentless and fast. She spoke runes quickly, seeming to pull more and more power out of herself as she advanced on him and it was all he could do to shield himself before she was upon him.

He couldn't even use the slicing spell to draw blood, he had to use all his magical focus on maintaining a flimsy shield between him and Kimber.

Kimber was bleeding from her left forearm, and the blood was incorporated into her hexes and attack spells as soon as it welled up, not a single drop left to fall onto the grass.

Alistair was backed hard against the wall surrounding the fountain, and he was considering stepping into the water to get further back. Kimber beat against the shield again and again and the force of her rage was almost overwhelming. A small part of him, which remembered how it felt to love her and want to please her, tried to tell him to stop, to let his guard down. He ignored it, gritted his teeth and used every scrap of knowledge he could remember to keep her back. The spells she used were far more complex and practised than anything the other Birches had used, they were beyond him, and he felt cold sweat on his forehead as he calculated how much longer he thought he could last.

"You should have stayed away," Kimber said. She spoke from between clenched teeth, forcing her wand into a crack that had appeared in his shield and slowly pushing it open. "The carriage should have been a warning to you, you should have been smart enough to understand it."

"What carriage?" Alistair sounded desperate now, pushing everything he had into keeping her from breaking through the crack in his failing shield. But even as he said it he knew what she meant. The night his parents had died, they were riding in a carriage.

"The runes had been there for years and years, waiting to pick up on their intention," Kimber said.

Then she cried out in triumph as his shield cracked into a thousand pieces and she was on him, knife flashing in the moonlight as she slashed at his face. Alistair had just enough time to throw an arm up to block her blow. It saved his eyes but he howled as she cut deep into the flesh of his forearm.

"If only you'd died with them, we could have saved ourselves so much trouble," Kimber hissed.

"That's enough!" The voice was deep, older, male. Professor Barlow?

A bright white light knocked Kimber off balance. Alistair rolled away, wincing as he rubbed his fresh wound in the dirt. He felt the energy of the earth below him and reached out for it, without thought. Beyond the advancing figures, Alistair saw the sundew grow large, as it had in his dream, reaching tendrils towards Kimber. He didn't know if it was something he'd done, or if the Garden was reacting to his need.

Professor Barlow and a fox strode through the meadow, the fox's hackles were up and it growled, going to pounce towards Kimber. Kimber started throwing spells at them, but was hit by another flash of light, this time cast by Medlock. She was flanked by Martha and Alexander. Alexander had a handful of something that he lobbed at Kimber, she shouted, deep and low and the ground under them all shook, setting them off balance. The thing Alexander had thrown exploded into aqua coloured sparkles over Kimber's head. She opened her mouth to speak and silence came out. She blinked, frowned and cut herself again a moment later she was back to casting runes. Barlow had constructed a magical net that he sent towards her. Medlock, grim faced, was flicking her wand as if it were a whip, accentuating and strengthening Barlow's spell.

William appeared beside Alistair, hauling him upright, with one hand in his armpit.

"Come on, we have to get you to safety," William said, voice low and urgent.

Alistair shook his head. "Wait, no. I don't know if she can access the wellspring but she's uncommonly strong. We have to help the others, make sure we win."

"Even with the wellspring, I think you've worn yourself out," William murmured. He turned to cast a rune of his own, slashing into Kimber's side. She whirled around, eyes flashing with something silver and dangerous. Alistair felt the urge to fall back under her spell, it would be as easy as going to sleep, her allure was so powerful. But William's hand steadied him, anchored him, and he resisted.

He looked within, tried to feel the traces of magic he could gather together to make a spell, but William was right. There was almost nothing left. Not enough to cast something useful at all.

But there was something else, something he was forgetting.

He blinked, of course! He was bleeding...

He dipped a finger into the wound and the power of his own blood pulled the magic from within himself. Kimber advanced on him and William. William was at this point mostly holding Alistair up. Alistair's legs were more than wobbly, they were buckling. Thomas dashed to Alistair's other side and leaned his foxy shoulder against Alistair's leg, bolstering him.

Alistair thought of the runes that would combine to make immobility, and cast them using blood magic. It hurt. It was like wrenching a breath out of dying lungs, the absolute last vestiges of power he held within him, but he had something, and he hurled it through the air at Kimber.

In the same instant, Barlow and Medlock's net wrapped around Kimber and with an aborted gesture, she fell to the ground, and lay there like a log, wrapped in Barlow's purple magic. The sundew tendrils surrounded her in a threatening manner, forming a barrier between her and Alistair. Alistair thought of the briars growing up around Sleeping Beauty, briefly. Then his knees gave out entirely and he crumpled backwards into William's strong embrace.

"I've got you," he said. "It's all right, it's over now."

"I hope so," Alistair said. It hurt to talk, his throat felt scorched and shredded.

Samal came down from the sky in a shower of golden light and Alistair knew it was safe to pass out then.

CHAPTER 30

*W*hen Alistair woke again, he was in midair, bathed in Samal's golden light and held securely in his arms. "Am I the Sleeping Beauty?" Alistair croaked.

Samal glanced down at him and smiled. "Just getting you inside to the infirmary, love."

Alistair closed his eyes. After all the things that had happened that night, and over the last few days, he didn't want to vomit from the movement of airborne transportation.

In the infirmary, Madame Waxleaf and Samal hit him with a barrage of healing spells until he felt normal again, if tired out. William and Thomas were watching from nearby, both of them looking drawn and worried. Thomas was in his human form and holding tight to William's hand.

Is Luis all right?" Alistair asked, once they'd finished the first wave of spells.

"Yes," Samal said. He picked up a glass bottle of milk and downed half of it in one swallow. "Once Kimber left with you, I was able to stabilise him and Madame Waxleaf appeared. She did the final healing. It..." He stopped speaking and pulled a face, considering his words before he continued. "It seems that

Kimber had used her power to somehow keep him from getting better."

"I've never seen allure used in that way," Madam Waxleaf said. She shook her head, her features pinched. "She had augmented her powers with something, a very complicated ritual and some other sort of magic."

"Maybe..." Alistair swallowed. "Maybe she used his blood against him? She did that to me."

There was a moment's silence as they all contemplated the ramifications of such an action. Finally, Madame Waxleaf said "Monstrous", and bustled off to check on Luis again. He was sitting propped up on his pillows, and he opened his eyes at her approach.

Alistair's bed was too far away to hear what they spoke of, but once Madame Waxleaf seemed satisfied she turned away, and Luis waved at Alistair. That was enough. His smile told Alistair that he didn't blame him. Alistair fell back on his pillow and let sleep take him once more.

The next time Alistair woke up, Councillor Rutherford had returned. He had a different attending officer this time, a young man who trailed after him and looked deeply nervous.

"What will happen to Kimber?" Alistair blurted, before any sort of pleasantries could be exchanged. Councillor Rutherford looked surprised, but went ahead and answered his question.

"Our courts will deal with her," he said. "You might be interested to know, though, that she isn't actually called Kimber at all. My officer here broke a particularly expert glamour which she has been using for some months. Her name is actually Amelia. Amelia Birch."

Alistair's mouth dried. "She's a Birch?"

"Eulalia Birch's godmother, and aunt to Everett and Eleanor."

Alistair rested his head back on the pillow and closed his eyes, remembering the letter they'd found in his father's hidden box of correspondence. Alice Birch begging for assistance to help her child, Elmer, who had died since.

"They hate me because my parents didn't save Elmer Birch," Alistair said without opening his eyes. "They could have tried, they could have sent me, but after Ambrose died trying to help William... Well. They cursed me to lock my magic up, and hid me away. They hid themselves as well."

"Yes, up until very recently," Rutherford said. "Once the glamour was broken, Amelia told us about the runes she and her sister had carved into the trees on the Lennox country house grounds, and on the cobbles outside the Lennox townhouse."

"She said something about trees and intention," Alistair said. "I thought she was raving."

"Apparently not. The night your parents died, Alistair, it was as a result of those runes. Years ago, soon after the tragedy of Elmer's death, they placed them there. Clever things, which could sense intention. As long as your parents continued to hide from their magic, and from magical society, they were safe. However, if they decided to return to it, as they did, the night of the accident, then the runes would trigger a fatal accident."

Alistair sighed deeply, rubbed his hand over his forehead and closed his eyes again.

"That's dreadful," Thomas said. He went to Alistair's side and took his free hand in his, rubbing his thumb against the back of it.

"We have a full statement from Amelia. With Luis's statement and Alexander's report of the ways she's used her allure on him, we will be able to prosecute with no problem. You don't need to worry about any more attacks or strange goings on. You have my assurance that the entire Birch clan will be under close supervision for as long as they remain on British soil."

"If they knew what was good for them, they'd go somewhere far away," William said. He was leaning against the wall with a blank expression but fire in his eyes. "My father will be livid, and well... it's not good when he's like that."

Councillor Rutherford raised his eyebrows in a way that indicated he understood the full implications of William's words. "In the meantime, if you could make a brief statement of what happened tonight in your own words, Alistair? I'll ask that your companions wait in the hall. We shouldn't be long at all."

It didn't take too long, Alistair was tired out, and he kept to the main points, trying to remember the exact words Kimber - no - Amelia, had said to him. Councillor Rutherford pronounced himself satisfied, and excused himself to interview William, Thomas and Samal.

Samal came into the infirmary about ten minutes later, checking Alistair's temperature with the back of his hand before searching his face. "You're tired, you need more sleep, Allie."

"I will," Alistair said. "I just need to know... the key for the Secret Garden, did anyone grab it? And uh... well, Barlow and Medlock know about it now, what will they say?"

"We'll find out and let you know in the morning, all right?"

He helped Alistair to get comfortable, fluffing the pillows and pulling the blankets up. "Just sleep, and we'll see you for breakfast."

"Thank you Sam. For everything, and thank the others too, for me? Everyone had a part." Samal kissed Alistair's forehead and was promising to do just that when Alistair fell asleep.

CHAPTER 31

Just like healing, the curse breaking was a slow process.

Alistair had been envisaging the breaking of William's curse to be one big event, the way the warding had been. But he'd learned from Professor Winterbourne, and ironically enough, from the Birches, that some things needed to be approached slowly and with methodical steps.

If the Birches had gone in, wands blazing and throwing curses right after Elmer died, his parents would have fought them and possibly defeated them. But by planting the runes with a slow release effect ... they could probably have evaded capture or repercussions. Well, if they hadn't decided they had to target Alistair as well.

But the lesson was this: Alistair took his time in the construction of the curse-breaking spell. He considered the puzzle from many angles, and came to the same conclusion each time. The spell was so old, so advanced, that one single approach simply wouldn't work to pull it apart.

When he emerged from the infirmary, two days after Amelia's attack, he sat at the breakfast table and looked at all his friends. William, whose stoic persona concealed a deep and caring heart, as well as a proficiency in magic Alistair aspired to.

Plus, a flair for the dramatic, which Alistair couldn't help but appreciate.

Samal, who had a heavenly talent for mending things, for taking what was broken and making it whole again. He had been so shy and awkward to begin with, but as he got more comfortable with Alistair and the others, more of his personality had shone through. He was a wonderfully caring friend, with a bone-dry sense of humour, who wasn't afraid to defend what was right, with violence if necessary.

Thomas, with his friendly, easy-going nature and ability to entirely change his form, the way he took things like the station of his birth in stride and attended Misselthwaite as his right. An honest and affectionate friend, who had made Alistair open up in the first place with his gentle understanding.

Then there was Martha, forthright and always ready to laugh, a loyal friend who took things in her stride and didn't judge. Alexander was there as well, a little awkward, but with a heart of gold. Standing at the end of the table, checking that they were all right was Zeta, who was certain in her beliefs and determined to use her impressive skills in the service of others.

Each of them made Alistair want to be better than he had been. He had come to know himself as a person through his interactions with each of them. Come to understand who he truly wanted to become. He knew how to get there as well. He had to keep being friends with these people, to listen to them, to trust them and help them in return.

That revelation had led to the way to solve the curse.

Alistair's plan was to use a little of everything he had learned. Mix up the styles and the techniques, and create something entirely new to combat the curse.

Alistair had Professor Barlow's reassurance that he had spoken to Lord Carlisle and secured the Secret Garden again. Apparently Lord Carlisle himself wasn't ready for the garden and his wife's memorial to be opened to the school at large, but he was content for his son and his boyfriends to make use of it, especially if the wellspring was able to cure William.

The key had been returned to Alistair.

Since the day he'd had an epiphany over breakfast, he'd spent a week honing his techniques with Professor Winterbourne, in between his other classes, whenever she had time to assist him they would work together. When she had other work, he would read and review his notes over and over.

He focused on the particular equations and delicate spellwork that would unlock a part of William's curse. This helped to clarify all the other parts of the curse which needed to be untangled and left Alistair with valuable notes on what needed to be solved next.

The next week he had spent a lot of time with April Quinn. Thomas and Samal had come around somewhat on blood magic, for although Amelia Birch had used it for nefarious purposes, Alistair might not have survived the fight with her if he hadn't been able to draw on it himself. They had been able to see the clear difference that intention made with the use of blood magic, and he had received their blessing to continue his studies.

Alistair and April dove deep into the ways that the life essence could be used to draw out extra power, and with a little sample of William's own blood, they unlocked another part of the curse and applied the solution directly to William via an injection.

Next, Alistair helped Thomas with his anatomy lessons, and then the painstaking and complicated work of deciphering that anatomy into something Thomas could transform into. They harnessed the power of the wellspring and Alistair assisted with his own magic, as Thomas transformed into a hawk for the first time.

They both crouched in the grass, jackets discarded and shirt sleeves rolled up as they cast the spell together. Thomas's light voice speaking the runes of transformation and Alistair's deeper, less expressive voice speaking the strengthening and support runes.

Alistair laughed and clapped when it was done. Sweat dripped down his face from the effort, even if the weather was beginning to turn chiller. Thomas wheeled overhead and then dove suddenly, approaching the garden with breathtaking speed before flaring his wings and banking to the left. Alistair held out his arm and with delicacy, Thomas landed on it, careful not to break his skin with his sharp claws.

"You are amazing," Alistair said. He gently stroked Thomas's soft feathered head with one finger.

What Alistair learned from his work with Thomas was the nature and technicalities of transformation. In application: how to stop William's curse turning him into a full blooded vampire, which it would if left unchecked.

Each night William and Alistair would sit together, both hands clasped, and meditate. Alistair concentrated on the puzzle he'd unlocked, and William on willing his body to listen and to stop the change from within. Their magic flowed between them in strange harmony, both of them so familiar with the feel of the other's magic that it felt simple to do so.

The following week, Alistair split his time between learning potions basics from Alexander and transformation with Martha. Both of these techniques resulted in physical things he could take back to William. A pomegranate flavoured potion full of healing and bolstering magic that William was to drink a little of each day and a ring which would slowly but surely break down the part of the curse that caused physical pain and transform it into healthy cells and healing blood.

Finally, he spent time following Samal on his rounds of the infirmary and the various things Madam Waxleaf called him in for. There was precious little Alistair could learn from the few days he watched, but he could hold clean towels, and he could bring fresh water, and he could remind Samal to take a drink and a rest if he appeared worn out. Between the two of them, they came up with a simple healing spell that would repair any damage the curse breaking did to William. Samal mixed a salve with the magical spell for William to use. It was a sort of slow-release magical medicine that William rubbed on his arm once a day that made him smell pleasantly of peppermint.

Finally, the day came to do the final parts of the curse breaking. Professor Winterbourne had offered her assistance and so had April Quinn, so together with Willam, Samal and Thomas, they made their way to the Secret Garden to do the ritual under the statue of Melusine.

Alistair made a protective circle, and set Samal and Thomas at the North and South points of it, to bolster the protection. William and himself were situated in the centre, with Professor Winterbourne and April Quinn just outside the circle, ready to assist if needed.

Alistair spoke the runes of protection, drew power up from the wellspring and began the ritual.

Because of all the pre-work he'd done and all the small components of the spell learned from his friends, which were already working, the ritual felt anti-climactic. He made a careful cut on his own forearm, channelled a little extra power, and placed his other hand on William's chest.

William gazed at him with so much love and trust, Alistair felt no fear at all. He simply pulled apart the last pieces of the curse, and sent them harmlessly back into the ground.

William took a deep breath, one that seemed to rattle through his throat, as if the first in a long time. His eyes were the same deep colour as always, and his skin was still pale, but when he smiled Alistair could read the relief as easily as a book.

"Is it done?" he asked, although he could sense that he had succeeded.

"I believe it is," William said. "I feel.. A weight is lifted from me. Something I've been carrying a long, long time."

"You look the same." Alistair reached up to tuck a little of William's black hair behind his ear.

"I feel the same, but better," William said.

Samal and Thomas hurried into the circle. Samal took a moment, his hand on William's shoulder, to sense if there was anything still affecting him, and then he nodded.

"It's done. I think perhaps, that William will still have some aspects of vampirism, there was some part of him that was too far gone to reverse, but theoretically he will age at a normal rate now."

"And you won't have any of the ill effects of the curse," Alistair said.

The four of them hugged. Joyful and awkward. Too many elbows, and too many bodies, making them all giggle.

Alistair broke the circle and went to Professor Winterborne and April.

"That was very good, Lennox." Professor Winterborne nodded her head once. "An exemplary example of using a prolonged and well-planned solution to a very complicated curse."

"And you did it with style," April added.

"You'll be passing my course with the highest of accolades, and I shall be recommending you for third level courses next term."

Alistair blinked. He hadn't even considered that what he was doing might be graded.

"Same," April said. "I don't know if my word as a visiting scholar will carry much weight, but I'll do what I can. You were brilliant, and it was wonderful to watch you. Good work, Al. Top marks from me."

"But I have barely done one year of study," Alistair protested. "Surely I can't-"

"You're doing brilliantly," Professor Winterbourne said. "You've showed fine dedication to your work, and a very mature approach to a complicated problem. I have no compunctions with recommending you for third year level curse breaking courses."

Alistair flushed warm, and felt acutely aware of his body as he struggled to respond to such wonderful praise. Part of him wanted to protest that he didn't deserve it. "Thank you Professor, but my friends and teachers really helped, I couldn't have done it without any of them, or you."

"That's part of it, too," April said. She nudged Alistair with her elbow. "Not a single academic scholar or professor got their working in solitude. None of us are heroes in a pulp novel, solving it all single handedly and before breakfast. You did good, kid."

"Thank you," Alistair said, with as much dignity as he could muster.

"Now, if you'd show us the way out of the garden?" Professor Winterbourne asked.

"I'm sure you lads have celebrating to do," April added.

"Just remember exams start soon," Professor Winterbourne said as Alistair walked the two of them up the path to the door. "And don't ignore your other classes."

"Thank you for all your help Professor, and you April," Alistair said. He hoped that they could tell that he really appreciated them. "Really, thank you."

He locked the door to the garden behind them and hurried back to his boyfriends.

CHAPTER 32

Alistair let the professors out and returned to find his lovers in the middle of shedding their clothes. William was kissing Thomas deeply as Samal tugged William's trousers down to reach between and stroke him.

Alistair had never go aroused so quickly in his life. "Starting without me?"

"Sorry, Allie," Thomas gasped. "William was just so relieved..."

Samal reached a hand out to Alistair and tugged him in for a long, lingering kiss that made Alistair forget his tiredness and the conversation with the professors entirely. All he knew was he wanted more kisses.

He got them.

Samal broke the kiss and passed Alistair to Thomas, who wasted no time in unbuttoning Alistair's waistcoat and shirt, and pushing both of them off his shoulders. Alistair kissed Thomas with a fiery passion, relaxing into the attention. William pulled them both down to the ground, and as Samal sank down to take William's hardness in his mouth, Alistair took William's mouth, kissing him hard, nipping his lower lip and exulting in his own ecstatic happiness at having achieving his goal of breaking the curse.

Someone stripped Alistair of the rest of his clothes, and in a moment he was surrounded by the bare skin of his three lovers, all crowding in on him, sharing kisses, hands touching all over.

Hands - he didn't know whose - caressed Alistair's rear and he unconsciously pushed back against the touch. He loved and trusted these men, and the arousal in him expanded his affection, wanting more of whatever they wanted to do to him.

He started when a hot tongue probed at him, teasing him open. It felt so good that he groaned loudly and turned his face. William bit his earlobe gently and Thomas claimed his mouth next.

Some part of Alistair's mind deduced that it must be Samal tonguing him, but he found the thought hard to keep hold of as the tongue was so good - gently pushing through the tight ring of muscle and making him moan.

He reached to touch Thomas, his hand sliding down the taut belly to find his hardness, pressing against Alistair's thigh. William's hardness was pressed against his side, so he moved to stroke him there too.

"Sex magic?" Thomas moaned. "Can you... William?"

"Oh, stars, yes..." William said the words and in an instant Thomas was flushed, his eyes starry and glazed.

Thomas moved then, pulling away from Alistair's hold to get on all fours. Alistair groaned at the sight of him like that. "Fuck me, Allie." Thomas's demand came out broken, his voice hoarse with need. Alistair would give Thomas anything he asked for, anything that would make him smile. He nodded, although he didn't want to move away from Samal's tongue.

"Will..." Alistair said, desperately.

William intuited his dilemma. "Sam, stop a moment, Tom wants Allie in him, what if you fuck Allie while he fucks Thomas, and then I fuck you?"

Alistair's heart sped up so it was thundering in his ears. "Please. Please do that."

"Stars, all right," Samal said, his voice higher than usual. "That sounds... overwhelmingly good."

William helped Alistair up to a kneeling position, and went to kiss Samal and open him magically as well. Alistair paused to lean down and plant soft kisses down Thomas's spine. "I'm gonna enter you now, okay, Tom?"

"Yeah," Thomas said. "I'm ready."

Alistair pushed inside slowly, his body aching to go quick, to reach his bliss and be done, but knowing what William had said, he knew he had to pace himself. He pushed in with a moan, feeling the way Thomas's body resisted and then gave, a delicious tightness around him.

"Oh, Tom, I love you," Alistair breathed. He wrapped an arm around Thomas's waist and kissed his shoulder blade. Thomas moaned deeply and rocked his hips, impatient for more. "Soon, love. More soon."

In a moment Samal was behind Alistair, and William did the spell again to make Alistair slick and ready, the stretching Samal's tongue had started, finished in a moment. "Oh merciful... I can't last!" Alsitair cried out. "It's overwhelming already."

"Then we'd better move fast." William's voice was breathless as well. Samal stroked Alistair's back, then gripped his hips.

"Allie, are you ready for me?"

"Yes, please, please, I need you." Alistair, if he'd been thinking straight, might have been embarrassed at the neediness in his voice. But he had given over to love and lust, and thoughts had little to do with those. He was all emotion, and the main emotions were affection and need.

Samal teased at Alistair's hole and gently pushed inside. Alistair tried to hold still, but he couldn't help pushing himself back onto the slow press of Samal's hardness. But that pulled him so he wasn't as deep inside Thomas. Thomas moaned and rocked his hips back, trapping Alistair between the two of them in the most stimulating way.

"Stars, oh stars," Alistair said. "Please, more."

William wasted no time in lining up behind Samal and pushing inside. "You all look incredible," William said, loud enough that Alistair could hear over Thomas's whining. Samal pressed his chest flush with Alistair's back and groaned in his ear and Alistair almost lost control and came from that. Instead he leaned forward as well, and nipped the back of Thomas's neck.

Thomas's arms shook and he lowered himself down to his elbows. This pushed his ass further up and Alistair got a deeper angle and moaned at the intensity of it.

"I can feel that," Samal murmured. "Your pleasure is making you constrict on me." His arm snaked around Alistair's waist, holding him steady, which was lucky as Alistair's leg muscles did not feel reliable.

Samal shoved forward without warning and Alistair cried out, forced deeper into Thomas by the movement. "Sorry, Will didn't warn me," Samal gasped. "Communication, please William."

Thomas whined and moaned. "It's so good, it's so good, it's almost... I'm so close."

"Me too," Alistair said. "I'm so full."

"I'm going to thrust now," William said. Then he did it without waiting for a response. Alistair cried out loudly, overwhelmed by the push of William sending Samal deeper into him, and himself deeper into Thomas.

It was too much, none of them could last any length of time like that. Which suited Alistair fine, they had been fast to start and this exultation in their mutual love didn't need to linger. They would take their time later on, back in the bedroom.

Thomas came abruptly on the next thrust from William, squeezing and milking Alistair with the contraction of his muscles until Alistair, barely able to move from his position, rocked his hips wildly and came as well. Samal jerked, bucking twice into Alistair as he filled him, his mouth fastened on Alistair's shoulder, sucking a bruise into his skin.

William was right behind, the slap of skin as he thrust once more into Samal echoing over their collective moans of pleasure.

They disentangled themselves slowly, gingerly, William ensuring that no one was hurt in any way, and using another spell to clean up the worst of the mess. He also chivvied them back into their clothes and up to Misselthwaite and their suite.

William ran a hot bath and they took turns soaking and cleaning themselves and finally piled into bed to cuddle each other and exchange soft kisses.

"Thank you, Alistair," William said, nuzzling his cheek.

"You're welcome," Alistair said. His head felt full of cotton wool again, but this time it was because of overstimulation and being surrounded by love, rather than a magical effect. "But what for?"

"Breaking the curse of course," William said.

"Well, thank you for suggesting we all fuck at the same time," Alistair said. "I liked it."

Samal chuckled. "So did I."

"Me too," Thomas said. He was curled on Alistair's right hand side, fuzzy fox ears tickling his cheek. "But maybe we save it for special occasions?"

"Yeah, agreed," Alistair said. He pulled William's arm closer around his waist, and reached past Thomas to cup Samal's cheek. "I love you all so much."

They all responded in kind, and before anything else could be said, they were all fast asleep.

The next morning, Alistair woke up warm and happy, snuggled in between William and Thomas, with Samal on Thomas's other side, one wing thrown over all four of them, although he didn't appear to be glowing or in angelic form aside from that. The air in the bedroom felt chillier than usual and Alistair could sense that the season was considering turning. Most classes were wrapping up in the next week to give students time to study for exams or to spend more time on their special assignment projects.

Alistair had been tired out after the spell, but he felt utterly luxurious, knowing that he had passed at least his two curse-breaking courses. He would need to work hard in the greenhouse, as his botany assignments had received the least amount of time, but he was confident that he could catch up there.

His other classes, well, they'd need a little time to be sure, but it wasn't enough to seriously worry him.

He wriggled, extracting his arms from where they were pinned against his lover's bodies, and stretched them over his head, letting out a contented sigh as he did.

A moment later he had a nose nuzzling into his neck - Thomas, and William yawned on the other side.

"Is it time for breakfast?" Thomas asked, his lips tickling Alistair's neck.

"Almost." Samal withdrew his wing and rolled over towards the edge of the bed. "How did everyone sleep?"

"Good," Alistair said. He turned to look at William. "How about you, Will?"

"Like I've never slept before," William said. His face was lit with a sweet, excited smile which Alistair had never seen on his face before. Alistair's heart fluttered in response. "I had dreams about toast and jam."

Samal laughed. "Doesn't everyone?"

"No, but... if I dreamed before, which I often didn't, it was nightmares," William said. "This was so pleasant. And now I want toast with jam."

"I'm glad for you." Alistair leaned in and kissed the tip of William's nose, delighted when he was rewarded with an even wider version of the new smile. 'We'll make sure you get toast at breakfast."

They got up one by one, took turns shaving in the mirror in the bathroom, and dressing for the day. Alistair, on a whim, chose a burgundy suit jacket to go with his customary grey pants and waistcoat.

"Looks like we're celebrating," Thomas teased.

Even breakfast felt like a festive occasion. In solidarity Alistair made sure he had a slice of toast with jam spread on it, and so did Samal and Thomas. Martha couldn't understand why they were giggling as they ate it, but rolled her eyes and decided not to ask.

Alistair and Thomas made their way to the greenhouse after breakfast, where everyone's microclimates were doing well. Professor Weatherstaff did a slow walk around the classroom, making notes on a grubby piece of paper about everyone's progress. Alistair had taken over Kimber's tray since the incident, so he and Thomas had separate projects, although they still helped each other with them.

Weatherstaff assigned a four page quiz, something that they could take away with them to be returned at the end of the week.

"It's just a formality though," he said. "You've all passed just fine, and I just need the paperwork to back up your grades, like." He gave them all a stern glance and then made a shooing motion with his hand. "Now put your lettuces aside. If you want to make up a salad with what you grew you're welcome to take it away with you, otherwise make sure you have the quizzes back by Saturday morning."

Some students took their lettuce, some stored them away. Thomas took his, citing some animal or other in the Garden that had a fondness for them. Alistair pressed him to take the lettuces he'd adopted from Kimber as well. Then he went up to Professor Weatherstaff. He felt like he was imposing somehow, as the Professor filed the unneeded quiz papers in an overstuffed drawer in his grubby desk. He cleared his throat.

"Professor, if I might have a word," Alistair said, suddenly shy.

Professor Weatherstaff turned to look at Alistair. "Go ahead, Lennox."

Things hadn't been quite right between them since the destruction of the microclimate spells, and although Alistair's name had been cleared, he had been so busy with breaking down William's curse that he hadn't taken time to make things right.

He cleared his throat again. "Professor, I wanted to let you know that I have the key to the Secret Garden here in the grounds," he said. "And... I want to invite you to visit it, if you'd like to."

Professor Weatherstaff's face crinkled up, his eyes almost closing, and for a moment Alistair worried that he had mortally offended the man. But then his mouth broke into a wide smile and he chortled.

"You found it, eh? I wondered if it'd be something of the sort. The way you were making so many advances, more than the other students, I figured there must be somewhere else you were working." He rubbed his hand on the back of his neck and breathed out slowly. "I reckon I would like to see it. I've heard so many stories."

"Barlow has said that I can keep it a secret for the time

being," Alistair said. "I hold the only key, but obviously he knows about it, and Medlock too. There's a wellspring, and a fountain and... well. I'd just really like you to see it."

There was a bustling from the front of the greenhouse and Alistair realised the second year students were coming in for their class. "Let me know when you want the tour," he said.

Professor Weatherstaff beamed at Alistair, which was a strangely craggy experience, with Ben showing off a couple of tooth gaps and his weathered face contorting, but it was no less wonderful for all that.

"I'll do that, Lennox. Now, you run along."

✦

The last classes of the term wrapped up and Alistair and his friends got down to the serious work of study.

He made amends with Kincade relatively easily with the explanation of what Kimber had one, and a promise to work some shifts shelving in the library to help ease Kincade's workload.

Some afternoons he was in the library, commandeering the armchairs by the fire, books spread over his lap, Thomas opposite with a huge book of animal skeletons open on the coffee table and William and Samal bickering over the correct translation of some ancient rune.

Sometimes Alistair needed more quiet, and he would situate himself in his suite at his desk, his back to the others if they were there.

And one day they just cleared off the breakfast things at their table, laid out all their notes and books and took turns quizzing each other on various pieces of esoteric knowledge for the whole morning.

✦

Lord Carlisle returned to Misselthwaite Manor the night before William's first exam. William had received word of his return, and went to meet him as he came in, insisting that Alistair accompany him to take credit for the breaking of the curse.

Lord Carlisle stepped down from his carriage, looking worn out and dusty from the trip.

Alistair had no idea where he'd even been, but from the size of the trunks the footmen were unloading it had been something of a long voyage.

"William," Lord Carlisle said. "You didn't need to come and meet me, I'd have sent for you once I settled in."

"Father, do you notice anything different?" Lord Carlisle looked him up and down and William practically bounced on the spot.

The realisation that the curse was in fact gone broke across Lord Carlisle's face like the sun rising. "By all the stars and Merlin himself, you've done it."

With a few strides and a great deal of travelling cloak swirling, Lord Carlisle caught William up in a hug. William stiffened, apparently he hadn't expected that as a reaction at all.

It took a moment, but William soon lifted his arms and hugged his father back.

After another moment they were both making aborted snuffling noises, as if trying not to cry. Alistair felt out of place, and very much as if he were intruding on them, so he took a discreet step back. The movement caught William's eye.

"It was Alistair," William said. His voice was muffled, speaking into his father's cloak. He lifted his head. "You were right, he was the one to break the curse."

"Of course he was." Lord Carlisle let go of his son, strode towards Alistair and wrapped him in a hug. "You are a brilliant boy, Alistair. I never had any doubt in you."

Alistair felt a sudden lump in his throat and blinked back tears. He patted Lord Carlisle on the back. He wanted to make this less awkward, so he said the first thing that came to mind. "I had plenty of doubts for both of us, sir," he said.

Lord Carlisle laughed and held him at arm's length, his pale face glowing in the lamplight. "The Carlisles owe you a great debt," he said. "You will always have a place here at Misselthwaite."

"Oh, I don't…" Alistair, flustered, looked at William and then back at Lord Carlisle. "That's very kind of you, but I love William, I'd have done it anyway."

Lord Carlisle's smile got even larger, and Alistair fancied he could see the pointiness of his fangs. "Regardless, my family is in your debt. You have given us hope, and brought the bloodline back to life. For that, I thank you from the bottom of my heart. You will be rewarded, many times over."

Alistair felt his cheeks and his entire face warm, so unaccustomed was he to being appreciated by such an impressive figure. He cleared his throat, nodded and mumbled a thank you. Lord Carlisle let him go finally, and they made their way into the Manor house together with William, to talk through how the curse breaking had gone.

"There's just one thing I don't quite understand," Alistair said, as they walked. "Where did the original curse come from? It was so old, and so complicated."

"Melusine's grandparents," Lord Carlisle said, his voice a little sad, and a little distant. "They didn't want us to marry. Her grandmother had seen in the stars that I would be turned, so they worked together to curse me to scare Melusine away… however it has long been my belief that the curse itself is what caused me to be attacked that night, and turned by a vampire. Melusine chose me even still. Of course, we didn't find out about the curse until later, until she was pregnant with you, William."

He sighed, the age old sigh of someone who has carried a burden too long.

"I'm so sorry, father," William said.

"It's behind us now," Lord Carlisle said. He managed a wan smile. "And now you can really concentrate on your studies, and make something of yourself. What do you really want to do with your life?"

William paused, stopping halfway up the stairs with his eyes going wide. "You know, I've been cured for a couple of weeks, but it had never occurred to me to actually plan for the future."

"We've got time for that," Alistair said. He took William's hand and encouraged him to keep walking. "And exams to worry about first."

On the last night of exams Misselthwaite put on an extra special banquet to farewell the students. Alistair, Thomas, William, Samal, Martha and Alexander all sat at their usual table, all a little more dressed up than normal.

Lord Carlisle proposed a toast to the students, and then another to the staff. The tables were laden with large platters of food so they could help themselves without getting up, and the mood was positively festive.

"So, Summer holidays," Thomas said. "What's everyone planning to do?"

They looked around at each other. "I had hoped to spend some time with all of you," Alistair said. "I got horribly lonely in the term break, even if it was only a bit over a week alone."

"I'd like to go to the beach," William said. He leaned back in his chair and patted his stomach, well stuffed with helpings of roast potatoes.

"The beach sounds divine," Martha said. "I'm travelling with my folks, out to Cornwall, which I expect will be dreary as ditchwater."

Samal rubbed her shoulder in commiseration. "I need to go

and see my mother for at least some of the break, but I would like to visit the ocean."

"How about I find us some rooms in a proper seaside hotel? Maybe out in Brighton?" William said. "You can all make your way there whenever you can, train tickets and rooms on me."

Thomas's eyes went round and wide. "Do you really mean it?"

"Of course." William made eye contact with Alexander. "You as well Alex, if you're interested. And Martha if you can find time to escape Cornwall."

"Maybe!" Martha sat up straighter. "I don't think we were planning on going for the entire break, Father has work after all..."

Alistair grinned, meeting William's eye. "I'd love that, I've never been to the seaside."

"Neither," Thomas said. "Maybe there'll be dolphins? I'd love to learn how to change into a dolphin."

"I've never been to the seaside for anything but health reasons," William said. "All right, it's settled. I'll sort out the details tomorrow, and you all send messages to your families and so on."

Alistair sipped his wine and took Thomas's hand, squeezing it. Thomas grinned and leaned his shoulder against his, his fox ears sprouting from his hair to tickle Alistair's cheek. William sat at the head of the table, on Thomas's other side, so Thomas reached out and took his hand too. William, his cheeks warm and rosy, tapped Samal on the shoulder. Samal had turned to Martha and was talking quickly, trying to make plans, when William tapped him he turned around, a little of the old irritation in his eyes. But when William held out his hand to him he softened, kissed the back of it, and took it as well.

Martha and Alexander rolled their eyes and smiled in a fond way, and Alistair knew that whatever came next, whatever the stars said the future would hold, he wouldn't be alone. He would face it together with the three loves of his life, and with the support of his dear friends.

~ fin

AFTERWORD

.

Thanks for reading Garden of Mysteries. This one didn't come as easy to me as its predecessor but the characters are such a joy to write, and I hope that shines through.

Find me on social media
   Facebook: Drake LaMarque Author
   Facebook reader group: Drake's Crew
   Tiktok: @jamiesandswriter

Thank you to my wonderful alpha readers/editor Z you are a shining star. Thanks also to the wonderful denizens of Drake's Crew and my stellar ARC reading team. You are all very much appreciated. Big love also to my spectacular spouse, without their support I couldn't have done this.

CABIN BOY - HIS PIRATICAL HAREM BOOK 1

Buy now

I've never been what I was supposed to be. Wealthy sons of Port Governors aren't supposed to be ejected from the British Navy after less than a year, they're not supposed to like pulp romances or daydream about the handsome heroes of the stories instead of the heroines.

When my Father issued me an order to marry a woman, I knew I had no choice but to make my own way in the world, and I found a berth on the first ship out of Jamaica.

I didn't mean to join a pirate ship, and I certainly didn't intend to find myself the cabin boy to an incredibly charming Pirate Captain. Or that I'd also be attracted to the mysterious First Mate, or that both of them would show me all sorts of unspeakable and salacious pleasures while on board. How can I choose just one of them when I want both?

In addition to confusion on board the ship, there's also enchanting genderfluid merfolk, a cat which seems to understand a lot more than it should, an unseasonable storm and a sea witch with a serious grudge... and with all these complications, I am definitely in over my head.

Come and meet the crew:

Gideon: an innocent with a lot of forbidden desires and a lot of love to give

Tate: a huge, muscular ship's captain with a sweet side

Ezra: a dominant and closed off first mate

Ora: a genderqueer, curious and affectionate merman

ALSO BY DRAKE

KIDNAPPED BY THE GENTLEMAN - GENTLEMAN'S BOUNTY BOOK 1

Buy Now

Cedric has been kidnapped by pirates.

...they have no idea how much trouble they're in for.

Cedric was living his best life, partying in the colonies, bedding whomever he pleased and trusting that his parents' money and affluence would get him out of any unfortunate scrapes.

Until he was kidnapped by the fearsome pirate Lucifer, who planned to trade him for a hefty ransom. Unfortunately, he's not the only one after Cedric, and the strange secret society who have Cedric in their sights might just be more dangerous than Captain Lucifer.

Now Cedric is trapped on a pirate ship with a dashingly handsome captain, a quartermaster who won't stop staring at him and an overwhelming desire to find some fun, all while saving his hide from an unknown organisation who will stop at nothing to track him down.

ALSO PUBLISHED BY GREY KELPIE STUDIO

OVERDUES AND OCCULTISM BY JAMIE SANDS

Buy now

A witch in the broom closet probably shouldn't be so interested in a ghost hunter, right?

That Basil is a librarian comes as no surprise to his Mt Eden community. That he's a witch? Yeah. That might raise more than a few eyebrows.

When Sebastian, a paranormal investigator filming a web series starts snooping around Basil's library, he stirs up more than just Basil's heart.

Between Basil's own self-doubt, a ghost who steals books and Sebastian, an enthusiastic extrovert bent on uncovering secrets, Basil's life is about to get a lot more complicated.

Overdues and Occultism is a sweet, no heat contemporary novella about a witch living in Auckland, New Zealand. MM romance, HEA.